Andrew K. H. Boyd

The Graver Thoughts of a Country Parson

SALZWASSER VERLAG

Andrew K. H. Boyd

The Graver Thoughts of a Country Parson

Reprint of the original, first published in 1863.

1st Edition 2022 | ISBN: 978-3-37500-381-4

Verlag (Publisher): Salzwasser Verlag GmbH, Zeilweg 44, 60439 Frankfurt, Deutschland
Vertretungsberechtigt (Authorized to represent): E. Roepke, Zeilweg 44, 60439 Frankfurt, Deutschland
Druck (Print): Books on Demand GmbH, In de Tarpen 42, 22848 Norderstedt, Deutschland

THE GRAVER THOUGHTS

OF A

COUNTRY PARSON.

THE

GRAVER THOUGHTS

OF A

COUNTRY PARSON.

BY THE AUTHOR OF

BOSTON

1863.

CONTENTS.

I.

SUNDAYS LONG AGO.

THERE is a subdued, silvery light on the sea to-day, and the hills across the water look like blue clouds. The air is so still, that you may hear the beating of the paddles of a steamer miles distant, unseen in the veil of mist. There has been drizzling rain at intervals through the morning; and the road by the sea-side, yesterday ankle-deep in dust, is pleasantly firm and cool; and the trees, just beginning to be touched by the Atlantic breezes of the early days of September, look green again as in May, in the glints of silvery light from the clouded sun. You may see many fair scenes within the compass of Britain: but yesterday morning, when the sky was sapphire-blue, and the sunshine was the brightest; — when that expanse of sea shut in by noble hills was glassy smooth, and the yellow corn-fields round, bounded by green hedges, looked so still and rich in the quiet air, not without a touch of bracing crispness; you would have said that there could hardly be anything fairer in the world than this bit of the homely Clyde.

Milton was wont to declare that in the autumn

days, when the leaves are changing and falling, his poetic genius quite deserted him; and he could not write a line. But in the spring-time, when the sap began to stir in the trees, and all nature to revive, the life around him thrilled his heart though it could not reach his eyes; and the amanuensis could hardly keep pace with the flow of unpremeditated song. One does not wonder at the spring burst; but it seems curious that the quiet, thoughtful days of autumn, which waken many old remembrances in most men, should have so chilled and disheartened the great poet. Many people can say, that there is hardly any influence that so stirs them to vague feelings and impressions which would be poetry in the hands of one who was able to give them expression, as the clear, still air, and the motionless autumn woods in the beautiful autumn sunshine. It is a season in which to recall the days that are gone: and sitting down here, on the steps which lead to this pretty Gothic church, let us think of Sundays long ago. The present writer, for a certain sufficient reason, has this morning been reading over certain pages, bearing truths and counsels which have been addressed to two Christian congregations, one in the country and the other in the town; and altering a word here and there. And in reading some of these pages, how strangely there comes back the feeling of the old quiet Sundays, far away! And the season has decided what kind of Sunday shall come most plainly back. It is the autumn Sunday, with its morning stillness: with the clear hills round: with the bright dew on the grass: with the yellow fields bounded by the green hedgerows: with the river murmuring by, under the gray churchyard wall: with the aged oaks round the little church just touched into greater beauty by the slight morning frosts: with an influence in the air that seems to brace up mind and body together: with the quiet country people sitting on the gravestones before service, resting after their miles of walking over the crisp rustling leaves. Turning a new leaf in life, my reader, you know how misty your former mode of living soon grows in your remembrance: it is only now and then that the old time comes over you; and you seem to breathe the air and to be surrounded by the little cares and interests of those departed days. And even when these come back most vividly, they serve only to make you feel the more deeply how completely the old days are gone.

I suppose that almost everybody feels that the Sundays of life are much better remembered than the series of any ordinary week-day. Sunday has always a character of its own: whereas Tuesday in one week need not be the least like Tuesday in the next week, in occupation, in scene, in feeling. Nobody can speak of the character of the Tuesdays in his history. A number of Sundays is like a flock of sheep, all very much like one another. A number of Tuesdays is like a drove of animals of the most varied aspect: as, for example, pigs, dogs, horses, lions, whales, giraffes, and peacocks. They form a heterogeneous mass. The peculiar kind of atmosphere that breathes from the Sundays of childhood, depends entirely on the bringing-up you have passed through. But most men, looking back upon the Sundays of childhood, are aware of a very decided character that invests them. The character may be pleasant, or it may be painful: but it is there, and you feel it strongly. Would that all parents were so kind and so judicious, as to have the will and way to make Sunday the day on which their children shall always look back as the happiest of all days! It can be done, very easily: and I believe that in these more enlightened times, it is very generally done. Let it be the day of little indulgences; which are very great in the judgment of the little men and women. I am well aware that many people in England entertain a most grim and repulsive idea of a Scotch Sunday. One of the present writer's most valued and revered friends says, on a page which has been read by scores of thousands, "In those fortunate regions they have not learned to make a ghastly idol of the Sunday." It does not matter where those regions are: but of course Scotland is the country aimed at by innuendo. No doubt, there are people in Scotland who make the Lord's day a ghastly idol: who compel their children to sit in church for three or four hours at a stretch, listening to two tremendously long sermons preached at the same service, in which Christianity is reduced to a system of the dryest metaphysics: and who, on returning home, devote the entire evening to questioning the poor little things upon the *Shorter Catechism.* That Catechism is a very admirable one: but one may easily have too much of even the best things: and the peculiar system which has been described, generally results in making the children hate both the Catechism and the Lord's-day as long as they live. And I have heard of a man who said that when he looked at a certain green expanse, on which on Sunday afternoon you might see many people quietly and decorously walking, before returning home from church, he was always reminded of Sodom and Gomorrah, and expected to see fire from heaven come down to destroy the wicked race. You have heard, too, of the Highland elder who spoke of the awful sight which may be beheld on a Sunday at Edinburgh. There, he said, you might see people walking along the street, smiling AS IF THEY WERE PERFECTLY HAPPY! But there are multitudes of men and women in Scotland who could tell you, that their Sundays, in childhood and manhood, have been the happiest days of their life; restful, thoughtful, cheerful days of elevation above the little cares and worries of week-days, when care and worry come: kept sacred, as far as may be, from the intrusion of these: and spent as in a purer air. You remember, my friend, how you used to think that all nature looked quieter and sweeter upon the day of rest: you remember the sunshiny evenings, so calm and bright: you could not wish, in this world, for anything happier or better! They are gone, indeed: and some who spent them with you are no longer here: but you may humbly trust that all that was good and happy about them will come back again.

But Sunday is especially interesting to the preacher. It is his most important day. And his work is a very solemn and anxious one; particularly in Scotland, where the clergyman feels that the entire service depends so much upon himself. The profit and comfort of the congregation, from the worship of that day, are too dependent, you know, upon your clearness of head and devotion of heart. But the preacher's work is always a solemn and weighty one: whether he walk in, one of four or five clergymen, surpliced, stoled, and hooded, following a procession of surpliced choristers, while the solemn tones of the organ peal through the long-drawn cathedral vault; or enter a little Scotch country-church, homely as homely may be, a solitary minister arrayed in robes of sober black, to do the whole duty of the day. For several Sundays past, the writer has been far away from his parish; and has gone to church daily with no feeling of responsibility for the conduct of the service. With what a different feeling one goes! However much you may love and enjoy your work, my friend, I am sure it is both pleasant and profitable for you now and then to go to a strange church merely as a worshipper, and to join in the service with unanxious quiet. It is a delightful rest and relief. If you hear a very poor sermon (which I am bound to say I hardly ever do, anywhere), you may be aware of some wish, or even longing in your heart, to be allowed to say a few sentences of comfort or warning to your fellow-Christians: you may vainly fancy you could give a better discourse; which in all probability is a fond delusion. But as for you, my reader, who never have to preach at all, you go to church on Sunday: you are there an hour and a half, or a few minutes more: all this is a little part of the week to you: it is but an incident in the week, though perhaps an important one: and as for the sermon, it is just half an hour's occupation to listen to it, which you do sometimes with interest, oftentimes with patience. But think how different a thing that sermon is to the preacher. I mean, to the preacher who is preaching in his own church on an ordinary Sunday. To him, if his heart be in his work, and if he be doing his duty, not merely to get through it decently, but to the best of his ability, that discourse is the culmination of all the week. His best thoughts for the entire week past have probably been running on that discourse which to you is just the occupation of half an hour. He fixed on that text, very likely, last Sunday evening, after considerable perplexity. Then he sketched out the sermon: and by day and night, its subject was always simmering in his mind. It cost many hours, possibly on three or four days, of steady work at his writing-table, to cover those pages which you see him turn over, one in every minute or two. And then, perhaps, he spent many hours more of toilsome drudgery, in committing all that material to memory, so as to give it without the aid of that *paper* which is the abhorrence of uneducated and stupid folk in many Scotch parishes. I have heard of good Scotch ministers, on approaching whose manse on a Saturday, you might hear a sound of howling, and of an occasional stamp on the floor. These noises signified that the minister was getting his sermon by heart; which in Scotch phrase used to be called *mandating* it: and that he was repeating it over in the fashion in which he intended to preach it from his pulpit. And no doubt, if the work of *mandating* was done so thoroughly, that the sermon could be given without a painful effort of memory, and a nervous fear of breaking down, the sermon gained greatly in its effect when preached. You had the accuracy of language and the deliberation of thought which can hardly be counted on in extempore speaking: with something of the fire and spontaneity of extempore speaking added to these. And I cannot admit that it is a mere vulgar prejudice, to prefer that a man in speaking to you should look at you, and seem to be addressing you, rather than that he should look at a written page, and read at you, or read in your hearing. But in many cases in which a sermon is committed to memory, and repeated without the aid of the document, you can see that the preacher is painfully reading from his memory: and that a very little thing would put him out, and cause him to break down entirely. And I can quite imagine that a man who could speak extempore with sufficient fluency if he had made up his mind to do so, might flounder and stop if suddenly cast upon his extempore resources by his memory failing him in repeating a written discourse. A good swimmer has been drowned when he has unexpectedly fallen into deep water. And considering the facts, that with most preachers, the sermon gained nothing in effect by being repeated and not read: and that the weekly labor of memorizing one sermon, and much more two, was the most irksome and depressing conceivable: we may rejoice that even in Scotland, the fashion of repeating sermons from memory is all but extinct. And in the most retired country parishes, where once upon a time many of the congregation would have risen in wrath and quitted the church had the preacher begun to read his sermon, you will find the rustics listening with the most decorous attention to a preacher who turns over his leaf at minute intervals. And no preacher now makes any secret that he reads: while I can remember, as a boy, the hasty and surreptitious fashion in which the leaf used to be turned over. You may imagine what a fearful mental burden a Scotch minister in old days had to bear, when he walked down to church with two long sermons in his memory. And any one who knows Scotland, must be aware of the great number of amusing stories current among high and low, turning upon the inveterate dislike to *the paper*, and the desperate and not always successful efforts of preachers to do without the forbidden aid. You are to understand, my English friend, that the reading of sermons was never forbidden by any law of the Church; but merely by popular dislike to it. A faithful clergyman, aware that to read his sermons would greatly diminish the good they would do his parishioners, would feel it a sacred duty to give in to a prejudice which he heartily disapproved. But even when a clergyman is free from the painful pressure of a sermon memorized to its every word and point: even when the fairly-written pages lie before him; we have all seen plainly with what nervous strain and anxiety the very greatest preachers begin their solemn and responsible work. And as for the ordinary run of men of fair ability, of whom their congregations expect less: the strain, my reader, is quite as great upon their moderate powers. And after all the labor of preparation, and the anxiety of the time of preaching, the hearer very likely thinks the sermon not very good after all. Depend upon it, my friend, the preacher feels *that* at least as much as you.

I have remarked that several preachers of great eminence are quite cool and unembarrassed before beginning their duty. I have seen such talking away on indifferent subjects in the vestry till the moment they ascended the pulpit; yet able instantly to call up the right feeling which becomes the solemn occasion, and to give very admirable sermons. I have heard one very distinguished man, of that happy equanimity of temper, declare that he could not understand it as possible that a preacher, in giving the same sermon on two different occasions, should give it on one occasion with great feeling, and on the other with very little. He said that surely any man might at any time express the same thoughts with equal perception of their force. Happy man! Many clergymen know that the self-same words are felt, and tell, very differently at different times. I have heard a great orator give a discourse, with a manifest effort, a painful and unsuccessful effort, to call up the corresponding feeling. The orator was at the moment quite out of sympathy with the mood in which what he had to say had been written. And such persons as have passed through this experience, I have remarked as specially nervous and anxious before their work. They know that though they have done their very best at home, many little things, physical and mental, may prevent their giving their sermon with comfort and effect. I am not going to mention names; but I can say that I have had opportunities of observing this in the case of several of the most eminent preachers both in Scotland and England. I have heard a very distinguished preacher say that he would think no reward too great for the man who would tell him how to come up to his work on Sunday in perfect condition for it. Body and mind should be at their best. And to secure any approximation to such an end, many things, little and great, must be attended to.

All past things, of course, are past; but one cannot but think how thoroughly past are the services and the exhortations of Sundays long ago. One has thought of this, going to hear a great pulpit orator. There is the church; the dense crowd of worshippers, or at least of hearers; the beautiful music; the audible stillness in which the telling voice poured forth its sentences of warning and comfort. But it is all over. There is the sigh of relief at the close, as if people had not had a full breath for many minutes past; and then the great tide of life ebbs away. And there is nothing to show for it all; nothing to be easily traced by sense. Robert Stephenson is dead, but there is the Menai Bridge; Brunel is gone, but there is the Saltash Viaduct and the *Great Eastern*. But now Chalmers is silent, a fading impression in many memories is all that remains; and in a few years, when all who listened to him are dead, it will be impossible rightly to understand what he was. It will be impossible to recall the almost awful impression of the moments in which you heard him: and in which you thought to yourself, that never before could you have believed that human words could have so thrilled through you and swept you away. Yet, there are enthusiastic recorders of all that. I have seen men, not easily roused to enthusiasm, warm into an unwonted glow of admiration and affection, in telling of that simplest-minded and noblest-hearted of great and good men. But the thing they always insisted on was, how vain it was by any description to make you understand the reality. You may go and visit the plain church where he preached: but his burning words have left no echo there. You may read the sermons in print; but to do that gives you no idea whatever of what they were when said by him. He could not publish that fire of manner, which made single words, and bits of sentences, tingle through you, which when you afterwards coolly looked back on them, seemed nothing particular. It seems to me, there is no more incommunicable gift of genius. An ordinary man may make a deep impression by saying something which is very fine and impressive; but he must have the divine gift who makes you start on your feet by saying *Mesopotamia;* or, *That is not true;* or who moves a crowd of thousands to tears by saying, *He did it, because Providence was kind to him.* Speaking of Chalmers, one is taking the extremest case; but it comes almost as touchingly home to one, to think how the thoughts and exhortations of ordinary men pass into entire oblivion. I once saw a great mass of old faded sermons of a good clergyman who was dead.

They were lying on the floor of an empty room in a house to let. I have little doubt they were ultimately used for lighting fires. You could not but think what a great amount of labor had gone to producing those neglected manuscripts. The good man who wrote them had for many years held the charge of a considerable country parish. You could not but think how the words written there, heartily spoken on Sundays in church, might be remaining (some of them) in the memory of a generation of rustics who had grown up under that instruction, and who had doubtless heard all the sermons several times preached. And in that case you might hope and believe that the exhortations remained not merely in the memory, but (better still) in the lives of the people of that quiet parish. You could not but think of a bright summer morning, when the people came along leafy ways, and listened (a little drowsily) to that faded sermon which, as you may see, was preached on the 24th of June, 1817. You thought of a clear frosty winter day, bracing and cheering, on which that other sermon did duty; which bears to have been given on a certain 24th of December. But our calculations are usually wrong; and it is probable that the June Sunday was cold and rainy, and that the Christmas time was a damp and green one. But how little trace remains of many things? All the work of preparing that sermon, and committing it to memory; all the anxiety of the Sunday morning; all the hearty tones in which it was given; all the warmth of heart it awakened in the people who listened to it; all the volume of simple but telling praise that preceded and followed it; have left no more trace than that inscription of *June 24th*, 1817. I see the people walking away home, by the various paths which lead from the church-door; I imagine how the poor little children in many homes were required to give some account of the sermon, and could not do it; I think of the good old clergyman going home from church, and having a quiet turn in his garden; and of the sun going down over each dwelling in the pastoral district which I can see; and here is what stands for all that: in faded ink, the date I have already told you. And when a clergyman who is still living and preaching turns over his stock of sermons, and looks at the inscription at the end of each, which states the churches and the dates at which each was given, he cannot but feel how little vestige remains of the circumstances in which it was preached, and of the impression made by it. There is nothing more completely forgot than the average Sunday sermon of even a very good preacher.

But a happy result follows. The preacher can use his discourses, even in the same church, a good many times over. In about four or five years, all remembrance of a sermon is gone, unless perhaps of its text, and of some odd sentence here and there. I have heard of a very excellent clergyman, who had charge of the same church for thirty years. His stock of sermons lasted just three years: so in that period each was preached ten times. Yet the people did not grumble: probably did not know. Here is an advantage which the preacher has over other producers and salesmen of thought. A man who writes leading articles for newspapers, or tales or essays for periodicals, must always go on, producing what purports to be new. He cannot republish an old article word for word, as the preacher can reproduce an old sermon. No doubt, literary men do reproduce themselves: it is the old material slightly rearranged and touched up: but it is their readers who feel this as an imposition and infliction; not the literary men who feel it as a relief. They fancy they are producing something new: there is all the effort of fresh production. The reader feels it is the old thing, but not so good. At least, it is not so fresh. It seems but a faint echo of the old days. But the preacher, after a suitable time is gone, takes out the old sermon, and preaches it exactly as it is. And if the sermon be fairly good, those who remember something of its tone, are quite pleased to hear it again. The person who likes it least, is probably the preacher himself: if his mind and experience be still growing. He feels he has got beyond it; and grown out of sympathy with it. And even besides this, he is aware of many defects and flaws. You look with great favor at a composition fresh from your mind: but after the lapse of years, you regard it much more coolly and more justly.

In the pages which follow, my friend, you will find certain of the graver thoughts of a writer whose lighter ones have been received by very many readers with a favor much beyond their desert. You will find some portion of the material to which the writer's best pains have been given, on many forenoons and many evenings in country and in town: which has been carried to church on Sundays in his pocket; and which has been spoken from the pulpit to the congregations given to his care. Many of these words have been said to a little handful of kindly country-people: and all of them to a large congregation of educated folk in a great city. It has been the writer's desire to make those who listened to him feel that religion is a real thing, with the most practical bearing on all the interests of life; and not a thing quite beside and beyond our daily experience. He has aimed at simplicity and clearness; and at that reality which comes of the preacher's saying what he has actually known and felt, and not merely what he thinks he *must* say. And he wishes for nothing better in this life, than to continue to set forth the blessed gospel of Christ, ever more simply and sincerely.

II.

HOW GOD FEELS TOWARDS MANKIND.

"If ye then, being evil, know how to give good gifts unto your children, how much more shall your Father which is in heaven give good things to them that ask him?" — St Matt. vii. 11.

I BELIEVE that one of the first and most important things that mortal man can do; I believe that the very first and most important of all things, for our spiritual welfare; is that we should get and keep just and right views of God. Many human beings, I say not only in heathen lands, where men have set up and worshipped as divine, stocks of wood, and images of stone, and fancied beings invested with every attribute of monstrous cruelty and foulness, — not only *there*, but even in this country of Christian light, — live under entire delusion as to what God is, and as to how God feels towards us His poor sinful creatures, — delusion which affects all their views, all their conduct, all their life. There is nothing whatsoever, which man can ever think or ever do, which will not be influenced, more or less, by the thought and the belief he has in his heart concerning Almighty God. Oh, then, how precious an attainment, how great a blessing it will be, if we are enabled, by the light of God's Word, and by the teaching of His Spirit, savingly to know God; to discern Him rightly; and (so far as may be here, where we see so dimly and darkly) to see Him as He is!

Now, here, in our text, we have words of authority concerning God. We might have doubted them, if we had heard them spoken by man: we cannot doubt them now. *He* said them, who spake as never man spake. *He* spake them, who could speak with undoubting authority of God, forasmuch as He himself was God. And you see the great principle which is involved in these words. The principle involved is *this:* that the way to judge of God, and of God's feelings towards us, and of what God will do for us, is to look at the best, and purest, and kindest feelings of human nature; and to think that God is like all *that:* only that He is infinitely purer, kinder, and better. *That* is the way to arrive at some faint notion of what God is, and of how God feels.

We are made in God's image, after His likeness. No doubt, the image is defiled and ruined: yet there are traces of the great, pure, happy original state. It is only because there is something in us, something in our spiritual nature, which resembles God, that we are able to form any conception of Him and His character. But for this, we could no more conceive of God's attributes, than a blind man, who never saw, can conceive of color. Of course, we are fallen creatures; and our blurred and blotted qualities bear only the faintest and farthest likeness to that Divine image in which we were made. Speaking as men speak, we may say that there are feelings which are unquestionably good in human nature; but we know that tried by the standard of perfect purity, the very best has some alloy, some lack, some flaw. And it is in these that something of God's likeness lingers: it is from these distant hints and indications of what God is like, that the Saviour would have us learn what God is.

And thus, in our text, Christ tells us what we are to expect of God, in His treatment of us. There is mystery about God's nature: we cannot fathom it: and we bow humbly before Him, taking up the prophet's words, "Verily thou art a God that hidest Thyself." And as God is thus mysterious, our kind Redeemer takes something that all men will know. He appeals to feelings which are lacking in very few human hearts. He goes to the love and care of parents for their child: something which is there, even in the most wretched and the worst. It is rightly thought one of the saddest and most miserable sights to be seen in this sorrowful world, — something indicating the loss of all that stamps a being as human, — the unnatural heartless wretch that does not care for his child: God be thanked that such heartless wretches are few, even among the most degraded of the race!

Now, says the Blessed Redeemer, speaking to you, and me, and all: If you want to know how God feels towards you, and how ready God is to give you everything that is really good; here is something to go by. You know how much you would do for your children: you know how anxious you are to care for them in every way. You know how a father will work, and how a mother will watch, all for the good of their little ones. You know how much of the work that is done by men in this world, and how much of the care that is felt, is not for themselves at all, but for their children: all for them. After the dream of fame is past, — after ambition is outgrown, — the man toils on as steadfastly and earnestly as in his most hopeful and most aspiring days,—that he may provide for his little ones; that he may see them in comfort and happiness; that he may push them on (as he trusts and prays) to be far better and happier than ever he was himself. The human heart is always the same: you do *that* now, my friends; and so you may be sure that people did *that* long ago, in the days when Christ was here. Well, says Christ, you know all *that*. You know all *that*, says His blessed voice: and now hear me and believe me when I tell you, that the great Father above is just like *that;* only a thousand-fold better. If even you, sinful and evil, would wear your fingers to the bone, would lose your rest, would cut off every selfish indulgence, that you might see your children's wants supplied, that you might see the little things happy and good,—then take this blessed truth to your heart, that in all you feel towards your children, you have a faint and far reflection of how the great God above us feels towards you. He feels for us just like *that:* cares for us, loves us, wishes us well, works for us. And if you know that when your poor little boy or girl comes to you, and asks you for something that is needful and right, they will not ask in vain; then be sure that when we go, with our feeble words and our many sins, and ask what we need from God, he is as ready to bend down from the throne of the universe, as with a smile on his kind face, and listen to our imperfect petitions, and help them out, and give us in answer all that is right for us, thoughtfully and graciously. And hear me when I tell you, my Christian friends, that even such is the picture we should have in our minds of the Christian's God! Not the grim tyrant, not the mere rigorous and inflexible punisher, that some misguided and gloomy religionists worship, and terrify their children with; not a being all severity and wrath and cursing and woe; not a being hard and cold as granite; not a being that damns little children that never sinned, and then asks us to thank him for doing it; not a being that made millions for sin and misery, and looks on in gloomy satisfaction as his poor creatures are consigned to hell, all for his glory. Call that black vision, conjured up by heartless and soulless logicians, as though they longed to drive man away from his Maker, — call it Moloch, or Juggernaut, if you will; but never dream that in *that* you see the Christian's God, — the God revealed to our love and hope in the blessed gospel of Jesus Christ! No; our God is one who, while hating the sin, pities and loves the sinner; one who wills not that *any* should perish; one who made a real sacrifice, the greatest, by sending his Son to die that we might live; one who would that his glory should be vindicated by our bliss and salvation; who "sent his Son into the world, that whosoever believeth in him might not perish, but have everlasting life;" who entreats us to come to him and trust him and believe that he loves us; who has manifested himself to us in no grim face, and in no cruel judge, but in the kindest heart that ever beat, and the kindest face this world ever saw; or where can we find a better and happier way of saying the truth than our Saviour's own way, — a kind Father listening to our prayers, with patience and love and care of which our best feelings are but the feeble reflection: "If ye, being evil, know how to give good gifts unto your children, how much more," — oh, listen to it, — "how *much more*, shall your Father which is in heaven give good things to them that ask him!"

If St. Paul had told me *that*, I should not have dared to believe it. If the greatest and most inspired of mere mortals had told me that, I should have said that *that* was too simple, kindly, and homely, to be a fair statement of the truth concerning the Infinite God. If any other had told you, that the way to know how God feels towards you, is to look into your own heart, and thinking how you feel, when at your best, towards your little child; you could not have taken it in. But you know Who said it. One, from whose lips you would believe anything; One, whose lips beseemed the best and most hopeful words; One, who knew God best, and what God is, seeing he is one with him; yea, One in whose face we see the invisible God. "The only-begotten Son, which is in the bosom of the Father, he hath declared him,"—and never in words more precious, or that come straighter to our hearts, than here.

And so, my friends, God feels towards each of us as a kind and wise father feels towards his child; and the difference is just this: that God, our Father in heaven, is infinitely better than the very best earthly father. And now that I have shown you the great and blessed truth which is taught us by the text, on the first glance at it, let us turn our thoughts to the further truth, that is brought out by the words in the text, "how much more;" the truth that God differs from an earthly father by being far kinder, wiser, and better. O brethren, there is an immense deal suggested by that "how much more!" It would be an unspeakable comfort to us, it would be a glorious and comfortable truth, that God was just as willing to give us all we need, as you kind-hearted people are to give what is needful to your little child. I think I know men and women who have hearts so good and kind; who are so ready to do what they can to make their own children happy, or to add to the happiness of any little child; that I should feel safe enough and sure enough in going, sinful, weary, to Almighty God, to ask for his mercy and his Blessed Spirit, even if I knew no more than this, that I should find such a welcome at his throne of grace as these good men and women would give to any suffering, helpless child, even if it were not their own. But "how much more!" What a silent reference to an inconceivable depth of love and pity in the heart of God! It is as if Christ had said to those whom he addressed, *You* cannot understand the difference; words cannot explain the difference; here is the kind of thing, in yourselves; but in God "how much more!" Yet not a different kind of thing; the same kind of feeling you bear towards your children, only heightened up to a pitch you can never know. And then, what a silent suggestion in the hint of what we are, even at our very best: "If ye, being evil;" *that* is what we are at our very best, in the sight of God. The man who bears on his kind face the unmistakable signs of the kind heart within, that make little children (those unerring physiognomists) hail him on short acquaintance as a congenial friend, — that kind good man, after all, is nothing better than *evil* in the pure sight of God. Far kinder, purer, wiser, better, is the care for all his children which dwells with the great Father of all. How inconceivably better is God than man at his very best! You, being evil, will do a great deal for your children; but God, "how much more!"

And so you see, my friends, that it is impossible for us fully to understand all the love of God for us; its essential depth and excellence are beyond our comprehension. But though Christ's words suggest that it is impossible for us to fathom the essential depth of our heavenly Father's love, still it may be comforting and profitable to think for a little of certain respects in which even we can understand how much better a father God is, than any earthly father can ever be.

And these points of superiority are so plain and simple, that they need very little illustration. For one thing, God knows what is good for us, as no human parent can know what is good for his child. Although no human parent, with a parent's heart, would give his child a stone for bread, or a serpent for a fish, many a human parent has done, and will do again, what really comes to *that*. With the kindest intentions, we all know how injudicious parents often are; how often they err on the side of over-severity or of over-tenderness; how completely they sometimes mistake what is to conduce to the true good or happiness of their children;—indeed, it is not too much to say that a very great proportion of all the sorrow that is in this world arises from the mismanagement of parents in youth, or from the consequences of that mismanagement in after-years. Now God knows us; knows what we are, and what we can do; knows what we are fit for, and how things affect us; knows all our peculiarities of temperament and disposition. He knows what we really need; he knows when to give us what we wish, and when to deny it; he knows how to make "all things work together for good" to such as love him. There is no caprice with him, no fretfulness, no passion. He never punishes merely because he is angry. Nor does he refrain from sending punishment when needful because he shrinks from giving pain. In short, he knows best what is good for us; and he has firmness to send us just *that.*

Another point in which appears the superiority of the great Father to whom Christ points us above all earthly parents, is his power. He is able to do all he wishes. He has all power to give us all good things; to help and save. You know how different it is with us; how well we often know what we should like to do for our children, to make them wise and good and happy; yet how very little we can do. When the ruler's little child was dying, what could he do but turn his back upon the house where was the darkened room and the little bed and the white little face laid upon the pillow and the cold lips laboring with the rapid breath,— turn his back upon all these,

— because *he* could do nothing to help, and hasten away along the lake side, — going in his despair to just the very best place where any of us can ever go, — going to the presence of our beloved Saviour, and saying, "Lord, come down ere my child die!" But, O brethren, think what a glorious combination: the kind Father's heart and the almighty God's power! Oh, how bright and happy and Christian a future would the wise and good among you picture out for your children, if you had the power to make them as good and happy as you could wish! But with human beings it is a commonplace ten thousand times repeated, how far apart are will and power. You have heard of the poor mother with her infant, who perished in a snow-storm crossing the hills on a wild winter night; there, in the dark night, and amid the waste wilderness, the mother died. They found her in the morning, cold and dead; but the little child was alive and well; for the poor mother had spent her last strength in stripping the clothing from her own stiffening frame and wrapping it about her child and clasping the little bundle to her breast. Ah, brethren, that tight clasp of the dead arms, and those poor garments, so carefully wrapped, — surely they spake from the world beyond the grave, and told the last care in the dying mother's heart; and told how her last thoughts had been with the unconscious little one that never would remember or miss her! Now *there* is the type of God's love; not more tenderly did the dying woman yearn over the little thing that must go through life and she far away than does God over each sinful soul in this place; and the grand difference lies in this, that our heavenly Father has infinite power to do all we ask or need!

Then God is always kind. There are unnatural parents — let us hope, very few. There are people who repel their children's confidence; who from mistaken principle or from a bad heart do all they can to make their children miserable; who point out with pride in the misery of a child, that things have come just as they said they would; who so act as to make us wonder that a trace of natural affection should be left in their children's hearts. I shall not dwell on a subject so miserable, save to remind you that our heavenly Father has anticipated such a case: "Can a woman forget her sucking child, that she should not have compassion on the son of her womb? Yea, they may forget, yet will I not forget thee."

And now the last matter I shall name, as to which our heavenly Father excels the best earthly one, is that he is always near. Earthly parents may be far away, just when they are needed most; there is many a father, away on Indian plains, thinking day and night of his children here; and thinking how he is losing their society just at the most interesting season of their life, — losing the years that change them from boys and girls into men and women, — losing those impressionable days, in which the soul is taking the character it is likely to keep forever. And earthly parents must often leave their children orphans; must leave the little thing, so pleasing and happy now, not knowing what things may befall it, — not knowing how years in this world, without a parent's care and love, may change that fresh young heart, and make the soul such that in the better world they may never meet again. You know, my friends, that with worthy people, it is not very long till the chief interest of life comes to be about their children, and about how it is to fare with *them.* Oh, I can well think that when the shadows steal from the sight this world and all its concerns; when the glazing eye of death can no longer see the faces round the bed; the sorest thought in many a parent's heart, is of how his poor little children are to fare when he is gone. The very bitterness of death to many a heart is in the words, "My little child, I must leave you! And who will care for you when I am far away?" The kindest earthly parent that ever lived cannot help or guide his little ones from the farther shore. They may go to his grave with their story of grief; but they might as well tell it to the winds. But, O brethren, our heavenly Father is always near! Always within hearing; always within reach; never leaving, never forsaking; Father of the fatherless, Friend of the friendless; yea, "When father and mother forsake me, then the Lord will take me up!" O Father of mercies, remember *this* word unto Thy servants, upon which Thou hast caused us to hope!

Thus kindly and graciously, my friends, does our Father which is in heaven give good things to them that ask him. Yes; and to them that do not ask, save by their needs. The good earthly father does not give good things only to those among his children who are able to ask; the mother's heart never warms more tenderly to any than to the little thing that cannot speak at all, — that cannot ask for anything, — most touching in its helplessness, and its incapacity to say or even to know what it needs. And even so with the better Parent above. He hears the voice of our wants; he gives us many a blessing that we have not the sense to ask for. Yea, when our race was asking nothing, and knowing nothing of its deepest wants, he gave us the best of all good gifts, — he gave us the Blessed Saviour and the Blessed Spirit! And well for us, my friends, that God did not wait to be asked; well for us that he supplied great wants of which we did not know; well for us that he treated us as the thoughtful mother does the little infant that cannot tell its needs; for true, as beautiful, are the words of the poet: —

> "So runs my dream; but what am I?
> An infant crying in the night, —
> An infant crying for the light, —
> And with no language but a cry."

There was a man who once said, that he was the best-abused man in Britain. I believe we may say, much more truly, that the most misrepresented and misconceived of all beings is Almighty God. You know that every syllable I have said of him has its warrant in his own Word. You know that the only right manifestation of him to our weak minds is in the face of his dear Son, our blessed and beloved Redeemer. And yet you know how many people think of God mainly as a grim punisher, mainly as the keeper of the dark prison-house below. I lately read, with extreme disgust and abhorrence, a book intended for little children, in which a mother was represented as asking her child, "What does God do for little children?" and the answer put in the child's mouth was, "God sends bad little children to hell." Think of *that* given as a fair account of God's character! It is as if a man, being asked, "What does the sun do for mankind?" were to answer, "Oh, he gives people sun-stroke and makes them drop down dead;" but not a word of his cheerful light and genial warmth, guiding the steps, ripening the grain, gladdening the heart! Oh, God does punish, but sorely against his will! He does not want to be glorified in the sinner's destruction; — he may be driven to *that* at the last; — but he wants to be glorified in the sinner's complete salvation. Hear his own words, as he pleads with his rebellious children: "Fury is not in me; who would set the briers and thorns against me in battle? I would go through them, I would burn them together. But let him take hold of my strength, that he may make peace with me, and he shall make peace with me!" The day may come, my friends, when that will not be so; but on this day of grace hear me when I tell you, that our God's right name is, "The Lord God merciful and gracious, forgiving iniquity, transgression, and sin!" It was because he loved us that he sent our Saviour to die for us; because God loved us, that our Saviour died. And freely and fully, through him, we can offer this day to all who will but receive them pardoning mercy and sanctifying grace. Let us all believe and live; God wills not that one should perish! And as I tell you these things, my friends, I come back ever to the blessed truth, whose preciousness and sublimity admit of no addition, that the self-same love which dwells in your heart, as you look on the rosy little face of your child, dwells in our Father's heart above, as he looks down upon us sinners; that he rejoices to give good things to them that ask him; and that when we go to ask the best thing, the good part in Christ, we may be as sure that he will give it us, as the child that runs confidently to a mother's arms can be of a mother's care. Surely there is not one among us who would not trust and love this God! Surely there is not one who will not join in the prayer, Our Father, keep us through life, thy poor wandering children; wash us in our Elder Brother's blood; and bring us to thy Home!

III.

THE THORN IN THE FLESH.

"And lest I should be exalted above measure through the abundance of the revelations, there was given to me a thorn in the flesh, the messenger of Satan to buffet me, lest I should be exalted above measure. For this thing I besought the Lord thrice, that it might depart from me. And he said unto me, My grace is sufficient for thee: for my strength is made perfect in weakness. Most gladly therefore will I rather glory in my infirmities, that the power of Christ may rest upon me." — 2 Cor. xii. 7–9.

I DO not know where we shall find words more touching, more comforting, more saturated with the deepest wisdom, more filled with the true spirit that should abide in the true Christian, than these words which you have read. They are touching words. I have no doubt at all but it cost St. Paul an effort to write them. You can see it was a sore subject about which he was to tell. Not often, I dare say, even to his nearest friends, would the great apostle speak of that heavy burden, of that sore infirmity, so humiliating in its nature, and so sure to last as long as he lasted, which he names as his "thorn in the flesh." And we seem to know him better, we seem to get at his inmost thought and heart in a way we seldom elsewhere do; when the good man thus takes us into his confidence, and speaks less like an authoritative and inspired apostle than like a tried and suffering man: frankly and fully telling us all about something to which *we* should not have liked to allude in talking to him; frankly and fully telling us about something he had to bear which was painful and humbling; frankly telling us how much he needed it, yet how earnestly he wished to escape it; thankfully telling us how God told him he must bear it to the end, but that the grace would never be wanting that would enable him to bear it rightly; and then humbly yet resolutely stating the determination to which he had come at last, of entire submission to his wise and kind Master's will. Yes, when St. Paul speaks to us in this brotherly manner, we feel a sympathy and a brotherhood with him which we cannot always feel with one so far above us and beyond us in all the graces of the spiritual life; and I think we could clasp the trembling hand of that greatest apostle, and tell him how well we understand him here; tell him that we too have our burdens, sore and crushing; that we too have our infirmities, of which it is painful to speak; that we too have had our disappointments; that we too have thrice and oftener than thrice besought God to do for us *that* which in his wisdom he saw it meet not to do; and then humbly pray, and ask him to pray with us, that the same needful grace may be vouchsafed while the trial lasts; and that in the end it may all prove to our true good and to our blessed Saviour's glory!

It seems to be God's way, and we may humbly and firmly believe a kind and good way, to give his creatures heavy burdens to bear; to make all, so to speak, carry weight in the race of life; and work and fight at a certain disadvantage. There is some little thing about every one which holds him back from being a far better, happier, and more successful man, than now he will ever be. There is something in our nature, something in our circumstances, which is as the additional pounds laid on a race-horse's back, preventing his doing his very best; greatly abating the visible results of his strength and speed. Now St. Paul had his drag-weight, we see; something that took him down and held him down; something that caused him suffering; something he would have given much to be without. You know, I doubt not, that much industry and ingenuity have been spent, to very little practical purpose, in trying to settle what St. Paul's thorn in the flesh was. It does not matter at all what was the precise nature of that trial. It may be stated, however, that the usual belief at present is, that the overpowering impression made upon him by that mysterious rapture, when he was caught up into Paradise, and heard unspeakable words, had so affected the system of his nerves as to leave a permanent infirmity; affecting, as we gather from various allusions in his epistles, his sight, his speech, and his hands. You remember how he could not write his own epistles, save a few tremulous lines at the end; you remember how kindly he spoke of those who did not despise his "temptation which was in his flesh;" and who listened with respect to one whose "bodily presence was weak, and his speech contemptible;" to one who in his worn features and his emaciated frame, was "always bearing about in the body the dying of the Lord Jesus." The material thing for us to bear in mind is just this: that St. Paul had to bear something humiliating and painful; painful as a sharp thorn ever pressing deeper into the quick flesh.

I need not say to you, my friend, that it is not merely to observe what the apostle did with his special cross, — how he felt towards it, and how he bore it, — that I have turned your thoughts to this subject. It is because all this is a matter of such deep personal concern to ourselves. It is because in all this we are not looking at St. Paul the apostle and the worker of miracles, doing things the like of which we could never do; but at St. Paul the suffering man, bearing his burden as we might ours, and feeling and acting under it as we might act and feel. It is because each human being has his own cross to bear; and because we ought to do with ours just what St. Paul did with his, — find out (that is) what God is seeking to teach us by it, and understand the way in which God may very likely deal with us as concerns the bearing of it. And thus applying the subject to ourselves, I take a large view of St. Paul's thorn in the flesh; I look at it, not in its specific and peculiar nature, but just as a great trial laid upon him for a certain end, and to be borne in a certain way. I take the thorn in the flesh as a type of any great trial which is daily pressing upon any one who shall read this page; bodily pain, perhaps, in some; disappointed hopes and ambitions, perhaps, in others; separation from dear friends, it may be, or their loss by death; the frustration of some cherished plan on which we have set our heart; domestic jars and discomforts, perhaps, with some; poverty and privations; heavy cares and anxieties as to the means of life, and the like; in short, by the thorn in the flesh I mean each man's especial trial and sorrow, — the thing which mainly detracts from the happiness of his life, — the thing as to which he would be ready to say, Oh, if *that* trouble were only gone, — if I were but delivered from *that*, it would be well with me. That is your thorn in the flesh, my friend; the thing you think you would be happy and right, if you could just get rid of. Each human being has his own peculiar thorn, whose painful pressure he himself knows best; many human beings are ready to fancy that they could bear almost anything, better than the particular trial which God has been pleased to send upon them. You will find people who speak as if they fancied that the Almighty knew just the sensitive place where they would feel a blow most keenly; and that his hand fell heavy there. It is just the most cherished hope that is blighted; it is just the thing on which you have set your heart that you are least likely to get. You may get something else; perhaps something better; but not *that.*

Now, my friend, the first lesson which is suggested to us by these words which St. Paul speaks, manifestly speaking from his heart, is this: that the thorn in the flesh comes for a specific end. Of course it does not come by chance; nothing does; it comes by God's appointment or permission. But more than this; God does not send it out of mere wilfulness, or caprice; He sends it for a certain purpose; and a purpose which we may in many cases find out. We cannot always, indeed, discover the design for which God's afflictive dispensations come, of the good that is to come of them. But in many cases we *can* discover all that; and whenever we feel the thorn pierce our flesh, we ought diligently and prayerfully to seek to do so.

Let us look at St. Paul's case. There are many lessons for us in it. Was it not hard that he should be weighted for the race of life with that which took so much from his usefulness and his happiness? It was not merely that the thorn in the flesh caused St. Paul suffering; that would have been a lesser trial to one whose heart was so entirely in his work; if the suffering had been something that made him do his work better, he could have welcomed it all; but the thorn was far worse than that: it was something that took from his usefulness; that faltering speech, those trembling hands, those weak eyes, that contemptible bodily presence,—all these things tended to make him a less successful missionary and apostle; ah, the thorn in the flesh pierced St. Paul just where he would feel it most bitterly! St. Paul did nobly for Christ, as it was; but how much greater and better things he might have done! Take off from him that burden he bore; give him the fluent, fiery words, that would convey the feelings of his burning heart; give him the swift hand that could freely trace upon the written page the message he so yearned to deliver; give him the dignified commanding port that should conciliate the respect and attention of the stranger; curb that hasty temper, that came of his shaken nerves; and who shall reckon how much more might have been done by St. Paul? And I believe that to many an earnest-minded man, the thorn in the flesh, or the crook in the lot, never comes in a form so painful as in the form in which it came to St. Paul; in the form of something that diminishes or destroys his usefulness; that keeps him from serving as he would wish his generation and his Saviour; that constrains noble powers, or the makings of noble powers, to rust sadly and uselessly away. Think of a heart, brimful of the longing to declare to dying sinners the unsearchable riches of Christ; but joined to a feeble, nerveless bodily frame that neutralizes all! Can you imagine a sorer thorn in the flesh? Or think of wonderful gifts of nature and training; cribbed and confined by circumstances to a sphere in which they are turned to no account. Think of Moses, wasting (as human beings would judge) the best years of his life, as a shepherd in the desert of Midian. *There* was the thorn too; piercing, and wearing, through a full third of his life; through forty long years! And yet, hard as the divine appointment appears in Paul's case, it was a divine appointment; it was something which the all-wise God deliberately and advisedly did. And the apostle tells us what the thorn came for; and tells us that he needed it all. It must have been a hard thing for him to say; but here it is. He needed it all, to keep down a strong tendency to self-conceit. Yes; with whatever effort, St. Paul will tell us frankly the unworthy weakness which the thorn in the flesh was sent to cut down. "Lest I should be exalted above measure through the abundance of the revelations, there was given to me a thorn in the flesh, the messenger of Satan to buffet me, lest I should be exalted above measure." The great apostle gives us just one reason why the thorn was sent: it was sent to take him down. There were many things which tended strongly to puff him up; and he had not got over that lingering weakness of humanity, — vanity and self-conceit. He had been especially and wonderfully honored; and all this tended to make him self-confident; to make him think how extraordinary a man he must be, who was thus distinguished above others. He had been early conspicuous for his learning, and for the strictness of his Pharisaic life; he had been especially called to the apostleship by the Saviour himself; he had been remarkable for his usefulness as a preacher of the gospel; doubtless he was held in the highest estimation throughout all the churches he had planted, and by many believers who felt that under God they owed everything to him. And above all these things, the apostle seems to have placed the wonderful revelations that had been especially vouchsafed to himself, which are mentioned in some preceding verses: how he had been, in the body or out of the body, caught up into the third heavens; how he had been caught up into paradise, and there heard unspeakable words, not lawful for a man to utter. And coming back again to this lower world, with these words yet ringing in his ears, and the light of that vision yet as it were in his face, we can well imagine how he might have been disposed to walk apart from his fellow-men, as one favored and honored as very few have been out of all the millions of the race. But then it was that God gave him something which should save him from high-mindedness and self-conceit; for though "the messenger of Satan," it was yet "given" by God; he would not cherish pride above others, when his special glory was known only to himself, and his special infirmity was plain to the eyes of all; and so the thorn in the flesh was given, "lest he should be exalted above measure!"

And so, the thorn in the flesh was sent to St. Paul by God; and sent for a certain specific purpose; and St. Paul knew what that purpose was. Of course St. Paul was an inspired apostle; and he was able to speak with an authority with which we cannot speak, as to the meaning and purpose of the divine dealings. When the thorn pierces *us;* when bodily trouble comes upon us; when sore disappointment is sent to us; when long seasons of anxiety and struggle must be slowly dragged through; when any painful and mortifying thing befalls us; we cannot be so sure as St. Paul was as to the precise end God has in view by all this. And more especially, when these afflictive things befall others; when we see disappointment and sorrow sent to our friends and neighbors; we should be most careful to avoid any such interpretation of these things as is only too common. You will hear some people say of a misfortune or disappointment which has befallen some man, Ah, *that* will take down his self-conceit; he needed it all; it will do him a great deal of good. Indeed I have never witnessed more manifest and disgusting indications of rancorous malignity and a thoroughly bad heart, than in people talking of the misfortunes and trials of their neighbors as providential visitations, and as likely to do their neighbors a great deal of good. I have remarked that people who never rejoice at the blessings of others when these blessings come in a pleasant shape, evince an immense delight at the blessings of others when these blessings come in the painful guise of disappointments and trials. And I shall venture to believe, that the real feeling of these people is one of pure malignity; and that what they rejoice at is not the ultimate good that trials and misfortunes *may* cause their neighbors, but the immediate pain that trials and mortifications are sure to cause. We have all known people who had no greater enjoyment, than to see an acquaintance taken down; the misfortune of a neighbor was a real blessing to these miserable creatures; and I have not the least doubt but that among people who knew St. Paul there would be a man, here and there, envious of the great apostle's gifts and usefulness, who would chuckle over the thorn in the flesh; who in his heart would rejoice at the suffering it caused the apostle; yet who would not venture to express his secret exultation; but would go about saying, "Ah, that Saul of Tarsus needs it all. Very conceited man; do him a great deal of good. It will take him down, teach him sense; and he needs very much to be taught that!" Cannot you imagine, my friend, how the envious, malicious, tattling gossips at Corinth would go about from house to house, saying that kind of thing? Now, my readers, let none of us here give way to this wicked and contemptible fashion of thinking and talking. What we are to do is this: each of us to try to understand the lesson which God is addressing to his own self by the thorns and trials that come; and leave our neighbors to interpret their own thorns and trials. It is beautiful, it is touching, it brings the tear to the eye, to hear St. Paul himself telling all about his thorn in the flesh, and about how much he needed it to keep him down, and about how humbly he desired to submit to God's heavy hand. But think how differently we should have felt, if anybody else had said the very same things about Paul; how different a thing it would have been, if Paul had told us about Timothy's weak health and often infirmities; and had said to us, You know Timothy was made a bishop very young; and he was growing quite insufferable, he was so blown up with conceit, till God sent him this failing health to take him down and keep him modest. Now, my friend, what would you have thought, if you had found words like these somewhere in Paul's epistles? You would have been astonished, I think. You would have said, This is not like St. Paul. You would say, No, no; Paul never wrote *that;* it is an interpolation; it is something foisted into the manuscript by some one who envied Timothy and hated him. Remember this then: that there is all the difference in the world between talking as Paul does in the text about ourselves, and about any one else. When trial comes to ourselves, let us humbly seek to find out the lesson God is teaching us by it; but let us not presume to say wherefore the trial has come to any other man.

Little we know of his heart; little we know of his special temptations, cares, and fears. I dare say we, each of us, may have formed a theory of the character of many a man we see every day, that is as far from the truth as the old astronomy was from rightly stating the nature and movements of the stars! You may have known men accused of self-conceit, by people who knew hardly anything of them, whom *you* knew well to be the humblest and most shrinking of mankind. You may have known men supposed to be very ambitious and self-confident, by those to whom they were almost strangers, who wished for nothing more in life than to slip unnoticed by.

But, my friend, while thus cautioning you against judging your fellow-men by what you see of God's providential dealings with them; let me ask you, when sorrow comes to you, or abides with you, prayerfully to inquire why it has come; and what God may be intending to teach you by it. You know, if you have indeed believed in Christ, you have God's own promise that "all things shall work together for good" to you; and the thorn in the flesh or the crook in the lot, just like everything else. And we can see various ways in which such things may work us good. Pain, trial, disappointment, may all be sanctified by the Blessed Spirit to wean our hearts from this world; to impress upon us that great fundamental lesson, that "this is not our rest;" to lead us with all our heart to Jesus, the only satisfying portion of our never-dying souls. And the thorn in the flesh may do us good also, by giving us a deeper and larger sympathy with others in their trials and sorrows. People who have not suffered themselves are very impatient of the sufferings and complaints of other people. We cannot properly understand a thing which we have never felt anything like. And you will find those who get positively angry with any one who is weak and ill, as if it were all his fault. But passing by these lessons taught us by the discipline of sorrow, let me turn your thoughts especially to the lesson the thorn taught St. Paul; the lesson which he tells us he needed; and one which perhaps each of us knows that he in some respect needs.

The thorn in the flesh was sent to keep Paul humble. And we may be quite sure it did what it was sent to do. It would be effectual. The apostle had many things to puff him up; but this one thing would keep him down. My friends, perhaps, in the case of each of us, most of those who know us would find it difficult to see any reason why we should be exalted above measure; we have not much perhaps to be vain about; yet who does not know how ready all human beings are to think of themselves far more highly than they ought to think; and to think of themselves as very different from what they appear to others? St. Paul, you see, was thinking especially about spiritual pride, and about temptation to be vain of his spiritual gifts and attainments; and probably there is no form of self-conceit that steals in more subtly than that, or needs to be more rigorously kept down. A man may feel a deep spiritual pride because he is (as he fancies) so free from spiritual pride. And indeed in all respects, — as regards our talents, our influence, our reputation, our general position, — there is in the heart of almost all a tendency, needing to be constantly held in check, to undue self-estimation. And this tendency is not one that will do to have corrected just once for all. It is not like a tree that you cut down once for all and are done with; it is rather like the grass of a lawn, which you may mow down as closely as you can, and in a little it will grow up again just as before. Now Paul's self-conceit, you see, was mown down regularly every day. If it was always growing, the influence was always at work to keep it down. If at any time the thought began to get the upper hand, how great, and useful, and highly-favored a man he was, — there was the sharp thorn piercing in, sorer and deeper; and *that* set him right. And it is so with us, my friend. As surely as you get to grow out of that humility which best becomes us; as surely as you begin to cherish vain thoughts and high thoughts; so surely, if God loves you, will something come to take you down; so surely will some thorn in the flesh bring you back to your better and lowlier self; — some fresh proof be given you, how weak you were where you fancied yourself strong; how little esteemed where you thought it far otherwise; how feeble, worldly, and imperfect a believer you are yet; how little grown up to that stature in grace to which you fancied you had grown. And painful as these lessons may be, we need them all. And if they be sanctified by the Holy Spirit, they will effectually do their work. We shall not think much of ourselves in the day of crushing sorrow. There will be a constant lesson of humility in remembrance of some sin into which we fell, or in even the remembrance of some act of weakness and folly. You look back, my readers, over your past life, and you remember many things such as we take to be symbolized by that humbling thorn of St. Paul. You have had many takings down. You have had many things tending to make you lowly; and they are coming every now and then; perhaps there is some humbling thorn from which you are never free. But was it not all needed? Very few can say that they are too humble with it all! Which of us can say that we feel our sinfulness and helplessness too much; and that we are clinging to our Blessed Saviour too earnestly? Which of us can say that we feel too deeply our utter weakness; and that we are praying too often and too heartily for the aids of that Holy Spirit who alone can bring us safely through? Ah, my readers, many as may have been our trials, our disappointments, our temptations, let us thank our God for them; for we needed them all!

And now we come to a most interesting part of the

subject. See what the apostle did about his thorn in the flesh; see what God did! St. Paul tells us that he did not like the thorn in the flesh; no man can like what is painful and humiliating; and three times he besought God that the thorn in the flesh might be taken away. "For this thing I besought the Lord thrice." Thrice, you know, is a number indefinitely used in Scripture; we may be sure Paul offered that prayer far oftener than the bare three times. Every day, I doubt not, when the thorn was first sent; morning, evening, noonday, would the earnest supplication go up from his very heart, that this heavy burden might be taken from him; surely it could never be God's will that through the long years of all his coming life he was to bear that heavy and crushing weight! My reader, have not you done the same? Have not you prayed in earnestness, yea, in bitterness of heart, that some cup appointed you might pass away;—have not you prayed in earnestness that some sore trial, that you thought would darken all your life, might be spared you; that some bodily disease would leave you; that some sorrowful bereavement you saw coming might be kept off; that the plans and hopes of years might not be frustrated; in short, that *your* special thorn might depart? And perhaps Paul's answer was yours. See what God said to Paul's prayer. The thorn in the flesh was not to depart. It was to hang about the great apostle, burdening and humbling him, till the last breath went out from that feeble frame. He was never again to be like other men,—that great apostle Paul! And yet, who shall say that his prayer was not answered; nobly, fully, sublimely answered! There are two ways of helping a man, burdened with what he has to do or bear. The one way is to give him less to do or bear; to take the burden off the back. The other way is to strengthen him to do or bear all that is sent him; to strengthen the back to bear the burden. In brief, you may give less work; or you may give more strength. And it was in this way, which even we can see is the better and nobler way, that the wise and almighty Saviour thought it best to answer his servant's prayer. "My grace is sufficient for thee: for my strength is made perfect in weakness." Yes, St. Paul's weakness was to be supplemented by God's almighty strength; the thorn was still to pierce, but patience to bear it all was to be sent; the load was to press heavy on the back, but the back was to be strengthened in just degree. And we do not need to go far for proof how completely God's promise was fulfilled. How thoroughly resigned Paul was; how sanctified to him must that thorn have been; how strengthened his heart must have been with an unearthly strength; when he could honestly write such words as follow his account of his Redeemer's promise! Oh, the thorn was there, piercing as deep as ever; marring his usefulness, making him seem weak and contemptible to the stranger; but he liked to have to feel, from hour to hour, that he must be always going anew to God for help; he liked the assurance of the Blessed Spirit's presence which he drew hourly from feeling himself kept up to bear without a murmur what he knew that by himself he never could have borne; and so he wrote, not perhaps without a natural tear, "Most gladly therefore will I rather glory in my infirmities, that the power of Christ may rest upon me!"

We cannot but think, drawing these thoughts to a close, how Holy Scripture sets before us two men, who were favored with very near revelations of God; and each of whom was visited with a thorn in the flesh to keep him down, and to keep him in mind. You remember the patriarch Jacob, by that stream at Peniel;— how there he saw God face to face, and won a special blessing through persevering prayer. You remember how he went away from that place, under the rising sun, as a prince who had prevailed with God; but you remember, too, how he went, not with the free and active step of former days; how as he passed over Peniel he halted on his thigh; and he went lamely through all his after-life, bearing about that thorn in the flesh in memory of that great spiritual blessing. And so St. Paul, caught up where living man has rarely ever been; and who heard words which mortal ears have rarely heard; bore always afterwards that thorn in the flesh to keep him humble. My friends, have you found special comfort in communion seasons; special joy in Christ; special sense of God's favor; manifold proofs of God's goodness in your daily lot; then seek to be humble with it all, that the sore discipline may not be needed, which, if needed, will (in some form) surely be sent. And should God be pleased to send us the thorn; if there be those who feel the thorn even now; if there be those bowed under bereavement, or blank with disappointed hopes; oh, my friends, do like St. Paul under his sore trial; learn the lesson of humility God is teaching you by it. We blame you not, if thrice, and more than thrice, you beseech God to take the bitter cup away. But if he see meet to deny that prayer; if he see meet to continue the trial even to the end of life; oh, pray for the better and sublimer blessing of grace sufficient for you, — of strength made perfect in the weakness of your feeble and sorrowful hearts. And so, by God's kind grace, and by the comfort of that Blessed Spirit whom we humbly desire for our closest companion; so it may come to this, that you shall never wish things other than they are; that you shall be content that the path be thorny and steep, so it lead at last to our heavenly Father's dwelling; and so that meanwhile, "most gladly shall you rather glory in your infirmities," — in your trials, disappointments, and losses, — "that the power of Christ may rest upon you!"

IV.

THE GIFT OF SLEEP.

"For so he giveth his beloved sleep," — PSALM cxxvii. 2.

WE shall better understand what is, in the first and most obvious force of the words, taught and suggested by this text, if we remember what is the general bearing of the psalm in which it stands, and what were the circumstances in which it is believed to have been written. The psalm bears the title, "A Song for Solomon;" and the usual belief is, that this psalm was written by David, and dedicated to his son; with the purpose of keeping Solomon in mind of a great truth, which every man should seek devoutly to remember, and which it was especially desirable that Solomon should lay to heart. That truth was, that God's blessing must go with all man's labor, in order that man's labor should be effectual. No exertion; no skill; no setting early to work, nor sitting up late at it; can make sure that our plans shall succeed, without the help and blessing of God. It is utterly vain for the creature to think to set up independently of the Creator. Now Solomon was a wise man; and he was likely to know that he was so; and there were sure to be plenty of people about him to tell him how wise he was; and so his father desired to caution him against undue reliance on his own wisdom. Then Solomon had much work before him when he should become king. He had God's temple to build; and it was well to remind him, that "except the Lord build the house, they labor in vain that build it." He had his city and his kingdom to guard against evil and invasion; and it was well to remind him, that "except the Lord keep the city, the watchman waketh but in vain." And the Psalmist seems to anticipate an answer to all this; he seems to anticipate his son's saying, What, will not my most diligent and self-denying labors suffice? If I toil early and late, if I cut off my enjoyments and recreations, and give my whole mind to it; may I not then please myself by thinking that I can build the house and keep the city for myself? No, the Psalmist says; all that is quite useless. "It is vain for you to rise up early, to sit up late, to eat the bread of sorrows." Not that David undervalued hard work; not that he did not know the virtue there is in hard work; not that he was ignorant that there are few things worth much in this world that can be had or done except by hard work; but still all those long hours, all that hard self-denial, would never make a man independent of God; would never come to any end but by God's help and blessing. And then, if that blessing be given, what is worth having or desiring of worldly or spiritual good may come without that life-wearing toil; the time spent in seeking God's blessing upon our work will be as profitably spent as the time spent in actual labor; our task will sit the lighter upon body and mind, if we cast the care of it upon our God, and do not try to bear it all ourselves; "for surely he giveth his beloved sleep." The word translated *so* ought to be *surely*. The proper meaning of my text is, "Surely the Lord giveth his beloved sleep." And I have told you the way in which it comes in.

It is known, I doubt not, to many of you, that a certain great genius who died not long ago, declared that there was no text, even in that book of Psalms whose sentences come so wonderfully home to our hearts still, though spoken to us across the ocean of three thousand years, that fell upon her ear so comfortingly and so sublimely, as this which tells us what gift it is that God Almighty gives, as a great and good gift, to such as he holds dear. "Surely he giveth his beloved sleep." You remember how one of the wisest of heathens wrote, as a great principle arrived at through the meditation of a long life, that "the end of work is to enjoy rest." And you will think of One, wiser than the Greek philosopher, who seems to have thought as *he* did as to what was the largest and best blessing which can be offered to man. You remember the blessed words of Him who made us and who died for us: "Come unto me, all ye that labor and are heavy laden, and I will give you rest." We must be somewhat subdued, indeed, by the wear and toil of this weary world; and we must have gained an insight into the deepest wants of our spiritual nature, such as comes commonly through fuller experience and longer thought; before we shall appreciate such words completely. It is the toilworn man that knows the worth of repose; it is the jaded pilgrim that understands best what it must be to sit down at home; and as we go on, year after year, till our hearts begin to grow a little weary, there is music, growing always sweeter, in the ancient words of the patient patriarch, "There the wicked cease from troubling, and there the weary are at rest!"

There are three shades of meaning in which we purpose to understand this text; and to rest for a little in its contemplation.

And first: take the most obvious meaning of the words. God "giveth his beloved sleep." People whose whole heart is set upon this world may rise early, and sit late, and eat the bread of anxiety and sorrow, in their eager pursuit of worldly aims and ends,—in their breathless quest of wealth, or eminence, or success in some of its many forms; and thus these men may be so fevered and wrought up, and have their thoughts so full of the perplexities of business, and of its manifold cares and worries, that when the jading day is done at last, and they lay their busy head upon their pillow, sleep may fly from them;

and they may seek its blessed refreshment and forgetfulness in vain. Now, this is not a small matter. Looking at its entire effect upon mind and body; looking at what it testifies as to the unhealthy and overdriven state of those parts of our physical nature which stand in closest relation to the immaterial and immortal soul; we can see that it is a most grave and weighty matter. There are few things more dispiriting, and more wearing out, than the loss of our natural rest. To count hour after hour in feverish wakefulness, seeking that forgetfulness which will not come; to feel the mind within stimulated to a preternatural activity, and refusing to recall any but the most sorrowful thoughts; to be stung by a host of painful and distressing remembrances of the past and anxieties for the future, — each (as it were) coming up and striking its little poisoned dart into your nature; many a one knows well how dismal a thing all that is. There are physical causes, doubtless, in many cases; we may be told of unhealthy excitement of the brain, and of undue sensitiveness of the nervous system; but I go beyond these second causes, and I say that as a general rule, the great cause of those weary hours of wakefulness, anxiety, and misery, is want of faith in God. It is because we are not able, as we ought, to trust ourselves and all that concerns us to his sure providence and his thoughtful care. You know quite well, my friends, that it is mental anxiety and worry that break your rest; that it is because you are trying to bear the burden yourselves, to build the house yourselves, to keep the city yourselves, that you have those anxious, miserable hours; it is because you *will* plan too far ahead, instead of letting each day bear its own evil, — because you *will* keep asking what is to become of you and your children if such and such an event takes place, — because you *will* try to take the reins of your lot into your own hands, instead of leaving the direction of it all to his wisdom and kindness, — it is because of these things that you so often rise unrefreshed from your weary bed, to take to the dreary round again. Ah, my friends, if you had all of you a stronger trust in God, you would have sounder sleep! If you have really sought and so found the good fruit in Christ; if you are sure that nothing can go amiss with you, — that all things are ordered for your good, — that "the Lord will provide," — that the daily bread and the daily strength will come with the day that is to need them, — that God will guide you by his counsel while you live, and receive you to his glory when you die, — that through all your way, in dark and in light, angels guide your steps and guard your beds, and that the Holy Spirit of God himself dwells within you from hour to hour; oh, how free from care and fear you will lay your head upon your pillow, and sink into gentle forgetfulness; to rise again with the morning light refreshed and cheerful and hopeful! You know, that when all is said that can be said of physical causes, it is the things that prey on our mind by day that break our rest at night. And you know, too, how in those still, waking hours, those thoughts of how it stands with him from eternity, and of the accumulated guilt of his past life, which the heedless sinner can keep off amid the occupations and the companions of the day, force themselves in, and demand that they shall be listened to. It is impossible, then, quite to suppress the question, where the soul is to be when the body shall lie down on its last lowly bed; when all earthly things have faded from around us like the fading light; and left us no other comfort but that which we may draw from things eternal! But if you can humbly trust that it is well with you; that amid your deep-felt unworthiness you are simply believing on the Saviour, and daily striving to grow like him; that your task is appointed you by God; that he is always ready to help you in it; that you and those dear to you are provided for by him, and *that* so effectually that you never shall want anything that is truly good for you, —and you remember the promise, "They that fear the Lord shall not want any good thing;" then, how pleasantly you may rest and how cheerfully wake! Surely God will "give his beloved, sleep!"

Now, in the second place, let us understand the text in a less literal way. We all know that healthful sleep is our most peaceful state. In the untroubled, dreamless, refreshing repose of health after fatigue, you see human nature in that state in which it is most thoroughly free from all annoyance or trouble. You all remember the Spanish proverb as to the comfort with which sleep wraps us round. And in this view, we read in the text something to remind us how amid all the anxieties and competitions of life, God has promised peace to his own. "Peace I leave with you; my peace I give unto you." "Thou wilt keep him in perfect peace whose mind is stayed upon God." But how little there is of *that* even amid such as profess to be true believers! How far is the peace from being "perfect" even of the best believers! You remember the single word in which the ancient schoolman hit what he conceived to be the great characteristic of this life. "I entered this world," he said, "in lowliness; I have lived in it in anxiety; I shall leave it in fear." And there can be little doubt, I think, that he was right. Anxiety, care, are the characteristics of most lives here. You need not go far for the proof of this. Look at the faces of the people you see upon the street; remark their expression. You will very seldom see a cheerful face. Almost every face you meet, beyond early youth, is careworn and anxious. There is no doubt that care sits heavy upon the majority of mankind. You know the anxious look and the inelastic step of most middle-aged people in this country. No doubt, there may be something due to the nation and the race. "They took their pleasure sadly, according to the fashion of their nation;" there is no need to tell you of what nation the old chronicler said *that.* And you know how the greatest physical philosopher of modern times tells us that far in the American woods, beyond the reach of civilization and the cares that come of it, he found an unwrinkled tribe, on whose smooth faces, fresh and young-looking even to the verge of life, anxiety seemed never to have drawn a line. And some of you will think of a sublime description, given by a great poet, of the fresh, serene, unanxious life of certain of the free foresters who were the pioneers of civilization in the wilds of the far western world. But still taking the life we lead, I think you will hold by the schoolman's "Anxious I have lived." You know how many people, even when they could not tell you of any particular thing about which they are anxious, do yet live under the pressure of constant vague forebodings of ill. If some hasty, unexpected messenger were of a sudden to come for any of you, your first question would be, What is wrong? You would be sure that something was amiss. And what testimony does that one little indication bear to the too well-grounded anxiety for the future under which most human beings live! Now, my Christian friends, *that* is not like the perfect peace which God has promised; that is not like the peace and the rest which the Saviour told us he would give to such as went to him in simple faith. But remember this; that faith in our hearts is as it were the hand which we stretch forth to receive all the gifts of God's grace. We receive salvation, you know, of God's free grace; yet we must believe that we may be saved; we must stretch out the hand of faith, and lay hold of the salvation freely offered us. And it is just the same with the promised blessing of rest and peace amid all the agitations of life. God has promised it; God is ready to give it; but we must receive it by faith. And we may confidently say, that the amount of peace and quiet that we shall experience in this turbulent and troublesome world, will be in exact proportion to the strength and reality of our trust in God. If we were able really to trust God with everything, and with a whole heart, instead of doing as most Christians do, — never trusting God more than they can help, and never feeling quite safe as to what he may do; if we were able truly to cast our cares and roll our burdens upon him, instead of trying to bear them all ourselves; oh, what a blessed fulfilment there would be of the promise in the text! Surely God would then indeed have given his beloved peace and rest! We should do our best; and then, with perfect confidence, leave the issue of all with God. And then, the lined face will grow smooth again; and the heavy heart would grow light; the mind, beset with anxious calculations and forebodings of evil, "careful and troubled about many things," would be buoyant and free once more; — for our heart would be "stayed upon God," and then we should be "kept in perfect peace!"

But I wish here to suggest to you, that probably the thing which is at the foundation of that vague disquiet and apprehension which in the case of many does so much to gnaw away the enjoyment of life, is one of which they do not think. Some people are disposed to say, Oh, if I could only be free from such and such a thing that vexes me and keeps me anxious, I should be all right; everything else is as I would wish, but that one bitter drop in the cup turns it all to bitterness! Now, any such idea is quite mistaken. I believe that the real reason of the disquiet of many hearts is, that they are not right with God; they have never truly and heartily believed in Jesus Christ. They may have thought a good deal about religion; but still they vaguely feel within themselves that they have never fairly taken the decisive step. Now, we cannot be converted to God unless it be heartily; we cannot go to Christ and at the same time hold by the world just as we used to do; we cannot put our hand to the plough, and at the same time look back, and hang back, and turn back. And if a human being thinks at all, he can never be otherwise than vaguely uneasy, unhappy, unsatisfied, restless, anxious, till he has really and heartily believed in Christ; till he is able, very humbly indeed, and with no vain self-confidence, to say, "I know Whom I have believed; and I am persuaded that he is able to keep that which I have committed to him against that day." I am not careful to explain the logical steps of the process;

there are many things in the working of our deepest consciousness which are beyond our logic; but let me say to every one who hears me, who is always vaguely foreboding ill, who trembles at the coming of post-time, lest it may bring some terrible bad news,— whose imagination is always running upon the sad contingencies and possibilities of evil which hang over our life here,—who carries only too far the wise man's admonition, not to "boast of to-morrow," because we "know not what a day may bring forth;" to every such person let me say, Try a different way of escaping from your cares and fears than perhaps you have been trying; the thing that is at the bottom of them all is the lurking fear that you are not right with God; it is *that* which is eating the heart out of your enjoyment of life; it is *that* which keeps you vaguely unsatisfied and fearful; oh pray to have *that* set right, and then it will be well with you! Do not foolishly refuse to examine into the truth of the case; probe your nature to the uttermost; it will not heal a deep, poisoned wound, just to skin it over; if you have been wrong till now, oh begin and be right from to-day! Go to God, and say, I am a poor, sinful, trembling creature; I fear I have been deceiving myself, and thinking of myself far too well; yet as I am I come to thee once more, and ask mercy and grace only through Christ! O brethren, get the great central stay made firm and sure; and all will be well. But if the keystone of the arch be wrong, or even doubtful, then all is amiss. The great step towards trusting all to God as your Father, is to be really persuaded that God *is* your Father; to be persuaded that he loves you, unworthy as you are; to be persuaded that he reckons you among those to whom the promise is given, "Surely he giveth his beloved rest!"

And I ask you, my brethren, to remark the kind of peace and rest which the Saviour gives his people; and will give us, if we seek and pray for it. If quiet and peace could be had only by withdrawing from the duties and occupations of active life, then quiet and peace for most of us could never be. Not many of us, perhaps, could escape from manifold work and care in this life. Where most of us are placed in this world, we are likely to remain to the end; it is not in our power to fly to some far and still retreat, in whose quiet we might escape the evils and troubles here. And the corner will never be found in this world, where care and evil shall be unknown by human beings. But the peace which the Saviour gives his own, is peace of heart and mind amid daily duties. It is that "central peace" which may "subsist at the heart of endless agitation." When you look at the believer's busy life, you may see no trace of his inward peace of soul. But you know that the ocean, under the hurricane, is lashed into those huge waves and that wild foam only upon the surface. Not very far down, the waters are still as an autumn noon; there is not a ripple or breath or motion. And so, my friends, if we had the faith we ought, though there might be ruffles upon the surface of our lot, we should have the inward peace of perfect faith in God. Amid the dreary noises of this world; amid its cares and tears; amid its hot contentions, ambitions, and disappointments; we should have an inner calm like the serene ocean depths, to which the influence of the wild winds and waves above can never come!

And in the third place, my friends, we come to a yet sublimer sense in which we may understand the text. Let us think of the last, deepest, and longest sleep, as given by God. "Surely he giveth his beloved sleep;" he gives it; and gives it to those whom he holds dearest; sleep; all sleep; every kind and form of it. You remember how God's Word names the violent end of the martyr Stephen; "he fell asleep." You remember how the apostle names the Christian dead; "them that sleep in Jesus." And you remember the words of One dearer and better by far; "Our friend Lazarus sleepeth." And that Blessed One liked the word; he used it more than once or twice; "She is not dead,"—not dead, as you mean by the word,—"not dead, but sleepeth." Thus kindly and hopefully does that kindest and most hopeful voice that ever stirred the atmosphere of this world, speak of our last change. And oh, how the very nature of death is changed when we thus think of it! Not the gloomy visitor, coming so unwelcome; but the kindly gift of our kind Saviour, gently soothing us to rest. When all is said, our hearts will never be quite free from troubles, fears, anxieties, forebodings, here; our feeble faith, and our many sins, clouding God's face, will make sure of *that;* but in that last repose we shall, if we be Christ's people, sleep into forgetfulness of all these. We never shall know a real, sound, untroubled sleep in this world, till *that;* till the weary head is laid upon the bosom of its God! "After life's fitful fever he sleeps well;" how literally, how gloriously true, the great poet's words are of the true believer! Let us bless God for the pleasant thought of death which is given us by this gracious text; we need it all. Gently as a mother soothes her weary infant, the kind Saviour calms away all our cares, all our fears and forebodings, in that perfect rest. We call to our remembrance the lowliness of death; we stand by the last bed; we see the weakness of mortality; we mark the sad signs of dissolution; and who that has ever seen them but knows how sad they are to see; but what a change comes over all *that,* over the parting breath, over the still face when the last pain is over, when we think it is but that God has "given his beloved sleep;" and gently soothed the unquiet heart to the dreamless rest of a child! He *giveth* it; it is not as if it were sent by even the sublimest messenger; he comes himself; he stands by his departing brother; it is he himself that composes the weary heart, and closes the glazing eyes. Not the fatal disease; not the days and nights of weakness and suffering; not those long years, perhaps, which have silvered the head and worn out the machinery of mortal life; look beyond these, my brethren; there is a Higher Hand here. "Surely God giveth his beloved sleep."

Yes, to his beloved. To those washed in Christ's blood, and sanctified by the Holy Spirit. We pray earnestly, this day, that all of us, that every one of us who are within these walls, may be so! We pray earnestly that we all may be led and enabled unfeignedly to love and trust him as we see him in Christ; and so that we may be loved by him; by him who first loved us, — who sought us in the wilderness when we had wandered away and were lost, and brought the wanderer home to his fold. And then, passing from this life, — closing our eyes upon this world of trouble, we shall rest in our Blessed Saviour; we shall sleep in Jesus; we shall win the peace of God! And in that rest, which remaineth for all his people, we shall be far away from all weariness, all anxiety, all care, all sorrow. And while the soul shall pass to God, to enter on the rest of glory, the mortal body has its rest no less, sleeping peacefully till the resurrection day. And when the green grass of another June waves over us; when the soft summer wind of another June sighs through the green leaves;

when the sunshine of some more genial Longest Day shall brighten cheerfully the stone which may bear our name and yours; what better can we wish, than that if we leave behind us those who may sometimes visit the quiet spot, they may be able to say, humbly and hopefully, Surely here, at last; and surely there, in a better place; the weary heart and hand are still; yea, surely God "hath given his beloved, sleep!"

June 22, 1862.

V.

JABEZ: HIS LIFE AND HIS PRAYER.

"And Jabez was more honorable than his brethren: and his mother called his name Jabez, saying, Because I bare him with sorrow. And Jabez called on the God of Israel, saying, Oh that thou wouldest bless me indeed, and enlarge my coast, and that thine hand might be with me, and that thou wouldest keep me from evil, that it may not grieve me! And God granted him that which he requested."—1 CHRON. iv. 9, 10.

THERE was a Hebrew mother, to whom a child was born in a season of special sadness and sorrow. We do not know what was her name; and we do not know the place or the time in which she lived; save that the time was many hundred years ago, and that the place was somewhere in the promised land of Canaan. We do not know what was the cause of the special sorrow which was in that poor mother's heart when her child was sent to her; though we may perhaps suppose, from what we are told as to the mother being the only one to decide what should be her boy's name, that her husband was dead; and so that the little one, half-orphaned from his birth, could never be met by a father's welcome, nor tended by a father's care. The sorrow of that Hebrew mother is all over now; and indeed we have reason to think that it was turned into gladness, if she was spared in this world, before many years passed on. But at the time, it had quite crushed her down; it had so overwhelmed her, that she seemed for the time to have lost even the power of hoping for better days. It seems as if she had thought that no good nor happiness could ever come of that little child that was as the memorial of so sad a season; and so she gave him a name that told of her present grief and her fears for the future. His mother called him Jabez; that is, Sorrowful. And he went through life bearing that name; and his memory has come down to us through all these centuries, linked with that name; Jabez, Sorrowful.

It is not much we know of Jabez; we have his entire biography in these two verses which you have read. But I think, my friend, that in this recorded history of that man, there is suggested to us something of as solemn warning, and of as blessed consolation, as you will find within the range of God's holy book. We know nothing of his childhood or his youth; nothing of the first steps by which he showed how little his name befitted him; nothing of the pride and delight, mingled with self-accusing for her lack of faith in a kind God, which would spring up in the mother's heart, if she was spared to see what her son became at last. We are only told that Jabez, Sorrowful, grew up to be a man; and rose to honor, — to special and superеminent honor. And we have preserved a prayer which Jabez offered, and which God granted him, which shows us that Jabez was as good and wise and energetic and devout as he was honored and renowned. *That* prayer we shall think of hereafter; it might be a pattern for ours; and every petition in it may serve to remind us of great religious truths, which we ought never to forget. But meanwhile, let us fix on this; the preëminent honor to which *he* rose, who came into this world at so gloomy a season, and who bore a name expressive of so gloomy foreboding for the days to come. "Jabez," we are told, "was more honorable than his brethren." You have nothing told you of the other members of that family, who perhaps came in happier days, and who perhaps received more hopeful names. We may well believe, from the way in which the story is told, that they were good and worthy too; but still, in fame, in holiness, in wisdom, in goodness, it was Jabez who was always first. And how strange a contrast it must have been, between the sorrowful name, and the honored and happy man who bore it; how strange a comment that life of honor and usefulness must have seemed, upon the mother's faithless forebodings, and her needless fears! Yes, it must have been curious to hear that name that sounded so sadly, mentioned by all men with such pleasant looks, and linked with so many deeds of kindness and wisdom and true heroism. For God, we are told, granted him the things he asked in that most comprehensive prayer; and oh, how good and wise and brave a man *he* must have been, to whom *that* prayer and all it asked was granted! And we say it must have sounded strange to hear it asked, Who was it that did that kind and noble deed? and to hear it answered, Oh, it was Jabez! Who was it that went out so valiantly against the enemies of his God, and "enlarged his coast," his portion of the promised land, by those rich fields and woods? Oh, it was Jabez! Who was it that comforted that despairing heart,—who cheered that house of sorrow, — who guided that poor wanderer back? Still, it was he whose name promised such different things; still, it was Jabez! Yes, it was Sorrowful who carried joy to many a desolate home; it was Sorrowful who made the dim eye grow bright again with hope; it was Sorrowful whose name was on the lips of multitudes of men, as their very ideal of all that was pure and good and true and happy. He rose above his fellow-men. He was "more honorable than his brethren;" and the words seem to imply that they, too, were honorable, — were good men, and happy men; but oh! there was none like Jabez! None like Sorrowful to gladden his mother's heart; none like Sorrowful for worldly success, and for spiritual wealth, wisdom, and happiness.

My friend, let us fix on this point in the history of Jabez to think of first; and tell me, is the lesson of all this far to seek? You see, it was to her best and worthiest son that the mother of Jabez gave the name, that implied how little hope of future happiness with him or through him remained in her weary, despairing heart. We can think of a contrasted picture; you remember the proud and hopeful name which the mother of our race gave to her first-born son; you know how much of confident hope was embodied in the name of Cain. *Possession*, she called him, — a great thing gained from God, — who was yet so sorely to wring her heart. For even thus vain are human anticipations, whether of good or ill; the first murderer welcomed with the hopeful name of Cain; while this wise and good and happy man was to bear the desponding name of Jabez. But without dwelling upon the vanity of all human calculations, — of all human hopes and fears, — let us now remember how often we all call by hard names, dispensations of God's providence which in reality are to prove great blessings. Probably in many cases those events in our history, those dealings of God with us, which we should call sorrowful at the time, stand us in more real stead, and do us more real good, than the brightest and happiest that ever come in our way. Even here, and now, we can understand, that *that* earthly trial or loss is not rightly called Jabez, Sorrowful, which works our spiritual good; which leads us with simpler and humbler faith to that blessed Saviour who is our only satisfying portion; and which weans our heart somewhat from those things of time and sense to which it so naturally cleaves. And do you not all know, how sometimes we can afterwards see, that even looking no farther than this world, it was good for us that we were afflicted; — good for us that we were disappointed, that we were tried, that we were bereaved? *That* turning you wished to take in life, you can now see was the wrong one; though it was a sad trial at the time when God hedged up your way, and bade you walk along a track so different from that which you would have chosen for yourself. Yes, even worldly success and advantage have come, because of dispensations which were disappointments and sorrows at the time they happened; and who does not know what precious spiritual blessing has often come out of dealings which when they came were Jabez; who does not know what blessed graces, — what purity, heavenly-mindedness, sympathy, kindliness, faith, and hope, — have beamed out, in modest loveliness, in the soul which has come through the sore discipline of sanctified sorrow, of disappointment rightly met and rightly used? If we be truly united to Christ, we may be sure of this, that nothing can befall us, which may not be turned to good, by God's sanctifying Spirit. Sickness, care even, bereavement; all may be like Jabez; dark and unpromising at the beginning, but brightened into glory and beauty in their result; and the believer, as he looks back on his past history, may be constrained to say, — God has been very good to me; he has sent me many blessings; but oh, never the blessing that was so good and precious, as when he sent me that trial which I felt so crushing;—as when he blighted the hopes so fondly cherished, or sent the bereavement which almost broke the rebellious heart!

And now, my friend, as we go on to consider the prayer which Jabez offered, and which God granted him; let us take along with us, to the consideration of the petition that stands first in it, the remembrance of these things which have been said, as to our little power to discern what is a blessing and what is not; as to the tendency in human beings to call *that* Cain which ought to be called Jabez; and *that* Jabez which ought to be called Cain. You see the all-comprehending petition with which the prayer of Jabez sets out. He "called upon the God of Israel, saying, Oh that thou wouldst bless me indeed!" Yes, Bless me INDEED! It was because Jabez knew that he could never certainly tell what was truly blessing, and what seemed blessing and was not; that he devolved upon God himself the charge and the responsibility of deciding what things were to come to him. What a wise, and what a safe prayer! "That thou wouldst bless me indeed!" Send me *that* which Thou knowest is blessing, though it may not seem blessing to me; and deny me that which Thou knowest is not blessing, however ready I, in my ignorance, may be to think it so! *That* is the spirit of the prayer. It was for the All-wise himself to decide what was the exact discipline which Jabez needed at the time; it might be a painful discipline, it might be a happy one; but whatever it might be, Jabez knew that the thing he needed was the true blessing; and all he asked from God was, that, pleasant or painful, God would send him *that!* Yes, my friend; put that prayer together with what we are taught by the entire history of Jabez; and see what a lesson it teaches us as to how we ought to pray. When we are praying for temporal blessings, we ought never to pray for them absolutely; we ought always to pray for them, if they be truly good for us; if not, God in answering our prayer would not be blessing us *indeed.* And even as regards spiritual blessings, though we may pray for them with more confidence and less reservation; — though we are quite sure that it must be truly good for us to have our sins pardoned through Christ, and our souls sanctified by the Holy Spirit; and though thus we are sure that God in giving us pardon and holiness would be blessing us *indeed;* — still, even as regards spiritual blessings, we do not know what is the exact dealing that may be most expedient for us at the time; we cannot be sure that in asking spiritual peace, joy, hope, or strength, we are asking the thing which would suit our present need the best. Perhaps humiliation may be the thing we need just then; perhaps the best thing for us would be to have our over-confidence rebuked, — to be brought back to a deeper sense of our own weakness, and a simpler leaning upon our kind Redeemer's strength and grace. You know, generally, the direction in which to steer; but you cannot say what little movement of the helm may be expedient from time to time, to suit each passing flaw of wind, or each crossing wave. And it is just because we do not know these things, that it is so wise to leave the decision of the precise thing to be sent us, as Jabez did, to God; and to pray, with him, that God would bless us *indeed.* Let him deny us *that* which is not blessing indeed, however like blessing it may seem; and let him send us *that* which is blessing indeed, though we might write against it, Jabez! Ah, my brother, you dare not pray, without a reservation if God sees it fit, that you may gain the worldly end on which you have set your heart; you dare not pray absolutely that you may live a long or a peaceful life; you dare not pray, without a condition, by the dying bed of your dearest, that they may be spared to you longer; you must always add, God's will be done, if God sees it good for you and them; but you can never go wrong, if you do like Jabez; if you go humbly and hopefully in Christ's blessed name; and call on the God and Father of our Blessed Saviour, saying, Oh that thou wouldst bless me indeed!

But let us go on with the wise and good man's prayer. The next two petitions in it let us take together. "Oh that thou wouldst enlarge my coast;

and that thine hand might be with me!" These two requests must stand together, as we shall see. No doubt the first of the two refers to *this:* that Jabez was an Israelite who had yet to conquer from his enemies some portion of the inheritance allotted to him in the land of promise. There were fair tracts round him, appointed to him by God; and he wished to win these from God's enemies; and accordingly he prays that God would give them to him; he prays, "That thou wouldst enlarge my coast!" And it was right, of course, to pray for this; but it was not enough merely to pray. It would not do, that Jabez should slothfully sit down, content to have merely asked God to give the inheritance he wished. You see from his prayer that he is going out to do what in him lies to accomplish the thing for which he prays. You see he asks that God's "hand might be with him," as he goes forth to do battle with the idolatrous race which meanwhile possesses the soil which is by right his own. In short, the wise man, in the exercise of a manly common sense, asks God to help him, because he is going to try to help himself.

There is a great and sound principle implied here; a great lesson for all of us. It is the duty of combining effort with prayer. When we, my friend, are desirous to compass any new attainment; — when we wish to enlarge our coast, as it were, by taking in greater fields of faith, of holiness, of patience, of humility, of all Christian grace, — in regard to all of which we may well take up Joshua's words, that "there remaineth yet very much land to be possessed,"—let us do like Jabez. It is not enough that we pray to God to give us more grace; we must labor to get more grace. We must diligently use the means that foster the growth of grace in us. We must cultivate Christian grace as we cultivate bodily strength and skill,—by exercise; all the while remembering that without God's help and Spirit we can do nothing; working, in short, like Jabez, as if we could do all, and praying as if we could do nothing. We may well and rightly pray for increase of spiritual comforts: for greater joy in communion seasons,—for greater heart and earnestness in prayer,—for more of Christ's love and life in our daily work and warfare,—for greater and happier elevation above worldly cares; but while for these things we pray, like Jabez, for these things let us also labor and strive, like him.

We may safely say, that if Jabez had merely prayed that God would enlarge his coast, and then remained idle at home, making no exertion for himself, his portion would not have been enlarged. God would have regarded such a prayer as a mere mockery. And on the other hand, if Jabez had gone forth against his enemies in his own unaided strength, he would likely enough have failed too. The wisdom of Jabez appeared in *this:* that he put prayer and effort together. You know how a wiser and greater than Jabez had done the like; how our Saviour bade us at once "Watch and pray." Now is it not a curious thing, that when God's Word and our own common sense tell us that these two things ought always to go together, and are (so to speak) the closest of allies,— we constantly find people talking as if they were things opposed to each other,— and as if by holding to the one, you sacrificed the other? But you just see here the narrowness and one-sidedness of man's view, as compared with the largeness and comprehensiveness of God's view. Jabez, you remember, prayed that God would enlarge his coast; and even as he prayed, he went forth to enlarge his coast for himself. Jabez was wise and right. But if Jabez had been like some people nowadays, he would have prayed that God would enlarge his coast, and then sat at home and done nothing; and finally wondered why his coast was not enlarged. And if Jabez had been like other people nowadays, he would have gone out to enlarge his coast without troubling himself to pray at all. You know how many among us take these one-sided views; and apparently cannot look at both sides of a truth together; or see that prayers and pains must go together; and that it is foolish to cry up either at the expense of the other. Thus, when pestilence threatens the land, you will find one set proposing to have a fast-day, and pray to God to avert the pestilence. And you will find another set proposing to flush sewers, and cleanse and ventilate close and filthy dwellings. And, strange to say, instead of seeing that *both* these things ought to be done; that you ought to drain and cleanse with all your might, and at the same time to pray with all your heart; you will find the advocates of the fast-day, and the advocates of the cleansing, abusing each other like bitter foes; as if the plan of the one set excluded the plan of the other. Why, of course, both should be done. Watchfulness and prayer must go together, alike in things temporal and things spiritual. And it is foolish to raise a question which is the more essential, when both are essential. It would be abundantly absurd to get up a furious controversy whether food or drink were the more necessary to the life of man. Both are necessary. And Jabez, wise and good man, knew it. And so, while he prayed that God "would enlarge his coast," he buckled on his harness and went down to the battle. Do you the like, my friend. Pray earnestly for more grace; and work heartily to get it.

And so we come to the last petition in this prayer; a petition comprehensive and wise as the first. The first petition, you remember, was for true blessing. The last is for deliverance from true evil, — and from the evil effects and influences of all evil. Here are the words: "And that thou wouldst keep me from evil, that it may not grieve me." You know that this is a world of evil, bodily and spiritual; a world of suffering and wrong; and through these, among other means, God works his ends on our souls. It is not God's purpose that we should never see or come in contact with evil at all. And you see the moderation, the acquiescence in God's appointments, the sound sense, which characterize Jabez's prayer. "And that thou wouldst keep me from evil, that it may not grieve me." He does not ask, you see, that evil may never come; but that evil may not be suffered to really harm when it comes. And so his prayer is in perfect harmony with that which was dictated to us by Christ: "Deliver us from evil;" for Christ's words do not lead us to hope that evil will never come; but that by God's grace when it *does* come, we shall be saved from its evil tendencies and results. Jabez did not ask, and we would not ask, that evil should never befall us at all; *that* would be too much; and if *that* prayer were granted, we should miss some of the most blessed and precious influences that ever helped to make the believer meet for the better land above. Evil coming, and trying us, may do us great good; we should not thrive without it; some of the heavenliest fruits of the Spirit would never grow in us if we never knew sorrow; patience, resignation, humility, sympathy, could hardly exist in the soul that never knew grief; and I think, my friend, that we should feel almost alarmed if we were never visited with trial; we should almost feel that our heavenly Father was not treating us as his children, — he who disciplines his children for immortality by the sad experience of sorrow and pain; we should feel it strange to be excluded from that training, so salutary though so sad, to which such multitudes of believers have been witnesses, — and which is embodied in that ancient declaration of St. Paul and St. Barnabas, that "we must through much tribulation enter into the kingdom of God." But Jabez prayed, and we may pray, that evil should not *grieve* us. We may pray that evil may never be suffered to harden us; to stir us up to wrath against God; to make us fretful, rebellious, impatient; to tempt us to sin; in short, to do us harm when God intends it always to do us good. It was for *this* that Jabez prayed.

Oh, my brother, we know that evil will come to us; it has come already, and it will come again. There is not a heart — not even the youngest — that has not had its share of grief; and *that* which has been is *that* which shall be. But if evil be sanctified to us; if it be met in a right and humble spirit; then, though it may come, it will not grieve; it will not offend us, — it will not prove a stumbling-block in our heavenward way. Nay; it will further us with a continual help! It will prove a blessing, — a blessing *indeed*. It will wean us from earth; it will purge away our dross; it will quicken our steps towards that peaceful home, where dwell such multitudes who "came out of great tribulation!" Let us then pray like Jabez. Let us prefer, not the unreasonable and extravagant request, that evil may never come; but the modest and Christian request, that when evil comes, as it surely will come, still that it may never grieve!

And such, my friend, was the prayer of that good man whose history so belied his name; and who, doubtless for our comfort and warning among other ends, lived and died, so long ago, and so far away. And see what came of Jabez. No wonder he was so honorable! You have seen what the things were for which he asked; and God's word tells us, closing the history of Jabez, "And God granted him that which he requested." God gave him all he asked! Oh, what a biography for any man! See what is taught us in the assurance that God granted Jabez his prayer. It tells us that through life, God blessed him indeed; that God enlarged his coast; that God's hand was with him; and that God kept him from evil, so that it did not grieve him. Think of *that*, my friend! Could you even pray for anything better? If God were this day to allow you to sketch out for yourself the kind of life which you would wish to lead, so long as you are spared in this world,—could you ask for more than that God would grant to you what he granted Jabez! Well, now for a comforting thought. It must have been a good and a noble life that Jabez lived; and perhaps you are ready to think that it is far beyond your reach; that it was all well in those distant days when men felt God's presence nearer them; but that only a specially-favored one, here and there, can look for such things now. But do not think *that*. It does not at all follow, from what we are told of that good man's honored life, that it was one of unmingled brightness; or that it was beyond what we may humbly ask through Christ, and humbly hope. God "blessed him indeed;" but *that* which is a blessing indeed, may not be what the worldly man would think a blessing at all. We cannot be sure, even of the man whom God blessed *indeed*, that his life was all sunshine. Likely enough, he had his share of the worries of life. Likely enough, he had now and then a great trial. Likely enough, there were days when the heart of Sorrowful was sorrowful enough; and when Jabez mourned beside the tomb where those he loved were sleeping. But still, he went on through life in such fashion that he drew good from all things that befell him; and so, through all, God kept his promise, and "blessed him indeed,"—for all that came was truly blessing. And then, though his "coast was enlarged," perhaps the portion he got, after all, seemed large only to his moderate desires and ideas; perhaps it was no such very great tract of territory after all; and likely enough, his neighbors would smile at Jabez for being so well pleased with it; and I dare say the ill-set people among them would try to put him out of conceit with it,—just as ill-set people do the same thing now. And then, when evil befell Jabez, all men could see the outward affliction, but none could see what was the inward result; all men could see that evil came, but only Jabez knew that it fell where it could not grieve. And so, to the eyes of ordinary onlookers, the outward lot of Jabez may not have seemed so much happier than the lot of other men. Perhaps his path in life may, to outward view, have appeared like the average one of ordinary believers. His lot was not beyond our reach; nor beyond the possibilities of what may come to ourselves. Perhaps there are people in every Christian congregation, who are very like what Jabez was. People who are more deserving of honor than most of their brethren of mankind, though they may not get it. People whom God blesses indeed, though they have their many cares. People whose coast is enlarged, though it be in fields of faith and holiness and peace, which are not visible to the passer-by. People to whom their share of evil comes, but is made by God's Spirit to conduce to their eternal welfare. And *we* may fitly ask for all *that;* and hope for all *that;* through our Redeemer, and for his sake.

Let us humbly pray, then, this day, to the God of our fathers, through that Blessed Redeemer who is our Elder Brother, saying, Oh that thou wouldst bless us indeed, and enlarge our coast; and that thine hand may be with us; and that thou wouldst keep us from evil, that it may not grieve us!

VI.

GAIN IN THE SAVIOUR'S LOSS.

"It is expedient for you that I go away." — St. John xvi. 7.

THE parting of friends, we all know, is always a sad thing, even if it be for not a very long time, and to not a very great distance; for it never can be quite forgot, in this uncertain life, that many things may come to prevent a meeting again. But partings sometimes are among the very saddest things that ever happen upon the face of this sorrowful world; partings of those who are very dear; partings of the playmates of childhood; partings of those who hitherto have kept close together in the race and the warfare of life, bearing one another's burdens, dividing one another's sorrows, sharing one another's joys, but who are now to be severed by long months and years of time, by long leagues of land and sea. I have seen an emigrant ship depart upon its long voyage; I remember the bustle and hurry which attended its departure; the crowded deck, thronged with old and young; gray-haired men bidding farewell to their native land, and little children who would carry but dim remembrances of Britain to the distant Australian shore. And who that has ever witnessed such a scene can forget, how, when the white canvas was spread at last, and the last rope cast off, the outburst of sobs and weeping arose as the great ship solemnly passed away! Doubtless that parting was to many of those who parted then, as complete as that which is made by death.

And why was it then, that those who felt the pang of parting so much, were yet content to part? Why, but because they felt it was better so. The emigrant felt that he was leaving a country where he was not needed, a country which would not yield him bread, for another where there were work and bread for all. And the friends who remained behind knew all that too. They knew that however keen might be the anguish of that day, brighter days would follow. They knew that it was best that the youthful son should carry his sturdy arm and his active brain to the young, fresh world across the Atlantic, and not remain to be hampered and held down through life in the over-crowd and over-competition here. "It was expedient" for all parties, "that he should go away." He would find a new home, far away. He would form new ties there. He might find there, perhaps, a path to fame and fortune. He would often think, indeed, in the thoughtful twilight, of the hills of his native land; and sometimes, perhaps, wonder whether, for all that he had gained by leaving the country of his birth, it might not have been as well had he saved his home-bred virtues in his father's lowly lot, and laid his head at last in his father's honored grave.

But after all, my friends, I do not doubt that you have found it in your own experience, that the thing to which people most naturally have recourse to blunt, in some measure, the pang of parting, is some such thought as is suggested in the text. The dying wife tries to persuade the husband she is leaving, that it is far better as it is. The poor, friendless young laborer, reckless and graceless once, but reclaimed by a kindness and a wisdom that were half angelic, said, as he felt life ebbing away, and thought of all the temptations he was saved from, — said in his own simple way of speaking, that "perhaps it was as well he should go home pretty soon." And just with that simple and natural thought did the Blessed Redeemer seek to console his disciples as he was leaving them behind. He is addressing them in those memorable words, in that last and most beautiful discourse, which we all know so well. It is the night on which he was betrayed. He has partaken of the Jewish Passover for the last time, and he has instituted that better Christian Passover which was to take its place; and now more plainly than ever before, he begins to tell his friends of his speedy removal from them. And as he sees the shadow fall deep upon their faces, and deeper upon their hearts, at the thought, he hastens to comfort them as a parent might the child from whom he was for a season of trial and training to be divided. I go, it is as if he said; and it is better that I should; I leave you, and though you may sorrow at first, you will gain more by my leaving you than you could have gained by my remaining with you. "I tell you the truth; it is expedient for you that I go away."

Now, we all know it perfectly well, that such words as these are oftentimes spoken, and spoken with a kindly intention too, when they are not really true. When some stroke of disappointment has fallen, when some cherished hope has been blighted, we are anxious to persuade ourselves that it is better as it is; we say so, and we try to believe it. And the dying father, who is leaving his little ones alone in this cold world, would try to make them think that it is better he should go in God's good time, although his anxious mind and his feeble heart belie the words he utters. We often say, and we often hear such words as those of the text, when they express rather what is wished than what is felt and believed. "It is expedient that we should part," we say; "it is better as it is;" when we could give no sufficient reason for thinking so; no sufficient reason, that is, save that one sheet-anchor of the weary and disappointed heart, the wise and kind decree of God. God orders all things that happen, we know; and whatever God does must be right; and so we may safely say of everything that happens that, in one sense, it is best as it is. But it is not merely in this general view, — and it is not merely by way of saying a kind word that might cheer up somewhat in a trying hour, that Jesus said to his disciples ere he left them, "It is expedient for you that I should go away." There must be good reason for his saying these words, or he would never have said them. And the reason, too, you see, must be one which related rather to his disciples than to himself. He was not thinking of that bright and happy home that was waiting for him, and of that glory into which he could enter only by bidding his earthly followers for the while farewell. He was not thinking of all the advantages which might thus follow for himself. "It is expedient for *you*," he says, "that I should go away." No doubt, to look at it selfishly, it was better for Christ himself to go away. It would be a change for the better, indeed, when the homeless wanderer, rejected and despised, who had not where to lay his head, should stand on the right hand of God, the centre of heaven's glory, the object of heaven's praises; but Jesus was not thinking of himself, or of what would be most agreeable to himself. He was thinking of his disciples, and he declared that it was expedient for them that he should go away. He was indeed their best and dearest friend; they never could find such another; and it must be some very strong reason indeed to make them believe that they would be as well or better without *him*. There must be much indeed to gain by his going, to outweigh what would be gained by his staying. And the Saviour himself fixes upon a single reason. His departure, he said, was the condition of another's coming, who would more than make up for his loss. Precious indeed, then, must that other be! Think of it, my friends; try to comprehend it; he was to be a better companion in that present season, a better friend than Christ! It was not merely that the new friend would make up for the loss of the old one; situated as they then were, the disciples would gain by the exchange. "It is expedient for you," said the Redeemer, "that I go away;" that is, You will gain by my going,— it is not merely as well, it is better for you that I should go. "For if I go not away, the Comforter will not come unto you; but if I depart, I will send him unto you."

We must all feel that although it is our duty and our privilege to "love the Lord our God with all our heart, and strength, and mind;" and although that pious affection ought to extend to each of three Persons in the Trinity: the Father, the Son, and the Holy Spirit; still there is one of these Divine Persons whom we cannot choose but single out for special love. It is our Blessed Saviour who has done the most for us; it is only he who has suffered for us; it is the remembrance of him that must always most warm our heart; and it is his constant presence which will make the Christian's heaven. And if the question were absolutely, whether we loved more the Saviour or the Sanctifier, and so which of the two we should absolutely desire to have with us; I believe that every Christian would feel his whole being answer, "Christ all in all," "Jesus the chiefest among ten thousand, and altogether lovely." And we should hardly be able to persuade ourselves that even the coming of the Blessed Comforter could make up for the absence of the Blessed Redeemer. Absolutely, this is so; but you see Christ's words are not uttered absolutely, but in a qualified sense. All that the Saviour declared in the text was, that for believers so situated as the disciples he was addressing, it was expedient and advantageous that the Comforter should be present with them, even at the price of his own departure. For you, it is as if he said,—for you who have to live in a world of work and warfare, a world of sorrow and temptation, a world which is not the heaven to be enjoyed, but the trial and training to be endured,—for you, so placed and so exercised, it is expedient that I should go away; for my presence with you holds away from you one whose society is, for beings placed as you are, even more important and more advantageous than my own. And it is not straining our Lord's words beyond their natural meaning, to say that they are spoken to the entire Christian Church on earth; that they make an assertion which holds good of the whole multitude of true believers; that they lay down the great principle, that for men and women like us, with our work to do, our sorrows to bear, our cares to bear up under, our sinfulness to strive against, it is better, so long as we remain in this world, to have the Holy Spirit of God constantly though invisibly present with us, than it would be to have Christ himself, in visible presence, still remaining here. Oh! if it had been good for us, surely he would never have left us! If it would really have conduced to our eternal well-being, then there still would be found on this earth a place, the centre of the Christian world, towards which, from all lands and climes, the streams of pilgrims would converge; and there we should even yet be able to behold the gracious face, and to hear the gentle voice, and to look on the beloved form of him who died to save us! We should even yet be able to touch the hem of his garment, to bring our troubles to his feet, to bring our children to his arms! But *that* is not to be; we must love him, while we see him not; we must mourn an absent Lord; we must wait till the fleshly vesture shall fall from around our spirits, before we shall see him as he is. And yet think not that the decree is made in severity; do not imagine that it is merely to deprive us of a privilege that we should dearly prize; it is for our own good that our Redeemer is unseen by us; it was the kindest consideration for our true welfare that dictated the law that looks so stern; it is far better, though it may be hard to think so, — it is far better as it is; "it was expedient for us that Christ should go away!"

Yes, my friends, it was expedient that Christ should go away, because unless he went, the Comforter would not come; and to the Christian Church, cast upon a world like this, the invisible Comforter would stand in even better stead than the visible Redeemer. But the thought naturally suggests itself, Why might the Church not have had both? Surely it would have been best of all to have Jesus still with us, gracious as of old; and the Blessed Spirit as well. Might not the Second Person in the Trinity and the Third have been both on earth together? Now, my friends, we must just take Christ's word for it, that this cannot be. We cannot tell how and why it is; but for some good reason, unknown to us, we cannot have both together. In this world, it is needful that we should do with one. The Saviour's words are perfectly explicit: "If I go not away, the Comforter will not come unto you." And so, receiving this as a truth which cannot be questioned, let us consider for a little how it comes to be, that it is better for the Christian Church to have the Holy Spirit, than even to have the Saviour personally present. Can it be made out that it was better on the whole to submit to the Saviour's personal loss, if *that* was the condition upon which alone the Comforter could come? We may not be able to make out all the reasons which were present to the Saviour's mind, when he thus exalted the Spirit's society above even his own. Yet it would be pleasing if we could in so far understand the matter; and it is a very fit use of our reason, to employ it in seeking to discover grounds for that which we receive by faith.

It is but the merest sketch of two or three considerations which it is possible for me now to present to you.

For one thing, then, let us remember that the choice lay between Christ as he then was, a person, dwelling in a human body; and a Divine Spirit, capable of being universally present at the same time. Christ, dwelling in flesh, could be only in one place at a time; while the Comforter, unbound by fleshly trammels, could be in a thousand places, working on a million hearts, all at once. And I think you will see, that for the grand end of carrying on the government of a Church that is to overspread the world, and to include within itself men of every country and every tongue, it was better to have one Divine Being, equally present everywhere, working with equal energy everywhere; than even to have Christ himself dwelling in visible form in some favored spot, and by the very fact of his being visible there, making those disciples in distant countries who saw him not, feel as though they were so far overlooked, — as though they were in some sense placed at a disadvantage. Far better, surely, to be able to think, as we can gladly think now, that there is *no* disciple who is far away from his Saviour's presence; and far better, surely, to be able to think, as we can think now, that *wherever* two or three are assembled in Christ's name, he is there in the midst of them; than even to be able to journey far away, till we reached the place of his visible presence; and there, entering some noble pile, the mother church of Christendom, to join in a worship, simple and sublime, wherein the visible Christ himself took part. No, it is the fancy of Popery, but it is not the purpose of the Redeemer, to have one fixed, localized, visible centre of the Christian Church. It is better to have a Divine Agent, everywhere present, everywhere exercising an equal power, than to have a living Sovereign, who by the very fact of his being seen at one place, clothed in a human body, is precluded from exercising an equal influence anywhere else. But as it is, the Divine presence is equally diffused over the entire Christian world. No believer can fancy that he is overlooked, no believer can feel as though he were kept at a distance; the empire of Christ, maintained on earth by the Holy Spirit, is able to afford equal and uniform blessings at all places and at all times. The Holy City has no preference above any corner of God's earth. We are no nearer Christ at Jerusalem than we are in Galloway or at Edinburgh. And if sacred places can even yet warm the Christian's heart; if not without emotion we can even yet pace the narrow bounds of Gethsemane, or climb the slopes of Olivet, or muse where stood the accursed tree; it is but the working of natural associations that awakens the feeling; it is not that Christ is nearer us there than here. And when you and I, my friends, call it to mind, how the cares and duties of life tie most of us to one little spot of this world; when we think how vainly most of *us* might wish to make a weary pilgrimage of thousands of miles, even though that pilgrimage should bring us into the visible presence of our God; shall we not be humbly thankful that *now* we have but to enter into our closet and shut the door, and we are as near our Saviour as we can be anywhere on earth; shall we not be thankful for the presence here of a Divine Being, Sanctifier and Comforter, who can make our very soul his home; and shall we not, as we think of all he can do in all places and all hearts at once, and remember that the price paid for his presence was the loss of a visible Saviour, whose visible presence would have blessed hundreds, but only tantalized hundreds of thousands, and who can still remain with us although unseen, — shall we not, as we reckon the gains and losses, agree, after all, with that Saviour's own declaration, that "it was expedient for us that he should go away"?

So much, perhaps, we are justified in saying, before we have thought at all of the special nature and work of the Holy Spirit. Even thinking of him merely as a Divine Being, whom Christ had deputed to fill his place, it seems as if his power of universal, though invisible presence, made him even more useful to the members of a Church scattered over all the world, than a bodily, visible Redeemer, limited by time and localized in space. But when we go a little farther, and think what are the peculiar functions of the Holy Spirit, — what kind of work it is especially his to do, — we shall see, I think, even more plainly, how fit it was that so long as the Christian Church is militant upon earth, he should take the place of the visible Redeemer. For what are the functions of the Holy Spirit? He is the Regenerator; he is the Sanctifier; he is the Comforter; he is the Prompter and Dictator of prayer. It is not for us to say how far such duties as these might be performed by other Persons of the Godhead; these are things into which we have no right to pry; but this we know, that it has pleased Divine wisdom to allot such work especially to the Blessed Spirit; and such work will be done, we dare not say better, but certainly more naturally, by him than by any other. Each Person in the Trinity has his own share in the great task of preparing man for heaven; and a certain work has been appointed to the Third Person, the Holy Spirit. Now, when you think of the several things which it is the Spirit's occupation to do, do you not see that this world is the place where they must be done? Do you not see that the Holy Spirit's work lies mainly with a suffering, struggling, sinful, tempted, imperfect Church? Do you not see, in short, a special fitness, a special relation, between the workings of the Holy

Spirit, and the condition of Christian people upon earth, till the day of judgment? Yes, placed and tried as we are, it is just the Holy Spirit we need; and so it is just the Holy Spirit that we get. It is in *this* world that his gracious work is to be done. We shall need him less, with reverence be it said, when we shall have entered upon the immediate presence of our God. For are we dead by nature, must we be quickened into newness of life, must we be regenerated? Then it is by the working of the Blessed Spirit that we are born again. And once new creatures in Christ Jesus, must we be sanctified day by day? Must we grow in grace, and become meet for heaven? Then it is by the working of the Blessed Spirit that we are sanctified. Christ's people are "chosen to salvation through sanctification of the Spirit and belief of the truth." And are we pressed with cares and sorrows? Has it grown into a trite commonplace, a tale a hundred times repeated, that this is a world of sorrow, that this is a world of care? Then the Blessed Spirit is the Comforter, who can make the Saviour's people bear up patiently, and sometimes even cheerfully, amid all earthly troubles; and who, not forgetting his other great work of sanctifying, can turn all earthly care into heavenly discipline; can make the path of tribulation serve to quicken the steps, and to purify the spirit, for the upper kingdom of God! And is this a world wherein the believer must live and breathe by prayer? Is this a world wherein prayer is the channel through which we can draw all needful blessing, day by day: daily bread, daily strength, daily guidance, daily pardon, daily comfort and hope? Then the Holy Spirit, Spirit of all grace and all supplication, is by us, to put upon our poor dumb lips the words of acceptable prayer, and to breathe into our cold hearts that fervency of devotion which shall make prayer effectual and prevailing, which shall make it at once profitable and delightful to pour out our hearts in prayer at our heavenly Father's knee. Oh for that blessed Spirit! Oh that his gracious, soft, beautiful influences, coming in showers of blessing, were poured out in tenfold measure, refreshing, reviving, comforting, sanctifying, upon this dry and dusty world, upon this valley of dry bones, crumbling and cold! Oh that his gracious influences, sanctifying, comforting, were poured out in tenfold measure, upon our own sorrowful and sinful hearts!

How beautifully, how admirably, surely you will say, the powers and influences of that Blessed Spirit, are adapted to all the exigencies of the collective Church and of the individual believer! There is not a point in the soul's better life, there is not an emergency in the Christian's earthly pilgrimage, at which the Blessed Spirit does not come in, the very thing we need! He begins, and he ends, all that the Christian counts of life. His gracious influences, indeed, were purchased at a dear price. He cost the early Church the presence of its Head and Lord. He would not come,—perhaps (who knows?) he *could not*,—till the last words of blessing had parted from the ascending Saviour's lips,—till Jesus, seen as he is, had quitted this world until that day when he shall come again. But yet, so precious was his presence with us, that the Redeemer's own words assure us that it was well worth all it cost; and in the prospect of his coming, and as the condition of his coming, our Blessed Saviour hesitates not to say of himself, "It is expedient for you that I go away!"

And so, for reasons such as these, it is better as it is. It is better to have the Holy Spirit, the Regenerator, Sanctifier, Comforter, Prompter of prayer, everywhere diffused over the Christian world, working on every Christian heart, than even to have the Saviour himself consecrating some spot on earth by his visible presence. It is better as it is, for this our life of discipline for immortality; and when our life of holiness and happiness begins, then we shall see him as he is, and grow like him through that beatific vision. We have not on earth, as yet, a fitting home for him, nor fitting friends for him; we are not yet pure enough in heart to behold with these eyes our God. His tempered glory beams upon us, his strong hand touches us gently, through the intervention of an unseen Spirit, who is truly and actually God. But still, if you are Christ's true disciples,—and to Christ's true disciples this sermon is preached, — the Saviour, although "gone away," is present in your hearts and in your dwellings still. He left us in visible form; it was "expedient for us" that he should; but even as he went, he said the hopeful words, "Lo, I am with you always, even to the end of the world!" And present in his spirit, in his house, in his ordinances, in his word, surely Jesus is with us still. Softened to our poor comprehension, mellowed like the setting sun to our weak sight, we have our Saviour with us yet, and we will never let him go! He is far away, yet he is very near; he "went away," yet he never left us; we cannot see him, yet he watches us night and day; and the hour is on the wing, when he shall return in glory; when the Comforter's mission will be fulfilled; and the Blessed Redeemer and his true disciples shall meet face to face, — meet, and never part!

VII.

SPIRITUAL INSENSIBILITY.

"Who, being past feeling —." — EPH. iv. 19.

IN the wilds of North America, amid vast prairies and trackless woods, there lived, through many centuries, the race of the Red Men. Encroached upon from all sides, hemmed in by settlers from Europe, and defrauded of their ancient territories, that race of men has almost disappeared from the face of the earth. They were a race of hunters; unsettled, cruel, and deceitful; yet not without many features of character which gave them a peculiar interest. Their hospitality was inviolate; and the stern gravity of their manners deeply impressed the stranger. But there was one thing about them, in particular, which they cultivated with especial care, and which was matter of especial pride: this was their power of absolutely repressing the slightest outward exhibition of feeling. If they were glad, they never looked it; if the most awful misfortune befell them, it wrought not the least change on their iron features and their impassive demeanor. From his tree-rocked cradle to his bier, the

Indian brave was trained to bear all the extremes of good and evil, without making any sign of what he felt. If he met a friend, the dearest friend on earth; or if he was being tortured to death at the fiery stake; he preserved the same fixed, immovable aspect. And you could not please him better than by believing that he *was* as completely beyond all feeling as he *seemed;* for he set himself out as "the stoic of the woods," as "a man without a tear."

And, indeed, it is curious to think how much, in this respect, the extreme of civilization and the extreme of barbarism approach one another. Greek philosophy centuries ago, and modern refinement in its last polish of manner, alike recognize the mute Oneida's principle, that there is something manly, something fine, in the repression of human feeling. A Red Indian, a Grecian philosopher, an English gentleman, would all be pretty equally ashamed to have been seen to weep. Each would try to convey by his entire deportment the impression that he cared very little for anything. And there is no doubt at all, that it might be unworthy of the grown-up man, who has to battle with the world for his family's support, were his feelings as easily moved as in his childish days, or did his tears flow as readily as then. Even the gentleness and freshness of womanly feeling would hardly suit the rude wear of manhood's busy life. And it must be admitted, that the highest pitch of heroism to which man has ever attained, as well as the vilest degree of guilt to which man has ever sunk, has been attained, has been sunk to, by the putting down of natural feeling. The soldier volunteering for the forlorn hope, must do *that* as truly as the desperate pirate who spreads his black flag to the winds. And yet St. Paul was right when he wrote these words of my text. When he was speaking of people who had become hopelessly and fearfully bad, who had broken through every restraint, who had flung off every obligation; he was quite right to mention, as something symptomatic of their case, that they were "past feeling." They were thoroughly hardened. You could make no impression upon them. They were beyond all sense of the foulness of the sin in which they were sunk; and it was vain to think to make them feel it. And *that* was the most hopeless thing about them. Say what you might, they did not care. You could not move them; you could not touch them; you could make nothing of them;—for they were "past feeling."

We all understand, then, that there is a certain pitch of wickedness at which moral insensibility comes on; and when *that* comes on, the case becomes almost hopeless. There is little prospect of repentance or reformation then. No matter how bad any poor sinner has been, there is still some hope so long as you can get him to feel. If when you speak kindly to the poor outcast, and point out to him the shame and sinfulness of his life, and remind him of his better days and of the home of his youth, and ask him what his father and mother would have felt, if they had lived to see him what he is, and tell him how Christ is ready to receive back even the chief of repenting sinners; if the poor outcast is touched by such thoughts as these, then there is still hope for him; there may be joy in the presence of the angels of God over that poor outcast yet. But if when the Christian minister presses such thoughts upon some unhappy being whom he has found in the course of his duty, they are all listened to with a reckless unconcern, with a total apathy; if the poor wretch shows that but for some miraculous interposition of God's irresistible grace, you might as well speak to a stone; if no tear flows, if no relenting is stirred at the heart; if your reception be just one of perfect indifference; then the Christian minister's heart sinks within him. Then he feels that he can do nothing, — nothing, at least, but pray for an influence that is beyond all human power. Then, indeed, it seems as if the poor sinner is past hope, — because he is "past feeling!"

Yes, brethren, St. Paul was right. It is one of the last and worst symptoms of the soul's condition, when feeling is gone. You know that it is sometimes so also with the body. Sometimes when disease has run a certain length, there is nothing which looks so ill as an entire cessation of pain. For that may indicate that mortification has begun, and so that all hope is at an end. So with spiritual insensibility; for *that* is arrived at by most men only after a long continuance in iniquity; and *that* is an indication which gives sad ground for fearing that the Holy Spirit, without whom we can never feel anything as we ought, has ceased to strive with that hardened soul, — has left that obdurate heart alone. O brethren, let us have sinfulness, however great, so there be with it the sensibility of life; rather than outward decency and propriety of conduct, and with them the insensibility of death. There is more hope of repentance, more hope of final salvation, for the very murderer, shuddering in the condemned cell, and wakened up to an awful, overwhelming sense of the black transgressions of his life, than for the decent respectable man, who, without ever heartily believing in Jesus, has, year by year, never missed a Sunday from church, nor a sacrament from the communion-table; and who has thus grown so thoroughly familiar with religious truths, that the mention of them makes no more impression upon him than a wave makes upon a rock. The guilty criminal is now, at least, brought to a state of intense fear, of intense alarm and concern about his soul; and God only knows what good may come out of *that*. But, oh! what movement can come of pure stagnation! What can you look for but *doing nothing*, from the man who has arrived at *feeling nothing!*

But while thus we remember that to have become "past feeling" is, morally and spiritually, a very hopeless thing; and, very generally, a thing which is not reached but slowly and gradually; let us not, therefore, imagine that our text describes a state of matters which can only be found among the most degraded and abandoned of the race. I believe, on the contrary, that our text names a spiritual condition which is too common a condition; a condition to which we have all a strong tendency; a spiritual condition which we must all daily be striving and praying against. We all run a great risk of becoming so familiar with spiritual truths, as that we shall understand them and believe them without feeling them; without really feeling what their meaning is, and without that degree of emotion being excited by them that ought to be excited. I am sure that even the very best Christians among us must often be surprised to find how coolly, how indifferently, they can listen to truths so awful, that, when we think of it, it seems almost impossible that men should ever remember them but with the hushed heart and the silent earnest prayer. That God is ever by us, and ever watching us; that death and the grave are before us all, we cannot say how near; that beyond the grave there awaits us a great eternity, in which there are but the two alternatives, heaven and perdition; that Jesus died to save us from hell, to raise us to heaven; and that we are invited and entreated to believe on him, and live forever; that the few years of our earthly pilgrimage are to decide the momentous question of our eternal state; — O brethren, do you not wonder to find that you can think of all these things, and believe them all, and yet *feel* so little? And if it be true, that even the converted man, in whom what we may call the organs of spiritual perception have been quickened from their native paralysis, and the capacity of spiritual emotion in some good measure developed, by the working of Divine grace, has to wonder and lament that he believes so much, but feels it so little; we need hardly be surprised to find that in the case of most unconverted men, living in a Christian country, and probably frequenting a Christian church, there is a perfect numbness of soul; as regards spiritual things, they are, in the full sense of the words, "past feeling!" They know already all that the Christian minister can say to them; they believe it all; it has been presented to them a hundred times in all conceivable forms, and pressed upon them by all conceivable arguments and considerations; but it produces no impression; you might as well speak to the wild winds; they never feel what you say to be real, — real in the sense in which trees and fields, home and children, friends and money, are real. You may remember what a faithful and zealous minister tells us, of a conversation which he had with an aged man in his parish, a respectable, decent man, who bore an unstained character, who never was absent from church or sacrament. That zealous minister, in his parochial visitation, went to that respectable man's house, and there, addressing him and his family, he told simply of the salvation that is in Christ, and urged those who listened to a hearty acceptance of it. The minister finished what he had to say, and when he left the house his friend accompanied him; and when they were alone together, said something like this: "Spend your time and strength upon *the young;* labor to bring *them* to Jesus; it is too late for such as me. I know," he said, "that I have never been a Christian. I fully believe that when I die I shall go down to perdition; but somehow *I do not care.* I know perfectly all you can say; but I feel it no more than a stone." And that man, we are told, died with the like words on his lips. He had lost the spring-time of his life; he had missed the tide in his affairs that might have borne him to heaven; his heart had, under the deadening influence of a present world, grown hard and unimpressionable; and saving only God's irresistible Spirit, there was no use in any one speaking of religious things to such as him. Oh, past feeling! Past feeling! Not past it in the mere sentimental sense in which the poet tells us that "it is the one great woe of life to feel all feeling die;" not past it in that mere sentimental sense in which youth has a freshness of feeling and heart which tames down, which passes away with advancing years; not past it merely in that sense in which as we grow older we grow less susceptible, less capable of all emotion; not past it merely in the sense, that when the hair grows gray, and the pulse turns slower, the tear flows less readily at the gospel story, and even at the table of communion we miss somewhat of the warmth of heart and the vividness of thought which we felt in earlier days; but "past feeling" in that saddest sense, that religious words fall with little meaning on the ear, and with no impression at all upon the heart; "past feeling" in that saddest sense, that now to all spiritual truths, to all expostulation and all entreaty, to God's abounding mercy, to Christ's blessed sacrifice, to the hopes of heaven and the fears of perdition, the understanding may indeed yield a torpid, listless assent; but the heart is stone!

Now, my friends, there is no doubt at all, that in the nature of things, by the very make of our being, we have to lament that we are far less impressed and affected by spiritual truths than we ought to be. We know them; we understand them; we believe them; but somehow we do not realize them; we do not, in short, *feel* them. And till we have in some degree "passed from death to life," — from death, with its torpor and insensibility, to life, with its keen senses and its quick perception, — we never can rightly feel spiritual things in their overwhelming reality and importance. And perhaps, indeed, so long as our souls are clogged by these mortal bodies, the true force and meaning of those grand realities which are discerned by faith and not by sight will never be felt by us as they ought. Oh, there would be no wicked men, if people realized what is meant by heaven and hell; there would be no worldly men, if people realized what is meant by time and eternity; there would be no heart cold to the gracious invitations of the Blessed Redeemer, if people realized to their hearts how kind and merciful and forbearing and gracious HE was and is; and realized to their hearts that in that gentle, sympathizing, loving Being, we see the visible image of the invisible God! But true as all this is; true as it is that at no period in our life, not even when the heart is softest and the head least sophisticated, do we naturally feel spiritual things as they ought to be felt; still it is true no less, that as we grow hardened through the wear of life, we must, apart from Divine grace, grow less and less impressible by them. Even in earliest youth we do not feel divine things as we ought; but in the common course of things, as we grow older, we shall always feel them less; because as we grow older, all feeling becomes less easily awakened, religious feeling and natural feeling alike. We grow so familiar with divine things, that they cease to strike us as they might strike a stranger. We know so thoroughly well all that the preacher can say to us, that his words fall upon our ear with the worn-out interest of a twenty-times repeated tale. What can we hear when we go to church that we do not know already? What argument can at this time of day be addressed to us, with which we have not been many times already plied? Oh for a return of the days when we first believed in Christ! Oh for a revival of the warm, fresh feelings of communion Sabbaths past and gone! Oh for a return of those early days when the tears flowed at gospel story; when, with the warm, touched heart, we traced the life of the Man of Sorrows from the manger to the grave, and listened to his comfortable words, and watched his deeds of mercy, and felt our souls burn within us at the recollection that all he did and all he suffered was done and suffered for us, and for such as we are! Oh for a revival of those better days, before years and care and hard experience had withered up the heart, and frozen the founts of feeling!

But, my brethren, while we never forget that in the case of even a true Christian, it is a sad thing when, as years go on, his religion appears to be always growing more a thing of the head, and less a thing of the heart; and while we are well assured that no one will lament *that* more than the true Christian himself; let us remember that such a train of thought must not be pushed too far. It would be very wrong if the aged believer were to fancy that because his religious feelings are growing less keen, less easily excited, than in former years, he must therefore conclude that he is backsliding from his God, and leaving his first love. He takes his place, shall we say, at the table of high communion; he receives into his hands those simple elements which mean so much; but he grieves as he misses something of that warm feeling which he remembers used to come over him in days gone by; and perhaps he makes himself unhappy by trying to awaken feeling which no longer comes spontaneous, and which, if it do not come spontaneous, will not come at all. He is causing for himself needless sorrow when he so acts and thinks. It is just that he has grown older, and so less capable of all emotion; but his choice of Christ may be just as firm, and his religious convictions as deep as ever. Religion in the soul has to do with both the head and the heart; it would be quite as false to represent it as entirely a thing of sentiment, as to make it entirely a matter of principle and resolution. We know that Christianity is such in its essential nature as to suit all sorts of men, those in whom the intellectual faculties predominate, no less than those in whom the emotional. True and vital religion is a plant which will grow in either soil; either soil may be good, and we cannot say which is best; and it may be that the calm, thoughtful mood, in which the old man covers his face, as he bends over the white cloth, befits as well our calm feast of remembrance, as do the young believer's tears. It seems to me as if some good divines go wrong, when they lead communicants at a sacrament time to fancy that feeling is the test and touchstone of worthy receiving; and that according as *that* is present or absent, the partaker of that consecrated bread and wine has made a worthy or an unworthy approach to the Lord's table. No doubt, warm emotion at such a time is much to be desired; no doubt we cannot but have a certain disappointment if it be lacking; but after all, it is of the nature of a luxury rather than of a necessary; and if it should please God to deny it to us, he may still be feeding us with the bread of life, though it may taste to us less sweet and refreshing than we have known it do. If, as years go on, the time comes, when even under the roof-tree of a long-parted father's house, even standing by his young sister's grave, the man of no more than middle age wonders that he feels so little where once he felt so much, we need not wonder if the same law extends to even the holiest emotion. And though we may think of it with sorrow, we need not necessarily think of it with remorse, if we have grown in some degree "past feeling."

But while it would not have been right, had I failed to mark this great exception to the general principle which seems to be implied in the text, it would be wrong, did I fail to add, that it is only to such as have really some good ground for hoping that they have believed in Christ, that all this should be any ground of comfort. If a man is truly a Christian, then the fact, that as time goes on, religious truths come to affect him less, and less than he could wish, may be explained by these two laws of mind: that when things grow quite familiar, they strike us less, and cannot but strike us less, than when they are new and strange; and also, that as we grow older, we grow, by the make of our being, less susceptible of the warm, lively feelings of childhood and of youth.

But if a man be not a believer; and if, when he listens to the declaration of the doctrines of the Cross, he understands them but does not feel them; if he knows thoroughly well that whosoever does not betake himself to the great atonement of Christ must perish eternally; and if he knows too that he himself has never gone to Christ, and never prepared to die; and if, with all this, he *does not care;* ah, *then* there is a sad and a fearful explanation of how he comes to be so! Ah, there is a sad and a fearful reason for all this insensibility! Is there not some reason at least to fear that this dead calm, this utter heedlessness, is because God's Spirit has let that man alone, has given him up, and is striving with him no more? Is there not something awful and strange, something beyond the mere spiritual insensibility of nature, in the calm recklessness, the cool apathetic indifference, of the man who knows perfectly that there is but a step between him and death, and that to him death means perdition; and yet who lives on quite quietly and comfortably, attending to his business, enjoying his home comforts, improving his estate — and *does not care!* Ah, has God indeed given him up? Is the black brand already, if we could but see it, on that composed and polite face! How else can we understand how he can come regularly, perhaps, to church; and listen to doctrines that should save, that should at the very least alarm him; and believe them all; and go away home and never mind! Surely there seems to be no other way in which it is possible to explain a state of things which exists in too many cases, — which is a sadly common one, — than by supposing that the decree has gone forth which we know went forth concerning ancient Ephraim: "He is joined to his idols, let him alone!" Surely you would say, that man is not sane! Surely he is under some fatal, mysterious influence, that paralyzes the soul's perceptions, and that deadens its feelings! And so he is, my friends. So are all of you, who weekly listen to the preached gospel, yet never seriously go to Christ, and never earnestly seek to make your peace with God. A faithfully preached gospel will act upon the soul in one of two perfectly opposite ways. It will either save, or it will harden. And if it do not save, it is sure to harden. If you listen to the declaration of the message of mercy, — if you come to know all about it, — if you grow familiar with all the arguments which the Christian minister can employ to impress it upon your heart, — and yet if after all you do not become a believer, — then if all this has gone on for years, it is less likely that the arrow of conviction will ever reach your obdurate, your hardened heart, than if you were a poor heathen in some darkened land that never heard of Jesus, and where, if that blessed name ever should be heard, it will come with the freshness of a surprise. The gospel has hardened *you!* The Saviour has knocked at the door so long, while you never opened it, that now you have grown familiar with the sound, and it is never noticed by your listless ear. We feel deeply, and right that we should, for the missionary laboring in distant lands, and seeking to convey the elements of the knowledge of Christ to the narrow understanding of the untutored savage; but narrow as is that untutored being's understanding, still he has a heart capable of deep feeling, and on his ear the glad tidings fall fresh and new. And perhaps the deeper sympathy is due, where we should hardly think of giving it, — due to the earnest minister of some beautiful country parish, whose congregation has listened to the gospel message so long, that many among it are thoroughly hardened; that all who are not converted are hopelessly hardened; and have been so often roused to inefficacious convictions, to passing concern that ended in nothing, that now you need speak to them no more, — that now they are "past feeling."

Then, brethren, let it be your earnest prayer and endeavor at once to go to him who came to seek and save the lost. There is deep philosophy, there is accurate knowledge of human nature, in the inspired warning, "To-day, if ye will hear his voice, harden not your hearts." For, speaking humanly, every day that repentance is put off, is making repentance more difficult. "*Now* is the accepted time, *now* is the day of salvation." With every succeeding day, your hearts are growing harder; you are becoming less capable of receiving any deep impression, or of making any vital change. You are leaving behind you, day by day, the more impressible season of your life. And if you live on, you are advancing to years in which the heart will always be more difficult to touch; and in which the care of religion, neglected so long, may become more than difficult, — may become impossible. The Holy Spirit, without whom you can do nothing, may be finally grieved away. You may reach at last that hopeless condition, that you shall know quite well that your soul is lost; and yet only wish to think of something else, and only feel that you do not care. You may live to know, that, as regards religion, you are "past feeling," and so past hope. It must be sad, indeed, to see the hardened criminal listen to the sentence of death, which the judge who utters it can scarcely pronounce, with utter insensibility; but all men think of *him* as of some monstrous exception to the common nature of humanity. And surely it is sadder by far to see a human being, a rational man, going onwards to a doom which Jesus wept to think of, which Jesus died to save from, — careless, heedless, feelingless as a stone. And yet there are some in every congregation who are doing all *that!* Oh, God have mercy on such, if there are any here! You have lived too long, my friends. You have outlived "the day of your visitation." What can we do but pray that the Divine Spirit may even yet speak to you, in sentences so telling, that they shall touch and penetrate even the obdurate heart, that, to human power, is "past feeling!"

VIII.

LIGHT AT EVENING.

"But it shall come to pass, that at evening-time it shall be light."
ZECHARIAH xiv. 7.

IT is when the day is drawing to its close, that most men have their hour of leisure. The season of toil is past, the task is laid apart, the strain upon bone and sinew is relaxed; and if it be the winter-time, we gather around the fire to enjoy the feeling of repose; and if it be the summer days that are passing over us, we wander forth in the declining light, and mark how nature sinks to slumber. We know, most of us, how nature looks at evening, better than we know how she seems in the busier hours of the day; we are too much occupied during them to have time for watching the aspect of trees and fields, the form of clouds and the azure of the sky. But in our evening leisure we have many a time had the opportunity of marking the sun's gradual withdrawal, the shadows as they darkened upon the landscape, the mist stealing upward from the river, and its murmur deepening upon the ear, the leaves so motionless, the silent fields, the universal hush and quiet. But after all, if we were asked what it is that makes the evening-time, — even the evening-time of summer, — we have no difficulty in singling out from the many features which we have remarked so often, that which is the essence of the evening, and the cause of them all. It is the gradual withdrawal of the light. It is the lessening light, after all, that makes the evening-time. It is because of *that* that the daisies close, and the birds fly to their nests, and this hush comes over nature. And it is just because evening is the time when, in the ordinary course of things, the light is going and the darkness is coming, that there is anything remarkable in the text which you have read. "At the evening-time there shall be light;" that is, light shall come at a period when it is not natural, when in the common course of things it is not looked for. It would be no surprise that light should come at noonday. We expect it then. It is just what we are accustomed to see. Hundreds and thousands of times we know that the sun has risen, and steadily advanced to his meridian splendor; and all this, we think, is only the usual thing. But if, when the twilight shadows were falling deeper and deeper, when the distant woods seemed in a slumberous trance, and the distant hills showed purple against the soft crimson, with a sudden burst the noonday light were to spread around, — that would be a surprise. It would be indeed only a thing which we are accustomed to see, but it would be coming at a time when we are not accustomed to see it. Yet nothing less than this is signified in that remarkable promise, given first to the Church of God and then to individual believers, that in their experience, in their day, " at the evening-time it shall be light."

That is, to state the promise in the form of a general principle, great and signal blessing shall come just when it is least expected. Evening, usually the season of increasing and encroaching darkness, is to be the season of special light. And this would be a noteworthy thing, if it happened at the close of the very brightest day. But it appears, from the words which precede the text, that this special light is promised at the end of a day which should be somewhat overcast and dreary. " It shall come to pass in that day, that the light shall not be clear, nor dark ; but it shall be one day which shall be known to the Lord, not day, nor night; but it shall come to pass, that at evening-time it shall be light." The day, you perceive, was not to be one of unmingled serenity, nor yet of unrelieved gloominess; there should be, perhaps, succession of light and shadow, and for great part of it, it might be, a subdued and sober gray; but however that might be, light should come upon the darkened way at last. And in all this, we have the picture set before us, of the ordinary Christian's ordinary life, and likewise of the history of the collective Church of God. As regards our daily life, my believing friends, how true it is that " the light is not clear, nor dark ;" childhood looks sunshiny when we cast back our glance upon it; and youth, too, has its bright blinks of light-heartedness and freedom from care; but as years go on, life turns but a matter-of-fact and commonplace thing; not much of the old gayety is left, not much of the elastic spring of spirit but is pressed out by the weary load of constant care; and yet it would be unjust to say that, except in exceptional seasons of deep sorrow, life is all gloom; there is usually something to enjoy, as well as something to bear; there is an equable sobriety, a sort of average endurableness, about this "pleasing, anxious being;" the light is "not clear, nor dark." And so, too, as regards our spiritual life. It is with *that* just very much as it is with our outward lot. There are times, indeed, when we seem to be upon the mountain's summit, and to feel the light of our heavenly Father's face beaming upon us without a cloud between, and to see the promised land almost as it were under our feet; perhaps on a Communion Sabbath, perhaps in a lonely walk, perhaps in an hour of solitary prayer; but oh, how fast these glimpses of sunshine leave us, and we may be thankful if it is no worse with us than just that the light is "not clear, nor dark;" for sometimes there come days of spiritual desertion and depression, in which it seems to us as if the Sun of Righteousness would never shine upon us more. It should seem as if God judged that neither in providence nor in grace would it be good for us to have either unvarying gladness or unvarying gloom; they shall come to us in succession; — or, if we are to have anything for a continuance, it shall be a sobered twilight, "not clear, nor dark." And so, too, in the history of God's Church on earth; it is but seldom it has known great extremity, whether of good or ill; there is for the most part mercy for which to be thankful, as well as judgment to which to bow. But however heavily the day might drag through, with however little of joyous light throughout its course, it was quite certain how it should close, so only it were a Christian day. There might be no great light where it might have been looked for; but *that* should be compensated by abundant light where men might have expected none. At the evening-time, if never before, — at the evening-time, there should be an end of that subdued twilight. *Then*, there should be light at last. When the Christian's little day has drawn to its close, when the Christian's earthly sun has set, then there should be to him the beginning of a day whose sun shall never go down, and whose brightness shall be lessened by no intrusion of the dark. Then a day shall break in which there shall be no anxiety, no care, no sorrow, no hiding of God's face, no struggle with temptation, no fall into sin; not one moment's darkness to mingle with that unvaried day. And so, too, with the Church of the living God, as with the separate members of it. When the world's day is closing in, when Time's evening is hastening on, then a light will be dawning upon the Church, purer and better a million times than that which led her forth from the ages which we call dark. At the evening-time there shall be light; and as for the season which shall follow the evening-time, we know that it shall find the triumphant Church in that country to which darkness can never come; because concerning that country, God's word assures us, that "there shall be no night there!"

We understand the text, then, first, in its most general and extensive meaning, as signifying that, in God's dealing with his children, it very often happens that signal blessing and deliverance come just when they are needed most, but expected least. "Man's extremity," we are sometimes told, "is God's opportunity;" it is when times are at the worst that they begin to mend. I purpose to show the prevalence of this law in the Almighty's treatment of believers individually; a thought upon days past will suffice to remind us how often the case has proved so as regards the collective Church. When was it that the first great promise was given, that contained the germ of so many more, "exceeding great and precious," but in the hour of that first sin which brought in so much death and woe? Surely it was in as dark a season as ever over-clouded this world, that the first beams of the Sun of Righteousness trembled upon the gloomy horizon. When and where was it that Abraham was called out to be the Father of the Faithful, but in a country and an age of the most degraded idol-worship? When did deliverance come to God's oppressed people in the land of Egypt, but when their slavery had grown altogether intolerable, — when the heavy task was doubled, and the first-born doomed to die? When did the Blessed Redeemer himself come, but in the world's darkest day? He, the "true light," shone upon our race just when "darkness had covered the earth, and thick darkness the people." And, not to multiply instances, was it not when, through centuries of ignorance and degeneracy, the better light of the glorious gospel was all but entirely eclipsed and hidden from men's eyes by falsehood and superstition, that men were raised up to clear away the accumulated rubbish of the Papacy, and set out gospel-doctrines in their saving simplicity again? The least acquaintance with the history of the world will bring before us a host of instances in which the oppressed and persecuted, sometimes the cold and apathetic, Church of God found better days dawn when they were least looked for, and so found the fulfilment of the promise, that "at the evening-time there should be light."

And now, when we turn to think of individual Christians, I might well trust the illustration of my text to the memory and the heart of each of you,— of those among you, I mean, who are able humbly to trust that you have given your souls to his keeping, who is able to preserve what is committed to him till the great day of account. Ah, no sermon that I could write will go home to the aged Christian's heart, like that sermon which is gently breathed to him from his own life's story. You do not need to tell *him* that in the experience of Christ's people, at the evening-time there often comes light; for he has found it so. He has learned it by experience. Many a time, through the years of his life, it has seemed as though darkness were settling down upon his path and his home; but when things were almost at the blackest, of a sudden his heavenly Father sent unlooked-for deliverance; the perplexity was unravelled, the cloud was dispersed, the falling stroke was withheld, the loss was compensated a hundred-fold, the bereavement was blessed and sanctified; the light came softly, beautifully, upon the benighted way. Yes, the humble Christian's life is the best sermon upon this text; and his own memory the best preacher. Each Christian has had his own dark seasons, to which God sent his own light; and these times of needfulness and of deliverance are known, perhaps, to no one but himself, — not even, it may be, to his very dearest. There is an inner world of thought and feeling in which each of us lives, wherein we are profoundly alone; and many a light and shadow may sweep over that little world, many a twilight gloominess may come, and many a heaven-sent light may scatter it, of which none save ourselves will ever know. And what reflecting person but must look with interest upon some thoughtful, aged man, as he thinks what an unread volume there is within that aged man's heart, in the remembrance of his own history, and in his reflections upon its changes and events? Yet, though I never can know with what peculiar force my text may present itself to each of you, my Christian friends, or from what passages in your own life you may draw your most impressive illustrations of my text; still, let us in that general way in which alone it is possible to discourse on a subject like this, in discoursing upon which the preacher is but drawing a bow at a venture, think of several occasions in the life of each of us, on which light has come, or may yet come, at evening-time.

And first, my Christian friends, has it been in your experience, that you did not feel the light of God's reconciled countenance lifted upon you, but after a dark eventide of anxiety and fear? We know that in the common course of God's grace, the soul must be awakened from worldliness and carelessness by fear; we must be convinced of our sin and misery by nature by God's Holy Spirit, before we feel our need of a Saviour, and surrender our helpless, sinful souls to him by simple faith. How many a one has never known what it was to find peace and rest in Jesus, till he had passed through a fiery trial; till he had been made to feel his sins a burden that was like to drive him to utter despair! How many a one can tell that the very darkest days of his life were the days of his spiritual awakening; that the terrors of the law laid their grasp upon him; that he felt himself a sinner above all other men; and that not till after a long and gloomy evening, say rather night, the happy light visited his soul! Not that in every case it is so. Not but that some happy souls may have been regenerated from their very birth, and, growing up under the pious influences of a Christian home, may have chosen Jesus as their portion from the earliest dawn of intelligence, and thus may have needed no conversion; for conversion means turning into another way. and wherefore should they do *that* who, trained up in the way they should go, are advancing in the heavenward path already? But though such cases are conceivable, we believe that they are very rare; that no holy training, however constant and kindly, can prevent the children of the most pious parents from being at least thoughtless and careless as to their soul's salvation; and who that has ever been aroused to a conviction of guilt and danger, but knows that *that* is a sin which sits heavy and crushing as any, upon the quickened soul? Yes, most men need conversion; and conversion is, for the most part, a dark and miserable time. But that is a darkness which is followed by a gracious light. The more heavily the burden of sin is felt to press upon the soul, the more heartily will the soul turn to him who alone can take it away. The deeper the darkness, the pleasanter the following light. It seemed to you, perhaps, that your sins were too great to be forgiven; that you had broken your purposes of amendment so often, and trifled with the gospel invitations so long, that now there was no hope for you,—that God's Spirit was quite grieved away. But at last you were brought to feel how free is the offer of salvation, how willing God is to receive the repenting sinner, how sure is that precious sheet-anchor of the despairing soul, "Him that cometh unto me I will in nowise cast out;" you were enabled with all your heart and mind to trust yourself to your Saviour; and then the gloom was scattered, and "at the evening-time there was light."

Let me further mention to you, as another occasion on which the gracious promise in the text has often proved true to the Christian, the season of great trial, —of losses, disappointments, bereavements. Every one knows that these are indeed dark seasons in our life; and the Christian knows that it has often happened that wonderful support and strong consolation have often been vouchsafed to him as he was passing through them,—that amid the dreary evening there stole in a strange, unearthly light. And I am not thinking now of those times when the darkness was, so to speak, entirely dissipated,—when the threatened trial was prevented from coming at all; when the hope, though long deferred, met with its fulfilment at last, when the dear one whose loss you dreaded was wonderfully restored and spared to you. I desire you to think of those sad seasons when sorrow did its very worst; when the cherished plan was entirely frustrated, when the possession you so prized was wrecked, and the friend you so loved died. Even then, have you not sometimes found it so, that a heavenly light has stolen into the bleeding heart, into the darkened chamber, into the house of death? No doubt, indeed, it was a sore trial when it pleased God to shut against you the way to that earthly eminence, honor, usefulness, on which you had set your heart; no doubt it was a miserable time when you were forced to turn your back upon the scenes and the friends you loved best in this world, and, pressed by the hard exigencies of life, to go far away; no doubt, it was a time not even yet to be remembered but with some return of the old aching desolation, when death made the first break in the family circle, and you saw the face that used to brighten at your presence, heedless, fixed, and cold. These were indeed the dark periods of your life; but still the darkness was not quite unrelieved. Did you not feel, with something like surprise, that now the worst had come, you were far less crushed down by it than you had expected; that whatever was taken from you, you still had much left to be thankful for; that as for the disappointment, — well, perhaps things were better as they were; that as for the bereavement, bitter as that was, you could bear it when you remembered how far happier it was to be a pure and blessed spirit in the perfect safety and peace above, than to be perhaps a poor sufferer in this evil world of sin and peril and sorrow and risk of endless loss; and when you remembered, too, that the same happy world to which your lost friend had gone before you was inviting you no less to enter upon its endless rest and quiet and union. And so, at the evening-time there came light; quietly, meekly, humbly, you set yourself to the duties that remained to you; you would do your task, you thought, though with a breaking heart; you would try to feel kindly towards all around you, though you never could care for any as for those who were no longer here; resignation and content might come, you thought, but cheerfulness and light-heartedness you did not look for; till, as the days and weeks crept on, you felt the revival of the old interest in life; you ceased to feel it a mournful contrast between the desolate feeling within, and the smiling face of the summer world; you felt the strength growing equal to the day, the strong consolation matching the need for it; the cloud was there yet, but the sunshine was breaking through; it was still the twilight, but *there*, in the distant horizon, you could see the dawn of brighter days; you had found, in a word, the fulfilment of God's blessed promise, that grace and strength and consolation should come when they were most needed but least expected; that "at the evening-time there shall be light!"

Thus, then, my friends, we have thought of several times in the progress of the Christian's life, at which he may find, through God's grace, some fulfilment of this precious promise; and now, in the last place, let us think of one time more, at which the evening may be darker, at which the evening will deepen into night, but at which the light that comes shall be perfect and never-setting. It is to that period, doubtless, that the text, when applied to individual Christians, makes especial reference; the evening-time of life, when the dark valley of the shadow of death must be trodden. The day of life, shall we think, is drawing to its close. It has been, on the whole, a sober day, with "the light not clear, nor dark;" there has been neither unvarying sunshine, nor unvarying gloom; there have been, no doubt, some great trials in it, and a host of little, insect cares, which do no worse than fret and annoy; it has seemed, perhaps, a dull and weary thing, yet we have grown to like even its dulness and commonness; it has had within it times of special elevation, love to the Redeemer, trust in God; and it has had, too, its seasons of backsliding, of coldness and worldliness, of lack of interest in spiritual engagements, of despondency, and almost of despair. For the day of grace goes by just such rules as the day of providence; and, save a few blessed and memorable believers, who have seemed to breathe the air of heaven even while they lived on earth, it is the general experience of even the earnest believer, that his inward feeling, like his outward lot, is a checkered one, is in the main a sobered one, — is shone upon by a light which is "not clear, nor dark." But the evening of the long day is drawing on at length; the day that dawned with the sunny cheerfulness of infancy and childhood, that went on amid the growing cares of maturity, that sloped westerly amid the enfeebled powers and the flagging hopes of age; and as the evening advances, as the hours go on in which the light that had lasted through the day might naturally grow less, — strange how it oftentimes is that *that* unwearied light does but beam brighter and clearer! It was but a cloudy day; but the Sun of Righteousness has broken through the clouds; the flaming west is all purple and gold; it is the evening-time, and oh, how fair its light! It has sometimes been as in that beautiful story, that the last steps before the dark river was reached lay through the land Beulah; — that already the brightness of the Golden City shone from afar upon the believer's face, and his sharpened ear could almost catch the fall of its ceaseless songs. I do not say that such a thing is common; all I say is that such a thing has been; and wherefore should it not be again with you or me? I shall not pretend to describe this happy state in my own words; I shall tell you about it in the words of one who spoke from his own experience, and who, shortly before he died, wrote as thus: — "Were I to adopt the figurative language of Bunyan, I might date this letter from the land of Beulah, of which I have been for some weeks a happy inhabitant. The Celestial City is full in my view. Its glories have been upon me, its breezes fan me, its odors are wafted to me, its sounds strike upon my ears, and its spirit is breathed into my heart. Nothing separates me from it but the river of death, which now appears but as an insignificant rill, that may be crossed at a single step, whenever God shall give permission. The Sun of Righteousness has been gradually drawing nearer and nearer, appearing larger and brighter as he approached, and now he fills the whole hemisphere; pouring forth a flood of glory, in which I seem to float like an insect in the beams of the sun; exulting, yet almost trembling, while I gaze on this excessive brightness, and wondering with unutterable wonder why God should deign thus to shine upon a sinful worm." There, my hearers, are words dictated by experience; *that* is what was actually written by a dying man. And, oh, what need I add to it, to make you feel how glorious a sermon it is upon the blessed promise, that "at the evening-time there shall be light!"

But then you will say to me, and say it truly, that it is not always so. Not only is it not the case that all who have "died the death of the righteous" have thus tranquilly, fearlessly, hopefully, triumphantly passed away, — but has not such a thing been known, as that one who was a true Christian, if true Christian ever breathed, died absolutely in despair? Oh, who can forget the story of that sweet and gentle poet, who would take nothing to himself at the last of the comfort his words have given to others; whose latest lines sadly tell us how his soul was whelmed in deeper than Atlantic depths; who regarded himself as doomed to everlasting perdition; and who shuddered at the very mention of the name of that Blessed Redeemer who was looking down in kindness upon his wayward child! But then, let me remind you, that fine as was that poet's mind, it was a mind unhinged and deranged; and however the Holy Spirit works upon the renewed soul, he no more sets himself to cure the hereditary diseases of the mind than those of the body. Religion does not alter temperament: it leaves the cheerful man cheerful; it leaves the anxious, desponding man still prone to look at the future through the haze of anxiety and fear. It no more pretends to cure that hereditary taint, that overshadowing gloom, that all his life had its grasp of Cowper's mind, than it pretends to weed out the family consumption or apoplexy from the Christian's body; and never let us forget, that constitutional temperament, and the depressing influences of many forms of disease, may make dark and distressful the dying bed of the very best believer. Perhaps, even with true Christians, the death is as the life was; the evening is what the day was, "not clear, nor dark," as the general rule. There are blessed hopes, but there are also distressing fears. And shall we say, then, that this text does not speak truth? No, far from that. The light *does* come; and it comes at evening; but evening is the close of day; and the light may perhaps not beam forth until day has entirely closed.

Not upon this side of time may the blessed promise find its fulfilment. The foot may be dipped in the chill, dark river, before the heavenly light has shone upon the face. The eye may be blind to dearest faces and forms, ere the Sun of Righteousness dawns; as in the natural world, the darkest, coldest hour is that before the daybreak. The tongue may never be able to tell surviving loved ones, how the shadows fled away when the dark valley was past, till they have passed through that darkness too. Yes, to the believer, true as that God liveth, "at the evening-time there *shall* be light;" if not in this world, then in a better! Bowing his head to pass under the dark portal, the believer lifts it up on the other side, in the presence and the light of God. It is but a single step from the darkness of death into the light of immortality; and if the evening should remain gloomy to its very end, all the brighter will seem the glory when the latest breath has parted. I told you how that Christian poet passed away almost in despair, — how the gloom that overshadowed his spirit endured all but to the end; but even in the last moment there came a wonderful change,—and they tell us how even on his dead face, there remained till it was hidden forever, a look of bright and beautiful and sudden surprise; the light at evening had been long in coming; but oh, it had come at last!

There is something very touching about the story of that eminent teacher, the most eminent of his time, who, when his mind wandered in the weakness of the dying hour, fancied himself among his pupils, engaged in his accustomed work; and whose last words, when the shadow of death was falling deeper, were, "It grows dark, boys; you may go." There is something touching too, in the parting scene of that great poet, dying as the sun was going down in its summer glory, who bade his friends raise him up that he might see the light once more,—open the window that he might look on the setting sun again, before his eyes should close upon the earthly light forever. And very strange it is, indeed, to stand, as some of us may have stood, in the chamber of death; and in the west to see the summer sunset blazing, and the golden rays shining upon the still face, and the closed eyes which never shall open more till the sun has ceased to shine. But it is only to us who remain that the evening darkness is growing,—only for us that the sun is going down. Oh! look on the fixed features of that disciple now asleep in Jesus; and think, as the prophet spake, "Thy sun shall no more go down; neither shall thy moon withdraw itself; for the Lord shall be thine everlasting light, and the days of thy mourning shall be ended." And oh, my hearers, tell me; as the evening falls on you, but not on him; as the shadows deepen on you, but not on him; as the darkness gathers on you, but not on him;—if now, at last, the glorious promise has not found its perfect fulfilment, that "at the evening-time there shall be light!"

IX.

A GREAT MULTITUDE A SAD SIGHT.

" And Jesus went forth, and saw a great multitude, and was moved with compassion toward them." — St. Matt. xiv. 14.

THERE is something, surely, that is remarkable in this statement of the evangelist. Our Saviour, we are told, looked upon a great multitude of human beings; and the feeling which that sight awakened in his breast was a feeling of pity and compassion. He saw the people; and he felt sorry for them. Now the general impression is, that a great mass of human beings collected in one place forms a grand and imposing spectacle rather than a pitiful and a sad one. Most people who have seen a vast crowd of many thousands of men, would tell us that they felt thrilled and awed at the sight; — that there was something in it inexpressibly awe-striking and impressive. Any one who has been accustomed to worship God in the presence of a very large congregation, could tell you how fine a sight it is when the great dark mass arises at once to the prayer, or listens as with one heart and mind to the exhortation. And no doubt this general belief that there is something grand and impressive about a great multitude is a true belief; but if we may draw a general principle from the words you have read, there is something farther and deeper about a great multitude, which suggests itself less immediately and less generally. We are not told whether when Jesus looked upon this occasion on the vast crowds that had followed him into the desert, he was impressed by their wide extent and their wave-like undulation, and awed by their mighty hum. We are not told whether he felt roused and stirred by the thousands of eager faces that were bent upon him, or whether he thought to himself that here was a congregation that was worthy of even his best preaching. But one thing we *are* told: that when he saw a great multitude, he was moved with compassion toward them. Nor does it appear that there was anything peculiar about *this* multitude specially to draw forth his compassion. He would have felt just as much pity awakened in his kind heart by the sight of *any* great assemblage of men. No doubt there were sick folk in that multitude, for we are told that the Saviour "healed their sick;" no doubt there were weary people there, for they had "followed him on foot," and they had followed him far; no doubt there were hungry people among them, for not without sufficient reason would our Lord have multiplied the loaves and fishes to keep them from "fainting by the way." But it does not seem that there was much, if there was anything, about that crowd to make it a sadder sight than any other. Hunger and weariness, sickness and sorrow, are not such uncommon things. Look at any great gathering of human beings, in any part of the world, and you may feel sure that there are many sad hearts there. No, it was for no accidental reason that the Saviour compassionated that multitude. If Jesus felt moved to pity in the sight of that crowd, it must have been because in some sense and in some measure, it is always a sad sight to look upon a crowd of men. And what we wish to do, in this discourse, is to consider what there can be in the presence of a great multitude that should move a kind and feeling heart to compassion. Why was it that when "Jesus went forth, and saw a great multitude, he was moved with compassion toward them"?

And to give us some little light on the subject, let us call it to mind that Christ was not the first who had felt that the sight of a great number of men was sad. It is now three-and-twenty centuries since a great monarch of the East, bent upon subjugating an independent race, collected together a force so large that it has hardly been equalled in the history of the world. His ships were ten thousand; his soldiers were three millions. When this incredible array was assembled, the king desired to see it all at one view; and he sat down, we read, upon a throne of white marble, whence, stretched along the shore, he beheld his fleet and his army. I will tell you the story in the simple words of the earliest of secular historians. "When he saw the whole Hellespont concealed beneath the ships, and all the coast of Abydos full of men, Xerxes held himself happy; but soon after he burst into tears. This being observed by his paternal uncle Artabanus, he, understanding that Xerxes was shedding tears, addressed him thus: 'Sire, how very different are your present actions, and what you did erewhile! For then you declared yourself happy, and now you weep.' The king answered, 'Yes; for when I consider how short is human life, pity enters my heart; since of these, many as they are, every one will be dead before a hundred years.'" That Persian monarch, knowing no immortality, looked abroad over his millions, gathered in proud array; and he knew that whatever might be their courage and their numbers, there was one quiet and sure adversary who would vanquish them at the last. The plains and the shores around him were warm with life. Millions of pulses beat; millions of strong hands and anxious brains were there; but before a century, they would be all dead and buried and forgotten. And at the thought, even the selfish and foolish tyrant wept. He acknowledged by the act that there is something pitiful to see, in a great multitude of men.

The Persian monarch, when asked why he wept at the sight of something so little likely to move tears as a noble army with gay banners and bright arms, thought he gave reason sufficient when he mentioned the shortness of the life to which each individual in it was destined. But the historian tells us that the man whom he addressed replied to him, that he did not think *that* the saddest thing in the lot of humanity. "Other woes," he said, "yet more deserving than this of commiseration, do we suffer during life. Indeed, the calamities that fall upon us, and the maladies that shake our frames, make life, short though it is, to appear long; death therefore becomes the most desirable refuge for man." It was not that life was so short, but that it was so sad, that the wise Persian counsellor thought the true cause for tears. The true reason, *he* thought, for looking with compassion upon a great multitude, was rather that the men who composed it were pressed by care and sorrow while they lived, than that they would die so soon.

But we may very well combine the two reasons for pitying human beings which were stated by Xerxes and by Artabanus; they are quite consistent each with the other; and there is truth in both of them. No doubt,—no doubt,—it is a reason why the feeling heart should be moved with compassion in the view of a large assemblage of people, to think how much suffering each of them must have gone through; — to look at the anxious faces, the thinned hair, the furrowed brow, and to reflect what weariness, care, disappointment, anxiety, sorrow, each heart there must have known; and no doubt, too, it is a reason why the feeling heart should be moved to compassion in the view of a large assembly, to think of the last solemn scene which lies before each of them, — to reflect upon the weariness and weakness, perhaps the pain and agony, in which every one of them must some day lie down and die. And no doubt such reasons as these for compassion may have been present to the gentle heart of Jesus, when "he went forth, and saw a great multitude, and was moved with compassion toward them." We can well believe that the kind Creator and Saviour, who "knoweth our frame" so well, who has proved for himself all our sinless infirmities, and who understands what sore temptations are because he himself has felt them, — we can well believe that as he looked abroad over that Eastern crowd, which would have seemed so strange to our eyes, he discerned the griefs, the cares, the bereavements, the privations, the fears, which were at home in each heart; he knew that all these things were as common under the Eastern sky, and within the Eastern dwelling, as they are now under our roofs and within our breasts; and how could one so kind and generous as the Redeemer look upon sorrow and suffering without feeling compassion for those who suffered and sorrowed? But we feel quite sure, that although Jesus, when he compassionated the multitude, was moved to that feeling by every reason which the eye of omniscience could see, and the heart of mercy be moved by, still that the strongest reason for compassion would be that which would touch him most, and he would feel the most pity for that which was the saddest thing in the lot of the human souls before him. And what, then, was the saddest thing in the lot of that great multitude? What is the saddest thing in the lot of any great multitude, gathered anywhere? Was Xerxes right, when *he* judged that it was that death is so near; was Artabanus right, when *he* judged that it was that life is so pressed with cares and sorrows? Nay, my friend, it was not either of these considerations that most moved the compassion of our blessed Lord. It was sin rather than sorrow that he was thinking of. It was not so much that the people were wandering weary in the desert, as that their souls and consciences were without a guide. It was not so much that they were faint for want of the bread that perisheth, as that they knew nothing of where they were to turn for the bread and the water of life. It was not so much that they were surrounded by griefs and troubles, as that they knew not how to seek the aid of that Holy Spirit, who can make of all these a heavenly discipline to prepare for a better land. It was not so much that they were hourly drawing nearer to death, as that they were deep in darkness about a glorious life and immortality beyond the grave. And in saying all this, — in asserting that such were the main and principal reasons, if not the only ones, of Christ's compassion for the multitude, — we are not speaking without due authority. True, in the story as related by St. Matthew, we are not told what were the reasons why the Saviour felt compassion; but, as you know, what is omitted by one evangelist is often supplied by another; and when we turn to the parallel passage in the Gospel of St. Mark, we find not merely the fact of Christ's feeling pity recorded, but the reason why he felt pity expressly stated. It is a striking contrast to the reasons for that feeling which Xerxes and Artabanus gave; it is a reason that goes far deeper, and that means far more. St. Mark tells us,* "And Jesus, when he came out, saw much people, and was moved with compassion toward them, *because they were as sheep not having a shepherd.*" So here was Christ's reason for feeling compassion. It was because the people were in spiritual blindness and ignorance. It was because they did not feel the burden of their sins, and had no one to point them to the only Saviour of sinners. It was because in sinfulness they knew not where to go for pardon and purity; it was because in sorrow they knew not where to go for comfort; in weakness where to go for strength; in death where to go for life; in dying where to look for immortality. It was, in short, their spiritual destitution that Christ regarded as the saddest and most pity-moving thing about that multitude. It was for *that* he felt the deepest compassion. It was the soul's disease that most touched the kind Physician of souls. It was the soul's darkness that looked saddest to him that came to be

* Chapter vi. 34.

the Light of the world. It was the soul's thirst and hunger that seemed most urgent to him whose flesh was yet to be meat indeed, and whose blood drink indeed, the bread and the water of life for the nourishment of our immortal part. And so the great reason why our Saviour felt compassion in the sight of that great assemblage was, that there were among it so many sinful souls. The great reason why our Redeemer would even yet feel compassion in the sight of any great assemblage of human beings is, that it is made up of sinful souls. Ah! he knows, as we cannot know, what is meant by sin! He knows how evil and foul it is in itself; he knows all that follows from it, — all that it ends in! He knows that this is the root whence all sorrow and suffering spring. He knows that if there be death in this world, death is the wages of sin. He knows that if there be care, anxiety, disappointment, pain, anguish, bereavement, in this world, they are all the result of sin. And so Christ's reason for feeling compassion in the presence of a multitude is one which includes in it all other reasons. It has within itself the ground of the Persian counsellor's sad estimate of life, and the ground of the Persian monarch's tears. All that ever has wrung the kind heart, — all that ever has darkened the comprehensive view, — every reason for pitying poor human nature that ever was thought of, — all are gathered up in the reason which the evangelist gives us for the compassion of our blessed Lord, —

who, when he saw a great multitude, "was moved with compassion toward them," "because they were as sheep not having a shepherd." Sinful, sorrowful, dying; yet knowing not where to go; wearied with this troublesome life; yet clinging to it because they knew of no better; orphan children, lost sheep, strangers and pilgrims on the earth, they had yet been guided to the right place for once, when thus they came to the feet of the Saviour.

Let me ask you to observe, my friends, that the Redeemer's reason for compassionating the great multitude is a reason of universal application. It was a reason for feeling compassion for that assemblage that day in Palestine; it is a reason for feeling compassion for any assemblage anywhere. Christ's pity was not moved by any of those accidental and temporary causes which exist at some times and in some places and not elsewhere. No; sinfulness, and the need of a Saviour, are things which press, whether felt or not, upon all human beings. If Christ were to look upon you, my friend, to-day, be sure he would look upon you with compassion. Many and great are the differences between you and the people who are spoken of in the text. You speak a different language; you wear a different garb; you live in a distant land; but oh! you are the same in being stricken with that disease which only Christ's blood can wash away. We are all by ourselves like lost sheep, wandering without a shepherd; we all need to be brought back from our wanderings into the fold of the Good Shepherd of souls. But how much easier it is to confess this with the lips than to feel it in the heart! Oh that God's Spirit might so effectually convince us all of our sinfulness, that we might deeply feel that the first and most pressing need of our nature, is the need of a share in the great atonement of Christ! May we feel that *that* is more to us than water to the thirsty, than food to the hungry;—in very deed the most urgent of all the "necessaries of life." For that spiritual malady of sin from which the Great Physician alone can save us is one that is wide as the human race. Ah, *he* sees in it the weightiest reason for compassionating any mortal, through every stage of his existence,—from the first quiet slumber in the cradle, to the rigid silence in the shroud.

Let me ask you also to observe, that the Redeemer's reason for feeling compassion toward the multitude was the strongest reason for doing so. One man, we have seen, said that death was the saddest thing in the lot of humanity; another said that the griefs and cares of life were sadder still; but Jesus fixes upon that which is the source and origin of both. He fixes, as the saddest thing, upon that which "brought death into the world, and all our woe." And when we just think what sin is, and what sin tends to, we cannot but feel how rightly the Saviour judged. For sin is indeed man's sorest disease, and man's greatest unhappiness. It means that man, the creature, is at enmity with the Creator; that man, the child, has rebelled against his Father in heaven. It means, that whereas, when things are right, all happiness consists in nearness to God, and in God's favor and friendship, man has now brought himself to this; that he shrinks away in dismay and dislike from God; — that he only feels it terrible and distressing to remember that there is a God; — and that he feels communion with God in prayer a weary and irksome task, by all means to be avoided. Sin means that God's handiwork is ruined; that God's creation is defaced; that God's glory is tarnished; that God's purposes are frustrated; all so far as such things can be. And sin, if unpardoned, tends to death, — death spiritual and eternal. A sinful soul is a soul stricken with the worst of diseases, leading to the most awful of deaths. Unpardoned sin leads to endless misery; and when Jesus looks upon a soul going on in sin, he sees at a glance all the ruin and despair to which, if unchanged from above, it is advancing. And O brethren, can you think of a condition so sad, and so fitted to excite compassion in a Being who is all kindness and mercy, and who sees things as they truly are? Surely, surely, if we saw things right, we should see that a soul going on in unrepented sin, and rejecting the Saviour's offered grace, is in the very saddest plight in which an immortal being can ever be. He may be gay and thoughtless now; he may never think of the doom that hangs over him; he may be surrounded with earthly comforts; and many a one may envy him; but in very deed, he is in a pitiable and wretched state. You feel compassion for the poor consumptive, whose hectic cheek tells you that the malady is at work which will lay him in his grave. And why do you feel compassion? It is not that he is suffering so very much now. Many a person, affected by some passing pain which we hardly think of seriously sympathizing with, is suffering perhaps twenty times as much. But we feel compassion, because we look forward, and remember to what end the slow decline is going forward. We remember that the headache goes, and leaves the man none the worse; but the consumption kills. And it is the serious ending that makes us think the disease serious, even in those early stages when it is causing little pain. It is because sin ends in eternal woe, that it is so dreadful a malady, even while the soul that is stricken with it is cheerful and gay. It was because Christ looked on into the unseen world, and discerned the wrath in which sin unpardoned would land the soul, that he felt so deep a compassion as he looked on the great multitude gathered in the Eastern desert. And just as ruinous as sin was then, sin is yet. This is a disease which has never worn itself out, as it came down to us through successive generations. It has lost nothing of its ancient poison, nothing of its power to bring down to death. Blessed be God, it is the most tractable and easily managed of all diseases, in the hands of the Great Physician of souls! There is a remedy for it which never can fail. It has healed millions of sufferers; and it can heal each of us. "The blood of Jesus Christ cleanseth from all sin!"

Let me ask you further to observe, that if Jesus thought the sight of a great multitude a sad sight,—if he could not look upon the multitude but with compassion,—it must have been because he could not look but with compassion on each individual soul in the multitude. And as that multitude was, so far as regards the circumstances which moved Christ's pity, a fair sample of the human race, it follows that Christ feels that there is something for him to pity as he looks on each of us,—on each separate human being. Oh, how it cuts down pride, to remember this! To remember that when that Being who cannot go wrong in his estimate of us, looks upon you and me,—whatever we may think of ourselves,—*he* feels compassion for us,—*he* feels sorry for us! Surely it is a lowly thing to be a sinful human being! How it pours contempt upon human self-sufficiency, to think that when Christ looks down upon the man of highest rank, and greatest wealth, and most extended power,—one before whom his fellow-creatures grovel,—one who carries a high head and a proud heart,—Christ sees in him only a poor, helpless creature, to be pitied, to be relieved! There are few things that people like less, at least after they have grown up to maturity, than to be pitied. They think there is something poor and contemptible about *that*. And this opinion has grown into the very construction of our language. We say that a thing is *pitiable*, when we desire to ascribe to it all that is low and contemptible. You cannot say worse of a man, than to say that he is a *pitiful* creature; unless indeed it be to say that he is a *poor* creature, which means much the same thing. Well, then, my friend, just remember this, whenever you feel any tendency to a haughty spirit,—whenever you feel any disposition to talk big, and look big, and speak about your position, and your influence, and what you are entitled to,—just remember this, that Christ thinks us all poor creatures,—pitiable beings,—beggars needing alms,—fever-stricken patients needing the physician,—helpless, hopeless, unworthy sinners, deserving of the deepest compassion because we are so devoid of help or hope. How humble we ought to be when we draw near to God; with how lowly a countenance ought we to address our fellow-men; how carefully we should avoid the least appearance of anything overbearing, or tyrannical, or haughty! The Bible tells us, as you all know, that pride is especially hateful to God. "God resisteth the proud, and giveth grace to the humble." "An high look, and a proud heart," said the wisest of men, "is sin."* And what wonder that it should be so?

* Prov. xxi. 4.

Is it not something besides sin; is it not the most outrageous folly? A poor creature, the object of Christ's kind compassion, — and fancying to himself how great and influential and dignified a person he is! — Oh, my brother, let us be humble! Let us be clothed with humility. It is the right frame of spirit for beings such as you and me. Let us go humbly to the foot of the cross; and feeling our helplessness, let us patiently wait till the kind Saviour shall look upon us with compassion, and take away our sins. We will admit no lingering trace of pride or self-righteousness: "After his loving-kindness, according to the multitude of his tender mercies," may he "blot out our transgressions, and remember our iniquities no more." "Like as a father pitieth his children," so may the Lord pity and compassionate us in all our sins. And take comfort from the gracious words of comfort to the humble-minded: "For thus saith the high and lofty One that inhabiteth eternity, whose name is Holy; I dwell in the high and holy place, with him also that is of a contrite and humble spirit, to revive the spirit of the humble, and to revive the heart of the contrite ones."

Yes, my friends, there is nothing degrading in bowing humbly, as sinful creatures, in the presence of our Maker, and in beseeching his kind compassion and his pardoning grace. There is no degradation in being compassionated by Almighty God; nor in being received as penitent sinners by that Best Judge of what is fit and becoming in human conduct, who looked with anger on the self-righteous Pharisee, and with approval upon the humble publican, standing far away with downcast eyes, and smiting upon his breast. It is a painful thing, and when it can be avoided it is a poor thing, to seek compassion from any human being beyond the circle of our nearest kin. We despise the man who is always grumbling and complaining to strangers about his griefs and troubles, whether these are great or small. We despise the man who is thus always seeking to excite compassion by hawking about the story of his ills, and always harping upon that tedious string. No; beyond the limit of nearest blood, let a man keep his troubles to himself. He may feel assured that his best friend will grow weary of hearing about them; he may be sure that the pity accorded to him will be in most cases mingled with something of contempt. Deception, of course, is never a right thing; but we are not required to wear our heart upon our sleeve; and ever since the days of that stern Spartan youth who kept a composed look while the savage beast was at his vitals, men have felt that there is something sublime in the unflinching resolution that waves off the stranger's sympathy, and that shows the world a firm face when the heart is weary and weak. But oh! when we turn to Jesus, who can read our inmost soul, — when we turn to him, who never will upbraid us or despise us, though we make bare to him every poor weakness, every sorrow, and every sin about us, — we feel that the need for that reserve is gone, and that it is no shame nor humiliation to tell out to him all we fear and suffer, with the same abandonment with which the little child sobs out the story of its little sorrows at a kind mother's knee. At the throne of grace, the man who, whatever he suffered, would never complain to mortal, may without reserve lay before the Redeemer the tale of his wants and woes. Ah, the dumb spirit that would dissemble and cloak its sins even before the heart-searching God, — *that* is one of the saddest symptoms of the soul's worst disease! Simple confession of sin to God is a part of true contrition; and if we go to God with the humble desire to confess our sins with a penitent and lowly heart, he will be ready to help us out with the sad recital, to anticipate our imperfect words, and interpret our contrite tears. "If we confess our sins, he is faithful and just to forgive us our sins, and to cleanse us from all unrighteousness."

And thus, my friend, we have meditated for a little upon St. Matthew's declaration, that Christ found something in the sight of a great multitude to move his compassion; we have sought to discover what it was about the multitude that made it a sad sight for Christ to see; and we have sought to draw some lessons from the conclusion to which we came. It was that the Physician of souls saw in that multitude an assemblage of souls diseased; it was that he saw before him souls stricken with that worst of maladies, sin; souls doomed, unless that disease was checked, to be drawn down by it to eternal death and woe. He felt compassion for that multitude, because he saw in it a host of immortal beings in the very saddest and sorest plight in which immortal beings could ever be. It is a sad and a sore sight, when some young one, smitten by wasting disease, is bidden, as the last faint hope, to leave the home of childhood, and to seek some milder clime, whose balmy breezes may perhaps fan the cheek to the glow of health once more; and we can think of few things more affecting than the last parting from parents and brothers and sisters, whose foreboding looks and sighs tell that they know that death may be delayed but not averted; that the sunbeams of Italy will smite in vain, and its climate can work no cure. And we can think of few things more sad than of that young exile, fading day by day in a foreign land; and pining, amid myrtle groves and glorious skies, for the well-remembered trees and sunsets far away at home. But if we saw things right, we should see a sadder sight in many a one who is a parent's pride and hope; we should see something that angels might weep over in the gay, thoughtless worldling that lives and acts in the forgetfulness of a Saviour and a life to come. For a direr malady is sapping that young life; a more deadly disease is wasting there. Yes, the compassion that Jesus felt for that multitude of common human beings, was just a little out-welling of that same kind and gracious compassion which had brought him to this earth at all! What was it that made the Son of God leave the glory and the brightness of heaven, and come down to this world, and suffer, and die, — what was it, but that looking upon this world, he "beheld a great multitude, and had compassion on it," — he saw the human race infected with the leprosy of sin, — smitten with the disease that ends in ruin, — and came to seek and save! Oh, may he remember now, when the travail of his soul is past, that it was for us it was éndured! As for us, may he not have died in vain! And if, when he looks down on us to-day, his kind compassion is stirred by the sight of sorrowful hearts, we ask that he may comfort *them;* but forasmuch as we know and are sure that when he looks upon us, his compassion *must* be stirred by the sight of an evil that is worse than sorrow, we would yet more earnestly ask that he would take away all iniquity, and receive us graciously, and blot out all our sins!

X.

THE RULING OF THE SPIRIT.

"Better is he that ruleth his spirit, than he that taketh a city."
PROV. xvi. 32.

EVERY one knows, and the most thoughtless can understand, that to carry a very heavy load for a mile, is hard work; or that to go through a long day's ploughing, is hard work; but not every person is able to understand and to take it in, that the things which cost a man the greatest effort and the hardest work that he ever goes through in all his life, may be done with no bodily exertion at all; may be done as he sits in an easy-chair with his eyes shut. Here is one great difference between the civilized man and the savage: a great part of the work of the civilized man consists of that which the savage would not regard as work at all. But every thoughtful person knows that the hardest of all work is that which puts the soul upon the stretch, though it may leave the body at rest; and that there is no wear like the wear of heart and brain. And all this wear and exertion may be without any outward sign, without any bodily effort, without any of *that* which the uncivilized man would understand by *work*. I dare say St. Paul never spent days of harder work in all his life than the days he spent at Damascus lying blind upon his bed, struggling to get free from the prejudices and convictions of all his past years, and resolving upon the course he would pursue in the years to come. Some of you, no doubt, have heard of that great English engineer who, when he was perplexed how to manage the construction of some new and intricate piece of machinery, would remain for days together in a darkened room, hardly stirring from one attitude, with his mind all the while strained to the top of its bent, till he had struggled through the difficulty, and had the whole plan of the machine clearly before his view. What tremendous work he went through in these days! But a stupid, ignorant person, if told that the great engineer had lain upon his bed without moving for three whole days, in a dark room, would very likely have said, What a lazy man that must be! Here he has spent these days, and done nothing! Done nothing! we might reply; you cannot tell what wearing, perplexing, bewildering drudgery he has undergone!

Now, my friends, the words you have read point us to an enterprise which makes no outward show; and boldly tell us that it is a better and nobler thing to accomplish *that*, than even to carry out another enterprise of the most showy and glaring kind. The text points out to us a certain work, very difficult to do, very noble when done, which yet is done with so little outward appearance or physical effort, that some might perhaps fancy that it is no work at all. Every one knows that he must be a skilful and a brave man who takes a guarded and fortified city. There must be much skill to devise the assault, — much bravery and exertion to carry it out. There is unmistakable work in sapping a way towards the beleaguered ramparts, in bridging over the deep moat, in shaking down the massive battlements; there are effort and daring needed for the final rush through the deadly breach, in the face of desperate foes, — for the hand-to-hand encounter, with its blood and din, till the central citadel is stormed, and the "city taken" at last. But the inspired writer is not afraid to set before us a companion-picture, and bid us contrast the two. He bids us turn away from the noisy triumph and the crowned conqueror; and he points us to a nobler and a "better" man. He bids us turn away from that wild exhibition of desperate energy; and he points us to a quiet labor that tasks yet more heavily all that is noblest in human beings. "Better," he says, "better is he that ruleth his spirit, than he that taketh a city!"

Now, my friends, every one of you who has sought to believe in the Saviour, and, by the Holy Spirit aiding you, to lead a Christian life, must have learned by experience how great a part of the work of an immortal being is mental work, is work that makes no bodily show, is work done by the soul without any corresponding exertion of the body. And I am not thinking now of head-work merely, as contrasted with hand-work. Of course, the man who sits at his study-table, writing his book or his sermon, is working very hard; the judge who sits in his easy-chair weighing the merits of the case which has been argued before him, and making up his mind what his judgment ought to be, is working very hard; far harder than the mason building his wall, or the ploughman following his team. But I am not thinking now of merely intellectual effort; I am thinking of the exertion of the whole spiritual nature, — of intellectual, moral, and spiritual effort, without bodily; and I say that all Christian people must know, that the most important work and labor which immortal beings ever can do, is of that kind. We have to "*work* out our salvation;" but the work is mainly to be done by the unseen exertion of the invisible soul. We have to "*strive* to enter in at the strait gate;" we have to "*labor* to enter into rest;" but the laboring and striving are all spiritual and not bodily. We have to repent; and it is not an easy thing to repent; but the strain to do it comes upon the soul. We have to believe; and it is difficult to believe; but when we go to God, and seek to believe, and pray for grace to "help our unbelief," it is the soul that goes and strives and prays. Our entire spiritual life; the entire path which we trust is to lead us to glory; is, in one sense, a "ruling of our spirit;" the idea of unseen exertions, of spiritual strivings and efforts, is one with which all believers are perfectly familiar. And *that* is the idea which the wisest of men sets before us in this text.

Of course, when the inspired writer tells us that "better is he that ruleth his spirit, than he that taketh a city;" he teaches us that to rule our spirit rightly is a difficult thing, and a thing from rightly doing which great and valuable results are to follow. And all this is as much as to say, that within the heart of every man there are many unruly tendencies; many impulses to do and to think and to feel wrong. There is a great deal in every human soul that needs to be kept down. If man's spirit were always ready to do right, it would need no ruling, or the ruling would be a very easy thing. But as it is, it is very difficult. It is very difficult to hold the path of duty, because there is so much within us that tends to lead us astray from it. And so long as we live in a fallen world, crowded with temptations and snares; so long as we bear a fallen nature, whose whole bent is towards evil rather than good, towards earth rather than heaven, towards the creature rather than the Creator; so long will the ruling of man's spirit be man's hardest and longest-lasting work; a work which no one who would not drift to degradation and perdition can avoid; yea, a work which but for the aid of God's grace and God's Blessed Spirit would foil and baffle and weary out the stoutest-hearted!

And now, looking more closely into the details of this solemn and most practical subject, let us think what are the things about our spiritual nature that stand especially in need of ruling. And we may arrange the evil impulses which in ruling our spirit we have to resist, under the two heads of *Impulses to think and feel wrong;* and *Impulses to do wrong.*

Let us look, in the first place, at those tendencies and leanings in our spiritual nature which would lead to think and feel wrong.

And this head of our subject, my friends, includes a vast field; and takes in little impulses, which to resist is no more than matter of worldly prudence; as well as grander temptations, to resist which is of the very essence of religion. If you look to the former clause of the verse in which the text stands, you will see that the special thing which the wise man had in view, when he spoke of ruling the spirit, was the keeping down of an evil feeling; he says, "He that is slow to anger is better than the mighty." He teaches us that it is a noble thing to hold in check this one bad tendency of anger, whether it may manifest itself in fretfulness, or in sullenness, or in violent outbursts of passion. It is in some men, no doubt, in a larger degree than in others, this bad tendency; some have a native amiability and sweetness of temper that makes it easy for them in this respect to "rule their spirit;" but there is none who will not sometimes be called on to do it; and remember this, that for any of you to give way to little spurts of petulance, or fretfulness, or general ill-temper, is not, as you may think it, a small matter; it is a symptom that something is amiss in your Christian character; that you are failing by God's grace to resist "the sin that doth most easily beset you;" that you are not striving by God's grace to "rule your spirit" as you ought. It is like the little leak which may make the gallant ship go down. I need not suggest how sadly this evil tendency in those who yet, as we would trust, have the root of the matter in them, goes to keep them from being epistles in commendation of their Saviour's cause, — goes to make them into stumbling-blocks and causes of offence. The sullen humors or the peevish outbursts of a professing Christian are not small matters, if they go to fix in the minds of the young a disagreeable and painful idea of what Christianity and Christian people are. Now, my friends, here is something in our spirit which we probably all of us have to rule: let us, honestly, praying for God's grace, seek to rule it. Let us not take up the impression that even the smallest temptation can be resisted in any strength of our own; or that the very least hindrance in our spiritual life is too small a matter to take to God's footstool, and to tell God about, and to make the subject of earnest prayer. I believe that there is hardly anything which does more to injure the spiritual life of ordinary Christians, than their getting into their minds some vague impression that it is all quite right to go and ask God's grace in prayer for performing great duties and resisting great temptations; but that really it would be something like profanation to make the little worries of life known at God's footstool, and to ask his Spirit to aid in ruling a little evil tendency in your spirit which you think you might really rule yourself. Let us get rid of that impression; it is out-and-out wrong. There is nothing that interests you, that is too little to confide to your God, in the solitude of closet-prayer. You may enter into your chamber, and shut your door, and, secure of a kindly hearing, you may tell your Father which is in secret of little things which worry and vex you, and retard you in your spiritual life, which are yet so little that you would be ashamed to confess to your nearest friend how great a space they fill up in your heart. Fix it in your mind, that there is no duty, however little, which we can do without God's grace; and no temptation, however small, which we can resist without God's grace. And do you need to be told, that little duties and little temptations make up, for most of us, the sum of common life? We are not called on to rule our spirit on a grand and magnificent scale; we are just to do the little task God sets us. You are not tempted to renounce your Saviour; but you *are* tempted to speak snappishly to those under your roof, or to dwell upon some little offence which has been given you. Your temptation is not the scaffold or the stake; it is no more than some little irritability of nerve or heart;

but it *is* your temptation, it is your besetting sin, it is the very thing which in *your* spirit needs ruling; and, whether in things great or small, "better is he that ruleth his spirit, than he that taketh a city!"

I need not tell any hearer, that it is quite impossible, and not even desirable, that I should make out a list, or attempt a description of all the varied tendencies to think wrong or to feel wrong that may be found in the human heart; — of all the things about our "spirit" which in this respect need to be "ruled," to be held in check, to be turned in the right direction. I aim at no more than setting before you such representative tendencies as may set your own minds thinking; I desire to say something which may make each of you remember *that* impulse to wrong or morbid thought or feeling which you yourself are especially called to resist and keep down. And now that we have looked at an impulse to wrong feeling or passion, let us look at another wrong tendency of a somewhat more intellectual cast.

I mean the tendency which exists, more or less, in most hearts, to discontent with the allotments of God's providence; to envy and jealousy as regards those of our fellow-creatures who are more favored and fortunate than we. The ruling of our spirit which I am now thinking of, is that which lies in reconciling our mind to painful things; in acquiescing in mortification and disappointment when they come; in feeling rightly towards people to whom we are disposed to feel unkindly and bitterly. And let me tell you, my friends, there is to many a man no harder ruling of the spirit, than that of reconciling his mind to the place where God has set him. The Hand above gives you your place and your work; and then there is the struggle heartily and cheerfully to acquiesce in the decree. And this is not always an easy thing; though be sure that the man who honestly and Christianly tries to do it, will never fail to succeed at last. How curiously people are set down in life; in all callings whatsoever! You find men in the last places they would have chosen; in the last places for which you would say they are suited. And such men, and all thinking men, have doubtless their own battle in making up their mind to many things, both in their own lot, and in the lot of others. I do not mean merely the intellectual effort to look at the success of other men and our own failure in such a way as that we shall be intellectually convinced that we have no right to complain of either; I do not mean merely the labor to put things in the right point of view; but the moral and spiritual effort to look fairly at the facts not in any way disguised, — not tricked out by some skilful way of putting the case; — and yet to repress all wrong feeling; all fretfulness, envy, jealousy, dislike, hatred. I do not mean to persuade ourselves that the grapes we cannot reach are sour; but (far nobler surely) to be well aware that they are sweet, and yet be content that another should have them and not we. I mean the labor, when you have run in a race and been beaten, to resign your mind to the fact that you have been beaten, and to bear a kind feeling towards the man that beat you. And this is labor, and hard labor; though very different from that physical exertion which the uncivilized man would understand by the word.

You know, my friends, that in all professions and occupations to which men can devote themselves, there is such a thing as competition; and wherever there is competition, there will be the temptation to envy, jealousy, and detraction, as regards a man's competitors; and so there will be need of that labor and exertion which lie in resolutely trampling that temptation down. It does not matter whether the prize be great or small; the temptation in all cases is the same in its essential nature. It does not matter whether it be two schoolboys, both bent upon the medal which only one can get; or two traders, each determined to be first in that street; or two statesmen, each resolved that he himself shall be Prime Minister; or two great lawyers, each set upon being Lord Chancellor. You are quite certain, my friend, as you go on through life, to have to make up your mind to failure and disappointment on your own part, and to seeing other men preferred before you. Now, when these things come, there are two ways of meeting them. One is, to hate and vilify those who surpass you, either in merit or success; to detract from their merit and underrate their success; or, if you must admit some merit, to bestow upon it very faint praise. Now, all this is natural enough; but assuredly it is neither a Christian nor a happy course to follow. It is natural enough; natural in inferior animals as well as in man. You have heard of the race-horse, running a neck-and-neck race with another, and beaten by an inch, which turned savagely upon his successful rival and tore him with his teeth. Natural enough, indeed; but just one of those wrong tendencies in our fallen spirit which it concerns the Christian man to rule and to put down. *That* is one way; but the other and better way is to fight these tendencies to the death; to struggle against them, to pray against them; to seek God's grace to put them down; to resign yourself to God's good will; to admire and love the man who surpasses and excels you. And this course is the Christian one, and the happy one. Rightly rule your spirit; and, oh, it is a noble thing! I believe that the greatest blessing God can send a man is disappointment, rightly met and used. There is no more ennobling discipline; there is no discipline which results in a happier or kindlier temper of mind. And in honestly fighting against these evil impulses we have thought of,—in thus seeking to rule your spirit fitly,—you will assuredly get help and strength and grace from above. And that ruling of the spirit which is needful Christianly to meet disappointment, brings out the best and noblest qualities that can be found in man. I have seen the homely features look almost sublime, when man or woman was faithfully by God's grace resisting and wrestling with wrong feelings and tendencies, such as these. It is a noble end to attain, and it is well worth all the labor it costs, to resolutely be resigned, cheerful, and kind, where you feel a strong inclination to be discontented, moody, and bitter of heart. It is not philosophy that will win in this fight; but the aiding, sanctifying, comforting Spirit of God. And when I would picture forth a noble conqueror, I turn from even the brave men who, with grim face and bayonets fixed, are climbing the slope slippery with blood, and raked by shell and shot, that leads to the scarce practicable breach; and of whom a bare remnant will in half an hour place upon the ramparts the unconquered flag that all the world knows,—I turn from even *them*, though the bravest of the brave, and I look to where the wisest man has shown us something more heroic; and I see it in the unsoured spirit and the kindest heart, which have gone on through many a care and disappointment, which have withstood many a mortification, and only been made the sweeter by many a taking-down; as I remember that no human wisdom dictated the words of the text, and told all men that "Better is he that ruleth his spirit, than he that taketh a city!"

But now, brethren, you will easily think of a host of tendencies to wrong thought and feeling, which the Christian man, in ruling his spirit, will need to hold in check. One of these, very powerful in many minds, is to procrastination as to our spiritual interests; it is *that* within us which would lead us, even when convinced that we must see to it that we make our peace with God, always to put off to another day, to a more convenient season, a work for which God has told us that "Now is the accepted time." Ah, my friends, how many a soul has dated its ruin to yielding to an impulse that ought to have been resolutely put down; to postponing till to-morrow a work which should have been done to-day! And after a reflection so solemn, we feel it is coming down to something almost trivial in comparison, though by no means trivial in its bearing upon the happiness of life, or upon the formation of our spiritual character,—when I mention as a tendency to be checked, that unhappy disposition which is in many hearts, to be always dwelling on and brooding over the little worries of life; to be unthankfully and querulously looking away from the hundred kind gifts God has given, and dwelling upon the crook in the lot,—the little vexation, the little cross, the little mortification, which he who would rule his spirit well would look away from, and try to forget. Suppose a man living in a pleasant home, in the midst of a beautiful country. Suppose that he has pleasing scenes all around him, wherever he can look; except that in one direction there is a bleak, uninteresting, ugly prospect.

Now, what would you think of this man, if he utterly refused to look at the cheerful and beautiful prospects which all around invite his eye, and spent the whole day gazing intently at the one ugly view, and at nothing else? Would you not say the man was mad? And yet, don't you know, possibly from your own experience, that there are hosts of men and women who, in a moral sense, do just that? Hosts of human beings who turn away from the many blessings of their lot, and dwell and brood upon its worries? Hosts who persistently look away from the numerous pleasant things they might contemplate, and look fixedly and almost constantly at painful and disagreeable things? How ungrateful to a kind God; how unhappy; how foolish; how detrimental to all that is noble and worthy in our spiritual being; how stunting to our growth in grace! O brethren, let us rule down this evil tendency; we cannot repress it entirely; but we can at least refuse voluntarily to encourage it; we should regard it as of the very essence of our religion to put it down; and by God's grace we may do so in a great degree. I do not mention, as another thing to be stopped, the giving the rein to impure and wicked imaginations, of things you would blush to speak of; for I trust that no one within hearing of my voice would wilfully do that; but I just name it as something which, indulged, has been to many as the opening of a floodgate which admitted the vilest excesses of degrading sin and shame. And I suggest to you, as my final specimen of tendencies and leanings in our spirit which need ruling, that great pervading tendency which is to most ordinary Christians the besetting sin; the tendency to keep this world and its interest first in the heart, and the unseen and eternal world only second; the tendency in our hearts to "cleave to the dust," — to set our affections upon things on the earth, — to live as if there were no other life, — to work as if food and raiment, as if worldly wealth and comfort, were the "one thing needful." O brethren, that God by his Spirit would in this matter rule our spirits to truth and wisdom, — help us to realize which is the substance and which the shadow, — and grant to us "the victory that overcometh the world," even a living faith! Oh that we might feel it, that not *this* is substance which we grasp, but *that* is substance which we believe; — that not the earth we tread on is the solid, enduring reality, but rather the unseen country which is very far away!

I have reached the end of my discourse, dwelling only on those tendencies to evil thought and feeling which were to have taken up only the first part of it; and there is not space to say anything of those impulses in our spirit, needing to be ruled with a tight and a strong hand, which would lead to express and open acts of evil. We need not turn *that* sad leaf; and I believe that in preaching to an intelligent Christian congregation, the other is the more practically important. We have thought of the angry passion which would use no deadlier weapon than a harsh word; of the envy and malice which rankle inwardly, rather than of such as would make an outward show. And indeed, it is when sins of thought and feeling are indulged, that they grow into sins of life and conduct; and after all, an actual fact, our great sins, — the main things *we* have to confess and seek pardon for, — are sins of thought and feeling rather than of life and conduct. We do not murder; but we may cherish that hatred of our brother which shall stamp us murderers in the judgment of God. We bow to no idol; yet we may cherish that covetousness, which is idolatry. We lead decent, regular lives; yet we may be so set upon this world, as that we shall be found guilty of crucifying Christ afresh, and grieving the Holy Spirit of God away! Our great sins, in short, are the sins of the heart; are sins of thought and feeling; and rightly to "rule our spirit," is the sum, the essence, of all our Christian duty. And to do *that*, what a noble work; how hard in its progress, how glorious in its results! All that shall make us like our Saviour; all that shall make us meet for heaven; lies in that work! No strength of our own is equal to it; but only *his* might, who regenerates and sanctifies, — that Blessed Spirit, who is promised without stint to all who seek him in fervent prayer. Oh, may he be poured down upon us, day by day! And so, through many duties, many trials, many temptations, many cares, we shall hold still that central peace of mind which is promised to the man whose mind is stayed upon his God; we shall be victors in a noiseless, bloodless battle, fighting day by day in many quiet places, — fought in by shrinking women, and by men that never drew a sword, — yet open, too, to the most daring and heroic; a battle which may leave upon the outer aspect no worse trace than the thin cheek and the sad smile; yet which is the heaviest strain upon human pith and endurance; and which may end in the most glorious rewards which can ever be won by human being. For "Better," said the wisest man, — inspired by wisdom beyond his own, — "Better is he that ruleth his spirit, than he that taketh a city."

XI.

BEARING ABOUT THE DYING OF CHRIST.

"Always bearing about in the body the dying of the Lord Jesus.'
2 Cor. iv. 10.

THERE is something striking and remarkable in these words; and it is not easy, at the first thought, to take in their exact meaning. St. Paul is telling of the persecutions and troubles which he and his friends had daily to endure, as they carried on their great work of preaching the gospel. "We are troubled," he says, "on every side, yet not distressed; we are perplexed, but not in despair; persecuted, but not forsaken; cast down, but not destroyed; always bearing about in the body the dying of the Lord Jesus." Now, it is likely enough, that there were things in this catalogue of sufferings which St. Paul would have avoided, if he had been able to do so with a clear conscience. He had no special liking for trouble, perplexity, or persecution, any more than we have; and if the kingdom of the Redeemer could have advanced as well, and his own growth in grace could have been secured as effectually, without these, doubtless he would have been thankful. It has been said, very truly, that tribulation is not a thing for us to seek, but for God to send. But there is something different about the peculiar trial which is mentioned in the text. It *was* a trial, or St. Paul would not have named it in thus reckoning up the troubles which he was called to bear. But it was a trial of such a singular kind, that the great apostle did not wish to be rid of it. It was a trial of that singular nature, that he prayed that it might be sent to him, and laid upon him. It is not here that he does so; but in another of his epistles he uses words which recall to us at once what he has written here concerning bearing about his Saviour's dying; and he tells us there, that there was nothing in this world he wished for more than *that.* He tells us *there*, that he counted all things as worthless, that he might "win Christ;" that he might be "found in him;" that he might "know him, and the power of his resurrection, and the fellowship of his sufferings; being made conformable unto his death." "Conformable unto the Saviour's death;" *that* is what St. Paul wished to be; *that* is what every Christian ought to be; *that* is what we should daily pray that *we* may be; *that* is something which implies difficulty, which implies suffering; yet which implies blessing so precious that you never could seek better for yourself, or wish better for your dearest friend; and what else does *that* mean, but that every true Christian should ever be doing what St. Paul tells us *he* always did:

"Always bearing about in the body the dying of the Lord Jesus!"

Now, my friends, we know the way in which St. Paul, and many of the first preachers of the gospel, had to do this. There is but one opinion, I believe, as to the first and literal meaning of these words of the text. It is understood that they mean that St. Paul and his friends were in daily peril of such a death as Christ's was; that they had daily to bear such stripes as had been laid upon that blessed Lamb of God; that their daily privations were wearing out within them the principle of life. It is understood that when St. Paul said that the apostles were "always bearing about in the body the dying of the Lord Jesus," he meant that all these trials and privations which they suffered had left their sorrowful trace upon form and feature; that these early Christians bore in their emaciated bodies the outward signs of the tribulation they were passing through. They may have been but a poor, puny race of men, in the matters of outward strength and outward comeliness, who yet were honored to convey to after centuries and to unborn generations, the very best tidings that ever gladdened man's weary heart, — the blessed gospel of salvation and immortality through a crucified Redeemer. They may have been but a weakly, dying-like company of men, in whose weakness God made perfect the martyr's heroic strength; and through whose instrumentality God told us of a Saviour in whom "whosoever believeth" "shall never die." It may be, that if you had looked upon the living form and face of the great apostle of the Gentiles, you would have seen in the pale, wasted figure, worn down by want and travel and scourgings and buffetings and aged before its time, — that St. Paul bore in his body the traces of such sufferings as wrote too early age upon the kindest face this world ever saw; that St. Paul bore in his body the traces of such sufferings as brought Christ himself to his grave.

That, my friends, was the apostolic way of "bearing about in the body the dying of Christ." It is not so that we are called to be "conformable to the death" of our Redeemer. The days of such martyrdom as that of the apostolic age are gone, in this part of the world. When St. Paul spoke of being conformable to his Lord's death, he probably meant that if need were, he was willing to die in like manner; and at that time, it was so likely that a professed Christian might be called to die a violent death, that the man who made such a declaration was likely enough to have his resolution put to the proof. Nor is it needful or right for us to seek by self-inflicted penances to rival the worn aspect of the early confessors; we are not called, by vigils, scourgings, and fastings, to macerate our bodily frames. You know that there are those among Christians now, who think to obey the injunction implied in the text in a fashion more literal still. There are persons who think to obey it by always bearing about with them the material representation of the Redeemer's death; the crucifix, where the artist's skill has sought to picture out the last agonies of our Lord, as he hung upon the cross; or the cross itself, the recognized emblem over the wide world of our holy faith, and of devotion to him who died for us on the accursed tree. Ah, my friends, *that* is not the way in which the believer is called to be "always bearing about in the body the dying of Christ." You might bear the crucifix or the cross with you wherever you went; you might have the dying Saviour's image placed where it should be the first thing to catch your waking eyes at morning, and the last thing to leave them at night; and yet you might be hundreds of miles away from any compliance with the spirit of the text. It is no mere bodily service which our Lord requires of us. The service *he* desires is the devotion of the heart; it is spiritually, and yet most really, that we, in these days, are to seek daily to do what St. Paul always did; even to bear about our Saviour's dying.

And now let us inquire, my friends, what manner of obedience to this unrepealed requirement remains for us. Let us think in what way we may still "bear about with us the dying of the Lord Jesus."

In the first place, we may bear about the memory of it. If it be true at all that our Redeemer died as he did die; and died so for us; nothing can be more plain than that we ought never to forget it. Even when we are not specially calling our Saviour's death to mind, the recollection of it should be latent in our hearts, and should be unconsciously affecting all our views of things. I am sure you know that such a thing may be. When you met some great bereavement; when some one very near to you died; even after the first shock was past; even after you no longer had before your mind's eye, wherever you went, the parting hour of the little child perhaps that was taken from you; even when you could once more with some measure of calmness set yourself to your common duties again, without having always breaking in upon you the picture you once thought never would leave you, of the lips of clay silent and still, and the little silky head laid in the last resting-place where *you* could ever lay it; did you not still feel, in the subdued spirits, in the greater sympathy with the sorrows of others, in the quieter and gentler mood, that you had not quite got over your trial; that you were still bearing about with you the dying of the dear one that was gone! The first shock was over; but its memory was there; and you were the kinder and the better for it.

Now, my friends, I say that in all our life, in all we are ever called to do or to bear, we ought to be, more or less consciously, "bearing about with us" the remembrance of our Blessed Lord's death, and of how he died. We should live daily in memory of his death; and that memory should influence and affect all our views and all our doings. You know, there is something that shocks one, when we see a new-made orphan, or a new-made widow, showing plainly that they have entirely and fast got over the death of the husband or parent who is gone. We have all, perhaps, been shocked by unseemly mirth, by revolting levity, in those who have been freshly bereaved; and most of us will agree in thinking that the rapid dying-out of warm feelings, and the rapid change of fixed resolutions, is one of the most sorrowful subjects of reflection which it is possible to suggest. We do not ask for any long continuance, even in the most tried, of extravagant grief; it is the manifest intention of the Creator that very strong feelings should be transitory. But it is a sorrowful thing when they pass, and leave absolutely no trace behind them. Let us be content, my friends, to look at the case temperately. Let us face and admit the facts. The healthy body and mind can get over a great deal; but there are some things which it is not to the credit of our nature should ever be entirely got over. And if it be a sad thing, and a shocking thing, to see any human being who has been called by God's providence to stand by the dying bed of many near relatives, showing by his entire demeanor that he has quite forgot it; if the tacit consent of all thinking people has decided that such a one may be, and ought to be, unostentatiously bearing about the quiet remembrance of their dying; is it too much to expect that we, whose

Saviour died such a death, and died it, in simple truth, *for us*, should not live quite as if he had not died! You would feel that you had a right to expect the friend you may leave behind you, to "bear about your dying" a little; especially if it were a death of special pain, and if you were to undergo it for his sake. The kind mother, who wore out her life in caring and toiling for her child, might well think that the child might sometimes come and stand by her grave; and remember her living kindness and her dying words, when she was far away. And, O brethren, when we do but try to think what our Saviour Christ has done for us; done for us by his life, but above all by his dying; when we feel how impossible it is for us to reckon up what he has done for us, and how impossible it is for us to understand and realise what he suffered for us; — when we think that every hope, every blessing, that ever can gladden our poor sinful hearts, was won for us by that great sacrifice consummated by our Saviour's dying; surely, surely, we might well determine that we never shall forget that death, — that we never shall live as if that death had never been! You hear people say, truly enough perhaps, that this world has never been the same to them since such a loved one died; that their whole life has been changed since then. Is it unreasonable when St. Paul suggests to us, that we never should look at anything now, just as if Jesus had not come to this earth and laid down his life for us; that we ought to look at everything, and specially at all spiritual and moral realities, in the light of his dying; that we should always bear about the remembrance of it! Oh, it is sad to see a Christian living in such a fashion as to show plainly that he has quite forgot how his Redeemer died! It is sad to feel in ourselves, that we spend many an hour just as if our Redeemer had never died! Surely it ought not so to be. It is not that we ought to be, or that we can be, always directly thinking of Christ's death; *that* is impossible; we must think of many a worldly matter, and think intently, too, or we shall do little good in this life; and no one, knowing anything of the laws of the human mind, would ever ask that the mind should be kept running ceaselessly upon any single thought. But what we ask is, that the remembrance of the Redeemer's dying should always be latent in our hearts; that it should, almost unnoticed, color all our views and doings; that even when other thoughts are uppermost, *that* should ever be at the bottom of our hearts; and more especially, that whenever we are called to think of spiritual things, and whenever we come to critical points in our pilgrimage-path,—places where we must go to right or left,—*that* remembrance should spring up into strong and vivid life, and be as a lamp to our feet and a light to our path. When we think of sin, let us see it in the light of Christ's death, and hate it because it nailed him to the tree! Let us, whensoever we are pressed by some pleasing temptation, associate it in our minds with the suffering and dying of Christ; oh, let us, whensoever and howsoever tempted to sin, call up before our memory the pale, drooping figure on the cross, anguished, bleeding, dying, — and let us think that *there* is the proof what sin is, and what God thinks of it; and thus, as a fence against temptation, as something to keep us always right in our views and feelings towards every form of evil, let us bear about with us the dying of our Lord! Or, is it suffering and sorrow that come to us; and are we ready to repine and to rebel? Oh, then, let us call to mind the agony and the dying of our Redeemer; and it will not seem so hard that the servant should fare no better than the Master fared? You may remember that good priest, in the history of our own country, who was subjected to inhuman tortures because he told a wicked king and court certain unpleasing truths. The pain was cruel, he said after it was past; but he thought how meekly the cross was borne up Calvary; and *that* thought enabled him to bear it without a murmur. And how slight and trivial all *our* endurances will seem, when we set them by the side of those of our kind Redeemer! Or, are we pressed with the sense of our sinfulness, and the fear of God's wrath for sin? Then let us remember how Jesus died for us, the just for the unjust; how his blood can take all sin away; how he was wounded for our transgressions; how our sins were laid upon his sinless head; how it must be in the salvation of such as us, that he is yet to see of the travail of his soul. And in days of doubt and fear for the way before us, let us remember how Jesus died; and think, he that spared not his own Son, but delivered him up to death for us all, how shall he not with him also freely give us all things? Oh, let us, by faith, bear that remembrance in our hearts! The Redeemer's parting hour, indeed, is passed away; but its remembrance should never pass from us. Yea, rather, as fence against temptation; as light to show the true dark colors of sin; as lesson of patience, faith, hope, and charity; we should be "always bearing about" with us "the dying of the Lord Jesus!"

But there is more than this. There still remains for us a further way of doing what St. Paul names in our text. We have seen that we may always bear about the memory of Christ's dying, and see all things by *that* light; but, secondly, we may show in our daily life the transforming power of the Saviour's death. Our whole life, changed, and affected in its every deed, by the fact that Christ died, may be a standing testimony to all who see us that there is a real power to affect the character in the sight of the dying Saviour; and thus we may, in a very true and solemn sense, be always bearing about with us the dying of the Redeemer; bearing about with us a soul which is what it is, mainly because he died. And there is nothing incomprehensible, nothing mystical, in all this. We are not asked to believe that Christ's death has a power to transform our nature, without seeing where that power lies, or how it is exercised. We have already, in thinking of the way in which we ought to be ever bearing with us the remembrance of our Master's death, had a glimpse of the rationale of the process by which Christ's death exercises its transforming power. To say that Christ's death has efficacy to transform the character, is just in other words to say *this:* that the remembrance of Christ's death is a practical thing in our hearts; that it will not rest in mere pensive recollection; — that it does not waste itself in *that;* but that it spurs on to action. It is impossible that we should rightly remember our Saviour's death; and yet live just the same as before. The remembrance of his dying; the view by faith of his cross; has something to say to everything we think, or say, or do. There is something in the mere contemplation of Christ crucified, for which heart and life, by God's grace, are the better, we can hardly say how; but we do not rest any weight on such a thought as that, because we know how natural it is for us all, when religious truths like *that* are presented to us, to feel somehow as if they were away from reality; and to fancy that many things are all sound and right enough in theology, but that somehow they fail to work in actual life. But, brethren, when in the view of the cross we see how bitterly and mysteriously evil and ruinous sin is, surely the practical lesson is plain: Is it not that we should dread sin, and battle with temptation, and resolutely tread it down; and earnestly seek for deliverance from the curse of that fearful thing which brought such unutterable agony upon our Redeemer; and constantly pray for that Blessed Spirit who will breathe new life into every good resolution, and vivify into sunlight clearness every sound and true belief? You cannot look upon the dying Saviour, agonized on account of sin; and then go and live in sin just as if he had not died! And thus, in a mind and heart all whose beliefs and affections are founded on, and take their tone from, the fact of the Redeemer's death; and in a daily life which is the outflow and result of these beliefs and affections; you will be showing that the sight of Christ crucified has a real power to affect and transform human nature; you will be "always bearing about in your" life and conduct and character, "the dying of the Lord Jesus!"

And this which has been said of the way in which views of sin, as beheld in the light of Christ's death, are carried into the life, and transform the nature, may serve as a specimen of the way in which the Saviour's dying should transform us entirely. Thus do right views of spiritual things, obtained by seeing them all in the light of Christ's death, pass into practice. When sorrow and suffering come, think of them as in the presence of the Redeemer's death; and you will learn the lesson of practical resignation. Under the deep conviction how sinful and lost you are, let the sight of your dying Saviour encourage you to go and confide your soul to him by a living, earnest faith. And in days of fear and anxiety, when you do not know how it will go with you, oh look to Jesus on the cross; and learn the lesson of practical confidence in God's disposing love and wisdom, as you think that surely he who provided *that* precious sacrifice will never fail to justify the hope and promise of the name the patriarch gave him; — that his name is still Jehovah-jireh, The Lord will provide; and that not in the mount of the Lord only, but over the wide world in the experience of all his people, *that* shall be seen. And to sum up all in one, let us be made conformable to Christ's death, let us daily bear about his dying, — by dying to sin and living to holiness. *That* is the grand conformity which is open to all of us; *that* is the fashion in which we may be "crucified with Christ!" In the perpetual mortifying of our corrupt affections and desires; in the ruling of our spirit; in the constant struggle against all that in us which is displeasing to God; all envy, hatred, malice, uncharitableness; all self-sufficiency, all pride, everything which there was nothing like in the mind of Jesus; we shall be crucified to the world, and the world crucified to us; and thus bear about our Redeemer's dying!

Yes, always bear it; never lay that burden down;

that yoke made so easy and pleasant by the precious communications of the Holy Spirit. Always bear it; not in sourness; not in that hard, severe type of religion which we may see in some mistaken and narrow-hearted believers, and which does so much to repel the young from religion; not in that stupid forbidding of innocent amusement, which is strange indeed in the disciples of One whose first miracle was wrought at a marriage-festival; and who, we may be sure, cast no damp over its innocent mirth. Yes; always bear the Saviour's dying; bear it in humility, in kindness, in charity in your doings and your judgments; in resignation to God's wise appointments, in faith in God's great love, in faith the simplest and in love the deepest towards that Best and Kindest Friend, transcending all thought and word, who died for us upon the accursed tree. Bear it, too, in hopefulness and cheerfulness, so far as these things are given to us in this life. There need be no change upon your outward aspect, like that wearing change which passed upon St. Paul, as *you* bear about in the body your Saviour's dying; no change wrought upon you save that wrought so gradually by advancing years and their many toils and cares; your brow need not be lined a day the sooner, nor your hair a day the sooner gray; but oh that all of us might be daily and hourly bearing that burden! it would be well for the world we live in, and well for ourselves; you would look with interest, and almost with awe, at a man concerning whom you knew, that all the while he was busied with the little business of life, there was a great, solemn, sacred remembrance at the bottom of his heart, ready to come up in the moment when it should be needed, and even now unconsciously giving its tone to all his thoughts; and oh, if a sand-grain looks small when you compare it with a mountain, think what petty, what inconceivably little, insignificant things the worries of daily life would be, to the man who was always bearing about with him the dying of Jesus Christ!

And thus, my friends, though to the end of our mortal life, we may never know what it is to bear physical sufferings like those of our Blessed Redeemer; though at the last we may lay our bodies in the grave, unmarked by stripes like those which he and his apostles bore; and though our cold hand, when it is cold at length, may moulder into clay, unpierced by such nails as pierced his merciful hands; we yet may, most truly and really, bear about his dying. It may go with us, that dying, in its remembrance and its influence, affecting all our views; leavening and transforming all our life. And when a few days or years are gone, and we are called indeed to die; when the heart, pausing for its long rest, beats feebly and slow, and the cold waters of the dark river seem stealing up and up to pass over us; oh let us think, to comfort and support us then, that we are faring only like our Master; that in this strange trial we are only being made conformable to our Saviour's death! And not, we may humbly ask and hope, — not quite conformable to *that*. For not, we may humbly ask and hope, not like him, in torment and in shame, may *we* be called to draw our last breath; but on our quiet bed; and with dear friends by, to moisten the parching lips, and to smooth the weary pillow. And oh, my friends, if it shall please God to grant us that peaceful departure, how light will our burden be to his; and how little a part of *his* dying shall we be called to bear!

XII.

THE INCONSISTENT WORSHIP.

"They feared the Lord, and served their own gods."
2 KINGS xvii. 33.

THE ten tribes which formed the kingdom of Israel, had at length wearied out God's forbearance; and God gave them over to the hand of the king of Assyria. That monarch took Samaria, and carried Israel away into the land of Assyria, where they remained as captives. But the Assyrian king did not choose that the land of Israel should remain without inhabitants; and so he collected a motley band of people from various portions of his dominions, and sent them to dwell in the cities of Samaria instead of the children of Israel. But these new-comers did not find themselves comfortable. Through the country having lain desolate for a while, wild beasts had multiplied; and lions came and slew some of them. They were a poor ignorant race, that mixture of people from Babylon, Cuthah, Hamath, and Sepharvaim; but though they were ignorant, and by consequence superstitious, they came nearer the truth in their idea as to the reason why the lions came, than some of our wise men nowadays, who regard any interference of God in the system of providence, as an unwarrantable intrusion. These poor ignorant people judged that God had sent the lions; and so far they were right. But they went wrong when they thought that the Being who sent the lions was a God specially connected with the land of Samaria; and when they fancied that this God had his own peculiar fancies, ideas, crotchets; and that he was angry because they did not know his particular way of thinking and feeling. They made their complaint to the king who had sent them; and a pitiful story it was. They sent him word that they were in a bad way; that they did not know "the manner of the God of the land;" and so that he had sent lions among them, who slew them; because they did not know the manner of the God of the land. Then the king of Assyria, feeling for their case; but with little sense, we may be sure, of the depth of meaning there was in that poor, sad, helpless wail of ignorance concerning God; gave orders to send back one of the captive priests, that he might give the new inhabitants of Samaria the information they needed; — that he might "teach them the manner of the God of the land." The priest went; and "taught them," we are told, "how they should fear the Lord;" but he must have taught them very badly, or they must have learned very ill; for the plan on which they fell was this. Each tribe continued to worship its own god, the idol which it had previously worshipped; and, in addition to this, all agreed in worshipping the true God as well. The men of Babylon worshipped one thing; the men of Hamath worshipped another; the Avites worshipped a third, and the Sepharvites a fourth; they kept up the worship of the old familiar gods to which they had grown accustomed away in their own countries; and then, in addition to *that*, they added a certain amount of worship to this peculiar-tempered "God of the land," with whose "manner" they had found it so hard to get acquainted. And the result was, that matters became what they are described as being in that short, but most suggestive sentence which forms my text. These new-comers to the land of Samaria "feared the Lord, and served their own gods." And so well pleased were they with this compromise between truth and falsehood, between God and Satan, that the historian that wrote this book was able to tell us they had kept it up for three hundred years.

If that singular race of men who lived many hundreds of years ago in the cities of Samaria had been the only race that ever did the like; if there were no such thing known among us, who are living to-day in Britain, as that men should "fear the Lord, and serve their own gods;" it would not have been worth while to found a sermon addressed to a Christian congregation upon such a text as that which I have chosen for this afternoon. No doubt, it would still have been a curious study, the conduct and character of those poor superstitious creatures, whom a vague undefined terror of Almighty God led to offer him a little share in that religious worship which they rendered with the heartiness of early training and old associations to various lying idols; but the study would have been more curious than practical; and I suppose that most of us have lived too long to be much surprised, however we may be saddened, at the sight of sincere, humble, earnest, honest delusion and folly. But it is different when we remember that in the errors and delusions of these poor benighted beings, we may see new foes with an old face; when we remember that among ourselves there are hosts of men who are doing the self-same thing which these people did; when we remember that in the heart of each one of us there is an inveterate disposition to do that self-same thing. Yes, brethren, this subject which the text brings up, is as fresh, and as practically important, to-day, as it ever was; and in asking your attention for a little while to the strange phase of religious feeling which the text sets before you, I know that I am asking your attention to a matter of personal concern to us all.

The first thought which I think suggests itself to our mind, in looking at the statement that the inhabitants of the Samaritan cities "feared the Lord, and served their own gods;" is of the curious inconsistency of their conduct. They worshipped the true God; and, along with him, they worshipped various false gods. Now, this seems strange to us. We cannot imagine a man being at once a Christian, a Mohammedan, a Jew, a Heathen, and an Atheist. You must make your choice what religion you will profess; you cannot profess several inconsistent religions together. But, my brethren, it is just because Christianity has so thoroughly leavened our ways of thinking, that there appears to us anything strange in the conduct of these inhabitants of Samaria. For Christianity, we all know, is an exclusive religion. It not merely calls men to believe in itself, but to reject every other faith. It not merely claims to be right and true; but it boldly says that every other faith is wrong and false. The God of the Bible not merely commands us to worship *him;* he commands us to worship no one else. His very first commandment is, "Thou shalt have none other gods before me." In short, the great characteristic of Christianity, and of Judaism which preceded it, is, that they are exclusive religions. This is their great characteristic as compared with all other religions. Christianity is a faith which admits no rivals, no competitors; it demands to stand alone. And the true God is not the God of this land or that land; he is the God of all the earth; he tolerates no brother near his throne. But it was not so at all with the gods of false religions; with the gods whom these poor Samaritans worshipped; no, nor with the gods and goddesses who were worshipped by the polished nations of Greece and Rome. It did not follow that because you held Jupiter to be a true god, you held Mercury or Apollo to be false gods. It did not follow because you worshipped Dagon, that you failed to worship Moloch. It did not follow that Beelzebub would feel himself slighted, because you offered a sacrifice to Rimmon. Each false god had his own province, and he held by *that*. One god was in prime favor in Philistia, another in Moab. One god ruled the sea, another the air, another the land, another the region under the earth. When the people at Athens or Rome heard of some new god, who was much esteemed in some distant country, and who was supposed to have done great things there; they took his claims into consideration; they inquired whether he deserved divine honors; and if they concluded that he did, they added him to their long list of gods; they built him a temple and appointed him priests and sacrifices; and all this without the least idea that they were trenching on the vested interests, on the rights and dignities, of the gods they already worshipped. And so you can see that these ignorant Samaritans, when they "feared the Lord, and served their own gods," had no sense at all of the inconsistency, — of the self-contradiction, — of what they did, such as that which we might feel. In all simplicity they imagined that in coming to Samaria, they had entered into the kingdom of a new god; and they judged that it was expedient to offer him such worship as might prevent his doing them mischief; but they had no notion at all of giving up the worship of the old, familiar idols, which they had worshipped in their distant homes. No; the gods would get on peaceably together. Tartak, Nergal, and Moloch, were still quite good gods, though it had been found expedient to add to their number one, who was evidently regarded as a rather peculiar-tempered god,— one whose "manner" it was not very easy quite to understand. It was upon this principle that these poor Samaritans went; it was thus they judged, and thus they acted.

A second thing worthy of notice in their conduct is this: the motive which led them to offer worship to the true God. You observe, *that* motive was pure and simple fear. They worshipped God, because they were afraid of him. They worshipped him, because they thought he had done them much mischief already; and because they thought that unless they did something to conciliate him, he might do them more mischief yet. They came, you see, from their various regions, to Samaria; they settled down in the abandoned homes which the mourning Israelites had lately left; they went on in their old worship of their old idols; and they never seem to have cast a thought upon the God of the tribes they had supplanted, till evil befell them. Good might have come, in any measure; and they would never have seen God in *that*. But when evil befell them, such was their conception of the Divine nature, they said, Now, *here* is the finger of God. The lions came prowling about their fields and dwellings; and this neighbor and the other was devoured by them; and then at once their thoughts ran up to a God as the sender of mischief; *that* was all they knew about him; and they determined to worship him, not because he was good and kind and deserving of all worship; but because unless they affected some measure of regard and respect for him, he might send them something worse than even the lions who had already come. They thought of God, in short, not as a being whose love they hoped for, but as a being whose wrath they dreaded. Their idea of the Almighty, was of an author of mischief; one who had sent lions already, and who might send worse if he were not kept quiet. And thus their worship was in truth devil-worship, and not God-worship; for the essence of devil-worship lies in offering worship to a being not because you love him, but because you are afraid of him; not because you hope any good from him, but because you fear much harm from him. They could not possibly, these men, have any love for a Being of whom their entire idea was that he had sent the savage beasts who had torn their friends and their children; they could not possibly join in his worship with any pleasure or any heart; the language of their hearts never could be, "How amiable are thy tabernacles, O Lord of hosts!" It would rather be, However disagreeable thy tabernacles, however unpleasant thy worship, we must perforce submit to *that*, for fear of something worse.

And this leads us to the third matter which I wish to suggest to you, as worthy of notice in the conduct of the people of whom we are thinking. It is evident from the entire account of them, that the worship which they paid to the true God was not nearly so hearty and real a thing as that which they paid to their old idols. "They *feared* the Lord;" they stood in a vague terror of him, which prompted them to offer him a sacrifice now and then; to meet for his worship now and then; but "they *served* their own gods;—they lived day by day in mind of *them;* they were not merely the *worshippers*, at long intervals, of these false gods; they were the *servants* of these false gods,—obeying them, working for them, from hour to hour. When the two things came together; the worship of a Being from whom they simply feared evil, and the worship of beings from whom they expected good; you can easily see which of the two would have the predominance. You can easily see which would always have to give way to the other, in case of any conflict between the two. You can easily see that the problem which the sharp-witted man among these Samaritans would set himself to solve, would be *this:* to find the minimum of worship which would satisfy the true God; to find the very smallest amount of reverence and service that would just keep him from doing them any mischief. The best they looked for from him, was to refrain from doing them harm; and the worship which would barely suffice to get him to refrain from doing them harm, was all that a prudent and economical man would think of rendering. But it was quite different with regard to their false gods. From *them* they hoped good, as well as feared evil. And in *their* case the astute Samaritan would think it judicious to offer a very great amount of worship, because he would think that, the more worship he gave, the more good he would get. A little worship was needed, for a beginning, to make sure that these gods should not harm him; and then any extra worship, beyond that point, would go towards making sure that they should bless him. In short, my friends, the worship prompted by fear will be the very least that *will do.* But as for the worship prompted by hope and love, there is no limit to *that.* No part of *it* could be regarded as thrown away; it would all be of use. Now, the great laws of human thought will in the long run sway the belief and the practice of even the dullest minds; and so these poor, ignorant, superstitious Samaritans had still penetration enough to see in what quarter, according to their ideas of Almighty God and of their own false deities, their worship would be most profitably invested. Accordingly, they carried out their views to their natural and logical conclusion: "They *feared* the Lord, and *served* their own gods."

Such, my friends, are the great characteristic features of the conduct of the people spoken of in the text. And in order that their way of thinking and acting might be set before you with greater clearness, I have pointed out to you these characteristic features without interrupting the line of thought by any reference to ourselves, and to our own ways of thinking and acting. But now, brethren, let us seek to give a practical bearing to all this that has been said. Let us look back upon the errors of these Samaritans, so many centuries ago; let us see whether human nature be not now very much what it was then; let us see whether we ourselves, and many around us, are not, day by day, falling into the like errors; or at least tempted to the like errors still.

The Samaritans did not see that it was inconsistent to worship the true God, and at the same time to worship false gods; they did not remember, because they never had been taught, that the true God claims to reign *alone;* that he does not regard himself as worshipped at all, if any other being is worshipped along with him. Now, my friends, we have not the excuse which the Samaritans had; we quite understand how exclusive is the worship which our God claims for himself; but is it not sadly true that day by day we are all too much disposed to combine his worship with other worship, — to "fear the Lord and serve our own gods"? Ah, brethren, many a professing Christian is trying in his entire life to do the very thing which the Saviour said could not be done, — to "serve God and Mammon." There is many a man who has that degree of superstitious fear of what God may do to him, that he dare not cast off God's fear altogether; while yet the love of money, or the love of pleasure, or the love of eminence and honor, really sits upon the throne of his heart! He "fears the Lord;" and at the same time he thinks to "serve his own gods," — wealth, pleasure, or ambition. Of course, the days of stock and stone idolatry are past, at least in this country; but who needs to be told that idols are worshipped in Britain yet, as truly as idols ever were worshipped at Babylon or Samaria? The essence of idolatry is there, whether a man casts his gold into an image and bows down to it; or only leaves it in the form of a balance at his banker's, or invests it in the Funds; and then makes it the first thing in his heart and thoughts. Not, my friends, that this view should be pushed to any fanatical extreme. Not that Christianity requires of us to set no value at all upon earthly good, or to refuse to give to those we love any affection at all. *That* is asceticism, monasticism; it is not Christianity. The requirements of Christianity are always characterized, among other things, by sound, practical common-sense. They are always *workable.* They will always *do* in actual life. What Christianity requires is, that God should be supreme in the heart; that nothing else should ever be put on a level with him; that he should reign in the soul as he does in the universe, *alone*, with all things else at an immeasurable distance beneath his feet. And the great practical test whether this is so or not, is, whether in the event of our duty to God coming in competition with our obtaining any worldly profit or pleasure or advantage of any kind, the worldly advantage has always and at once to give way. Say you have it in your power to gain some money by doing something dishonest; by telling what is not true to your neighbor, or by overreaching him in any way. Now, my friend, if you admit for one moment the idea of doing the unfair thing for the sake of the profit that may come of it; you are for that moment weighing with yourself whether you may not succeed in doing what the Samaritans did, — "fearing the Lord," and at the same time "serving your own god," — your god in this case being Mammon. The fraudulent trader who adulterates his wares, and yet is never out of church on a Sunday; the greedy farmer, who will tell many lies to get a sound price for a lame horse, yet who would not on any consideration be absent from a sacrament; and I say it with sorrow, brethren, I have known several such; what are such men doing but what the Samaritans did: "fearing the Lord, and serving their own gods!"

And this brings us to the second thing we remarked

as worthy of notice in the conduct of the Samaritans: they worshipped the true God, because they were afraid he would do them harm unless they worshipped him. Their motive in worshipping God was not love, but fear. And, O brethren, is it not sadly true, that there is too much of the same thing among ourselves? Are not very many professing Christians constrained to make some little profession of religion, and to pay some little regard to religious duties and observances, just by a superstitious fear that something will happen to them if they do not, — that God will send some evil upon them if they do not? Is it not so, that all of us have known what it is to do some religious duty for no better reason? When we were weary and had little heart for it, and would rather have escaped it, have we not sometimes uttered some formal, heartless words of prayer, because we were afraid to omit them; because we feared something ill would happen to us, if we did not interpose this perfunctory performance of duty — a duty that is worth nothing if it be done perfunctorily — between us and the anger of God! Ah, brethren, it is deep-set in human nature, the disposition to serve God from the wrong motive, and to regard him from the wrong point of view. It is deep-set in our fallen nature, the disposition to think of God as a being from whom we dread evil rather than as one from whom we hope good; and the disposition to worship him rather from fear than from love. But surely you do not need to be reminded what an unchristian way *that* is of looking at God; what a heathenish motive *that* is for serving God! Who can forget what Christ told us was the first and great commandment of God's law? Not, Thou shalt dread God, be afraid of God, crouch and tremble and shudder at the name of God; no, far from that: "Thou shalt *love* the Lord thy God with all thy heart, and with all thy soul, and with all thy mind!" *That* is Christian worship; *that* is the grand motive that should prompt to the worship of the Christian's God! Under the dispensation of the Cross, the terrors of the law may still be rightly used to awaken men from utter carelessness as to their soul's salvation; you may rightly impress it upon them, that away from Jesus, God is to the sinner "a consuming fire;" but once driven to "flee from the wrath to come;"—once led to Jesus;—once united by living faith to that kind, loving Saviour,—oh, it is love and not terror that leads the Christian on! The mere dread of hell, I make bold to say it, has in the heart of the earnest believer, walking humbly with his God and leaning simply on his Redeemer, really no appreciable weight at all. It is not because sin ends in ruin, that he hates sin so much; it is because sin bound his gracious Saviour to the accursed tree! It is not because he dreads final perdition, that he strives daily against sin, and seeks daily the aids of the Holy Spirit, and strives ever to lay up his treasure on high; it is because he longs for his blessed Lord's gracious presence, because he pants for the day when sin and sorrow shall be done with, because he thirsts for the time when he shall enter on the blessed rest of God! We did not come here to-day, my friends, because we were afraid of God; we "worship him in fear," indeed; but it is no slavish fear; we are not within these walls, a crouching, panic-stricken, shivering crew, as driven by the slave-driver's lash, in pure abject terror that God would send some terrible judgment upon us if we failed to present ourselves in his house, and to go through some form of his worship. No, we have come to the kind merciful God who loves us, as children might gather at a parent's knee; we have come to One who so loved us as to give his son to die for us; we have come to worship One who wills not that any should perish, but that all should believe and live; we have come to tell of all our wants that he may supply them, and to confess all our sins that he may wash them all away; we have come to ask strength for our work, and comfort in our sorrows, and heart for our weary way. And when we look up to him, we see nothing of which to be afraid. The invisible God, indeed, eludes our sight; but we can see him in a gracious face we know well; with the eye of faith we can see a gentle, loving countenance looking down on us, with eyes that for us have been dim with tears! We see the "glory of God in the face of Jesus Christ;" we can trust our souls to his blessed keeping; we can worship and serve him "whom having not seen we love;"—and love without a fear!

And finally, my friends, you remember that the last thing we remarked in the conduct of the Samaritans was, that it was plain they were far more hearty in serving their own gods, from whom they expected good, than in serving the Almighty, from whom they only dreaded ill. And who needs to be told that in *this* respect, too, many professing Christians exactly resemble them? Indeed, my brethren, by the very nature of things, the three things mentioned as remarkable in the Samaritans will always go together. If you, like them, try to combine the worship of God with the service of Mammon, or Pleasure, or Ambition; you will soon find that any worship you can spare for the true God, you are giving, just for fear that some mischief will happen you if you do not take means to pacify him; and you will soon find, too, that your worship of God is a very chilly and heartless thing when compared with your service of your worldly idol. The avaricious man; the dishonest man; the over-ambitious man; even if for fear of evil he keeps up some kind of worship of God,—will find that God is always growing less in his heart, and money or eminence growing more; will know quite well that if he were free to act as inclination leads him, he would give up the sham of worshipping God at all, and openly give his worship where he has already given his heart. It is a fact about which there can be no doubt, that if a man tries to worship God and Mammon together, Mammon will always have the advantage; Mammon will always have the preeminence, and the chief share of service. If you try to "fear the Lord, and serve your own gods," then in the long run, your own gods will get all your service, and the Almighty will get none, — or, if any, then the very least thing that you think will keep him quiet. You know that, my friends. Your prayers will always get shorter, — your attendance at church more irregular and more heartless, — your reading of the Bible a more wearisome task. Your conscience will always become more easily pacified; the worship of your earthly idols will eat up the worship of your God; and some day you may remember with a start, that weeks have passed since you knelt in prayer, or since you opened God's word; that the care of your soul and of eternity, long pushed as it were into a corner of your time, can now find no time at all!

O brethren, may God grant to us, to make religion the first thing; to give God the first place! We *may* work, we *must* work, for many things; but may we never forget that there is "one thing needful!" And so shall we be enabled to escape that error described in our text; an error as natural to human beings now, as when men six-and-twenty hundred years since "feared the Lord, and served their own gods." So shall we be enabled, in a nobler sense than that in which he wrote them, to take up the poet's words: to "fear our God, and know no other fear!"

XIII.

THE VAGUENESS AND ENDLESSNESS OF HUMAN ASPIRATIONS.

"And I said, Oh that I had wings like a dove! for then would I fly away, and be at rest." — PSALM lv. 6.

I DO not know, my friends, where I could find more convincing proof of the essential identity of human nature now, with human nature thousands of years since, than we find in these words. The words are very ancient; but their spirit is perfectly modern. These words were centuries old, in the days when this country was a savage wilderness, peopled by more savage men; and yet, they have quite the ring of the latter half of the nineteenth century after Christ. Here we find David, king and psalmist, involved in some of those many sorrows and troubles which we may be glad he passed through; some of those many sorrows and troubles which fitted him for writing those sacred poems which come so home to our hearts, and which seem to suit our own case and describe our own feelings so well. Here we find the psalmist and king in great perplexity and grief and fear. The first of modern essayists has said that the great characteristic of modern life is worry; but it should seem from the text that it was the great characteristic of ancient life too; for if there ever was such a thing in this world, here we have the utterance of a thoroughly worried man. And see what he says. From the midst of endless and countless cares, fears, and griefs, he wearily looks up; he plainly sees that where he is, the day will never come in which cares, griefs, and fears will not still surround him; and so he bursts out into a vague, hopeless, yet passionate cry, — he cannot clearly say for what, — but only that he might get away to some place, — he does not know where, — in which these should be done with forever! Ah, the vague aspirations and longings of human nature, — only to define them, only to try and get them into a tangible shape, makes us feel how vain and foolish they are. The psalmist wanted, he did not well know what; — but only to get away from here. He knew he was not at rest where he was; he felt that he never would be at rest there; and he breaks out into words which seem mistily to mean that he fancied there surely was, somewhere, some happy island where he might find peace and rest at last. My friends, I spoke of the essentially modern tone of that fancy as proving how-like *we* are now to what King David was centuries ago, — as proving that man is always essentially the same. Do you not remember that when the greatest living poet wishes to set before us a human being of this age, restlessly dissatisfied and disappointed, he puts upon *his* lips words which look almost like an expansion of the vague aspiration of the psalmist; he represents *him* too, as confusedly wishing that he could get anywhere away from where he was; he makes *him* vaguely long to burst all links of civilized habit, to leave all traces of civilized man behind him, to fly to distant seas where an European flag never floated, as though thus he could cast off the burden of his cares and of himself! And no doubt, we can all sometimes sympathize with the fancy. No doubt, it must be accepted as an unquestionable fact, that the many advantages of civilization are to be obtained only at the price of countless and ceaseless worry. No doubt, we must all sometimes sigh for the woods and the wigwam; but the feeling is as vain as that of the psalmist's wearied aspiration in the text. The modern poet, indeed, shows us one point of difference between ancient and modern modes of thought; he makes the man whom he describes analyze his feeling and his wish, and see for himself how vain they are; he makes him confess that his words are wild, and that they set out no more than a dream and a fancy. Here, indeed, we can discern that the psalmist was of an earlier age, and an earlier period in human development. He merely records what his feeling was; he does not stop to analyze and examine it; for all he tells us, the vague feeling might have remained with him yet, that once you gave him the swift wings, he would know where to fly with them; — that once he had "wandered far off," he could "remain in the wilderness," and be quite peaceful and content at last. But it is just this thing, which makes the aspiration in the text one so practically profitable for us to think of; it is just because in its vagueness, its unreasonableness, its endlessness, it is so accurate a type of the endlessness and the vagueness of human aspirations. Oh, give the psalmist the swift wings; and whither could he fly? Give him all the universe to choose from; and where would he find the place where he could be at rest? Give men all this world could yield them; tell men that for the naming it, they shall have every wish gratified to the utmost, that begins and ends on this world and this life; and they will be as far from rest for their weary souls as ever. And, thank God, we know the reason why. It is because "this is not our rest." It was because God had unalterably fixed and appointed, that worldly things alone can never make the soul of man permanently happy. You think to make yourself content and happy without the good part in Christ, and the reconciled love of God in him; you cannot; it is impossible. God says *No* to that; it cannot be done. If you think and try to find real rest for your soul away from God in Christ; if you think to be really happy away from Christ; you are thinking and trying to do what, by the make of your being, is impossible. You might as well think to quench the thirst of the parched throat with sand, as to satisfy man's thirst for happiness with anything merely worldly. You are in the wrong course altogether, when you try to do *that.* And when you think to do it, you are doing something as natural, as endless, as hopeless, as the Jewish monarch thought to do, when in a world which has no corner, no field, no seclusion, no station, no life, that could give him rest, he fancied he could find rest if he could but fly far enough away from the sorrows that were plucking at him where he was; when he said, "Oh that I had wings like a dove! for then would I fly away, and be at rest."

Yes, my friends; it is a most practical, and a most important subject, for us to think of to-day, that this text brings before us. For it would be our salvation, if we could only feel and realize the fact, that this world is not our rest; and that only in God, as we see him in the face of Christ, can we find rest and peace, and that which shall truly satisfy our weary and thirsting souls. For, after all, it is the love of this world that stands between most men, and their seeking to go to Jesus and believe in him; and if you could only get them to feel it in their hearts that this world will not do, — that this world cannot give us rest, — it would be a vast step in the direction of honestly seeking to lay up their treasure in a better. Now it is just by vague fancies, like that of the psalmist, that men encourage themselves to go on setting their hearts on earthly things, and never really striving to win the good part in Christ with the same real intention and industry with which they strive to gain some worldly advantage. When human beings meet with disappointments, cares, anxieties, bereavements; when they find how different a thing daily worry has made of life from what they had anticipated in the bright dreams of childhood; when they are constrained to feel, day by day, that they are not happy, that they cannot be happy, that there is always something happening to vex them, and keep them from being happy, — instead of learning the lesson which God is teaching them by all this, that they ought not to set their heart on things here, that they ought to seek for that one thing needful which will never disappoint, that they ought to seek for rest in Jesus, where alone it is to be found,—instead of doing all *this*, they do something exactly analogous to what the psalmist did; they fancy that there is some time if not some place in this world to which if they could fly away, they would be at rest; they bear up under the worries of present time in some vague hope that better days are coming, — days in which there will be no more of these little fretting cares, these heavy disappointments, these crushing bereavements, that weigh upon the present; days that shall pass unanxiously, peacefully, happily; and in which this world will, not perhaps satisfy our early anticipations of it, but at least come up to the moderate hopes of maturer years, and afford the soul something like content and quiet happiness at last. Oh, brethren, that we could once for all get rid of this false notion,—a notion which does so much to keep our hearts in slavery to the things of sense and time! Oh that we could really feel that it is as vain a fancy, to believe that future years will bring rest with them, as the psalmist's, that once far away in the wilderness, he would be at rest! The days to come will do no more for us, than the dove's wings and the desert would have done for him. Coming days may and will do for us just what the wings would have done for the wearied monarch;—they will no doubt bear us away from the trials and troubles that now surround us,—that are present now;—but they will only bear us to other trials and troubles that are awaiting us then. Oh, brethren, that we could lay it to heart, that the day will never come in which there will not be something to vex and weary; the day will never come in which everything will go as we would wish; the day will never come in this world that will make the soul happy and complete; and all this just because God does not intend that such a day should ever come; all this because this world was never meant for our rest; and whenever it is beginning to grow too like our rest, God will send us something to remind us that it is not; all this because these immortal souls within us are not to be put off with any worldly aim or worldly enjoyment,—but will ever reach and blindly long after something as immortal as themselves! It was not a piece of mystical piety, but a plain, certain, philosophic truth, that sentence of the ancient African bishop, written more than a thousand years since: "Thou madest us for Thyself," — thus he addressed his Maker, — "and our souls are restless, till they find rest in Thee!"

The wings and the wilderness would not have made the psalmist happy; and no imaginable worldly blessings will ever suffice to make us so. The only real rest that the soul of man can ever know, is that which is given by him who said, "Come unto Me, all ye that labor and are heavy laden, and I will give you rest." And not even *that* rest, given by the Redeemer to his own, is perfect in this present life; the best believer's heart will be many a time disquieted and perplexed, so long as he abides here. "There remaineth a rest for the people of God." It *remaineth;* it is waiting for them; far away. My dear friends, this is not our rest; our rest is beyond the grave. We are but "strangers and pilgrims upon earth;" and heaven is our home. And it is only our Saviour's presence that can make us happy. God has made us so that we never shall be right, till we are "forever with the Lord!" It is not the quiet country, that will give all the rest he needs to the jaded man of business in the great city. It is not the longed-for breathing space, the longed-for leisure, that is all which is needed by the over-driven brain. It is not the home fireside, and the cheerful domestic circle, that is all the lonely wanderer needs to give him rest. It is not money that will really satisfy the soul of the man who works hardest for it; it is not high station and eminent fame that will truly enable even the most ambitious man to sit down and feel himself perfectly content at last. There will always be something wanting; always some vague idea like the psalmist's, that if he had but wings, he would fly far, far away. There are rest and peace to be found in God, — in God as we see him in the merciful face of Christ; and no other where!

Now, brethren, we remember that it was a king who wrote these words of the text. It was one who had attained to the highest position which can be reached by any human being. It was one who had experienced an extraordinary degree of what men esteem as good fortune. He was at first nothing more than a shepherd-lad; but he came out from that lowly estate, and rose to fame and power and wealth. He actually reached all those things after which most human beings are striving in vain through all their lives. You know how men labor and pinch year after year to gain money, and possibly after all can do no more than get the ends to meet, of what they get, and what they must give away; here was a man who attained wealth without limit. You know the silly way in which people scheme and plan, to gain a little advance in social position; to get recognized as fairly belonging to a class a hair's-breadth higher than that in which they were born; to get admitted to good society; well, here was a man who had undeniably risen from a humble origin to the very top of the social scale. And is *this* the man, we are all ready to think, who speaks so poorly of a world which has used him so handsomely? Yes, the very man. All these things he had attained failed to make him happy; there were many thorns yet in the pillow; his heaviest sorrows befell him after he was an anointed king. You remember, too, how his more famous son, Solomon, the wisest and greatest man of his time, summed up the result of all his experience of life in the mournful declaration, "Vanity of vanities, saith the Preacher; all is vanity!" Now, brethren, it is good for us to listen to such words, from such lips. You cannot say that Solomon or David cried down this world because they could not get it; you cannot think that *they* said the grapes were sour because they could not reach them; you might have suspected something like *that*, if you had heard a man who had failed in life declaring that "all is vanity," or wishing for the dove's wings, that he might fly to the wilderness, and get far away from a world of which he was sick and weary. This was not Timon, giving up the world because the world had given up him. Here were men who had got all that life could give them; and who yet declared that all would not suffice to give the soul rest. And not merely is there here for us a lesson not to envy the rich and great; not to seek great things for ourselves; not merely is there something here to remind us, that we may be as happy in a lowly station as anywhere on earth, — that in the Valley of Humiliation, as Bunyan said, we may have as much of the herb called heart's-ease in our bosom, as anywhere; but there is a lesson of yet deeper spiritual import read us by the history of those great men who stand out like beacons for our guidance as we steer over the sea of life. Very few men indeed ever reach all the specific objects they seek; and so come to such vague aspirations as those of the psalmist. Very few men, whatever may be their occasional feeling, ever reach that point, that the serious and constant wish of their heart comes to be after the undefined end, the vague rest, of our text. For it is of the essential nature of human objects of pursuit, that while each is in view, it shuts out the view of the rest; it concentrates our thoughts and wishes upon itself; it creates some confused impression that we should be happy, that we should be right at last, if we could only reach it. We fancy that something would make us happy if we could get it; and if we never do get it, we go on under that fancy; we keep thinking that it would make us happy; while if we had got it, we should have found that it would not. As for instance: a man wants to be rich; he sets his heart on wealth. Well, year after year, he toils for *that.* He never reaches it. And so he still thinks that if he had but reached it, however much it may have failed with others, it would have succeeded with him; and he goes down to his grave still fancying that if he had been rich he would have been happy, — still thinking within himself, No doubt I knew So-and-so, and such another man, who were very rich, and they did not seem to be very happy; but *that* was their own fault; they did not know how to manage; if I had been in their place, I should have been perfectly content! Yes, the next end shuts out all the rest; as when you ask a drowning man what he wants, he says, Save me from drowning, — *that* is all he wants in the mean time; he never thinks of anything more till he has got that. But here in the text we find a man who had actually gained all the ends after which men seek and strive; here is a man who has actually gained wealth, rank, fame, empire; and now he vaguely wants more. He has got past the stage in which we fix on something near, — on some specific end, — as money, or position, or the like; he has got past that, and reached the farther stage at which we look up, and take a general view, and ask ourselves to what all this is tending; and *then* comes the vague, confused wishing and reaching on for something which we cannot define; then comes the "Oh that I had wings like a dove! Then would I fly away, and be at rest."

And now, my friends, let me remind you, that it is not God's word alone that tells us how this world is not our rest. Other voices chime in, and tell us the same sad story. "Vanity of vanities;" "The world passeth away;" "We all do fade as a leaf;" O brethren, is not *that* the strain of very much of the best part of the literature of this day, and of all days? Do you not know how one of the most brilliant authors of the age has devoted all his writings to the illustration and enforcement just of Solomon's famous text? But, brethren, what a wretched blank we feel, when genius tells us the story of this world's vanity, — and stops short there! Oh, surely those who have, with an eloquence that far surpasses the theologian's, told us of the unsatisfying nature of all this world can yield us, were especially bound to point us to him in whom alone the weary, thirsting soul can find all it needs! If you *will* point man's poor soul away from this world, oh, point it to Jesus; direct its faltering steps to *him* who has promised the rest to which the speediest wings would not bear you, and which you could not find in a wilderness far more remote than that remote seclusion to which the wearied monarch would fain have fled away! Never say that "this is not our rest," without remembering the blessed "I will give you rest," — without remembering thankfully that "there remaineth a rest for the people of God." But how different the case often is! You find it set out, sometimes with all the bitterness of the cynic, sometimes with matchless pathos and tenderness, that "here we have no continuing city;" well, and what then? You wait in vain for that which would complete that half-sentence and half-truth: "but we seek one to come." No; in many cases you will hear what virtually comes to this: "Here we have no continuing city; and it does not much matter." It *does* matter! If this world be so blank, so vain, so unsatisfying, what could we do, but for the blessed hope of a better; what could we do but for that blessed gospel which tells us of a Saviour who will guide us thither, and wash away our sins in his blood, and send us a Holy Spirit to make us pure as he is pure! This is far too serious a case for mere sentimentalism. Nothing will stand us in stead but the faith of Christ, with its present strong consolations, with its substantial hopes for days to come. There is nothing real upon earth, but that good part, that saving interest in Christ, which never can decay. Everything else, even if it could satisfy while it lasts, is passing away so fast, and will be passed away so soon! We feel this sometimes, when sudden vivid glimpses come back upon us of tranquil days, gone forever; or when we realize it plainly, that all the blessings which now surround us, — home, friends, children, strength and life, are going too, — changing, decaying, ebbing away from us, withering in our grasp. Oh! dear friends, where shall your portion be? Here, amid the cares and changes of time; or there, amid the satisfying and enduring joys of immortality! Oh that we might each choose, for our soul's portion, him in whom there is pardon for the guilty soul, holiness for the sinful, rest for the weary, and peace for the disquieted! He made us for himself; he redeemed us with his blood; his blessed promise is of rest; oh, may our souls, by nature restless, find rest in him!

XIV.

COMFORT TO SODOM.

"When I shall bring again their captivity, the captivity of Sodom and her daughters, and the captivity of Samaria and her daughters, then will I bring again the captivity of thy captives in the midst of them: that thou mayest bear thine own shame, and mayest be confounded in all that thou hast done, in that thou art a comfort unto them." — EZEK. xvi. 53, 54.

NOW, first, what is the meaning of this text?

We find that Jerusalem is said to have been a comfort to Sodom and Samaria; and this is mentioned as if it were a fault. Jerusalem was to be punished, we are told; Jerusalem was to be ashamed and confounded; because it had been a comfort to Sodom and Samaria. Jerusalem was the chosen city of God, we know; and Sodom and Samaria were places remarkable for their wickedness. But still, we are a little surprised at the first glance at our text. Is it not a Christian's duty to do good to *all* as he has opportunity? Are we not bidden to love even our enemies, and to do good even to them that hate us; and can it then be wrong to be a comfort even to the worst of mankind, — even to Samaria and Sodom?

Yes, in such a case as this it is wrong to be a comfort to a bad man or a bad city; because in such a case it is the very reverse of a kind turn to be a comfort to them. It is doing harm to them, and not doing good to them, to be a comfort in this particular way. For Jerusalem had been a comfort to Sodom and Samaria, in such a manner as had encouraged them in their sins. When the wicked men of these cities were ready to be frightened and anxious about their sins, then the men of Jerusalem had behaved in such a way as tended to keep their minds easy, — to smooth down their anxieties and fears. Jerusalem had, so to speak, kept Sodom and Samaria in countenance. When the people of Sodom and Samaria were growing ashamed and alarmed, and were likely to repent of their sins, they looked across to Jerusalem; they saw it was just as bad as they were; and so they said to themselves, If Jerusalem, God's own chosen city, goes on in these evil courses, there can be no great harm in our doing so too. If we are going wrong, we are going wrong in good company. We, who never pretended to be better than our neighbors, need not mind much if we are no worse than people who profess to be the chosen people of God. And so, Jerusalem encouraged Sodom and Samaria to go on in sin; and so, in this blameworthy sense, Jerusalem was "a comfort to them." It was a comfort, even as the flapping wings of the vampire bat make a cool current of air which is extremely comfortable to the sleeping man whose blood it is drawing fast away. It was a comfort, as it is comfortable for the weary man, out in the snow-storm, to sink gently down in that slumber from which he will never wake below. Bnt the comfort of that sleep which will shortly end in death is far from a desirable thing. The true friend of a man in such a case would be he who should rouse him up, however rudely, and compel him to push on his way, however unwillingly. And in like manner, if Jerusalem had wished to do a kind turn to Sodom, the course to follow would not have been that of soothing its fears away, and encouraging it to go on peacefully and cheerfully in the road which would end in woe. The best and kindest turn which a good man could render to a bad man, would be, to be by precept and example a constant gnawing discomfort, — to keep his conscience always uneasy, — to give him not an hour of rest, — to keep him ever anxious, unhappy, fearful, — till he had turned him into the right and safe path. It was sin and shame for God's professed people to live in such a way as encouraged those who never professed to be God's people to persevere in their sin and thoughtlessness; and very fitly might Jerusalem be threatened with shame and confusion, "in that it was a comfort" to Sodom.

Now, my friends, I am sure you will all readily see, that there is a great and important principle suggested to us by the words of the text. The text suggests to us, that it is very blameworthy in those who profess to be Christians, to do anything which may comfort a sinner in his sinfulness, and encourage him to go on in his evil ways. You know, every Christian is solemnly bound to do all he can to make other men Christians. The knowledge of the gospel is not a thing which a man may have, and without blame keep to himself. No; all Christians, and not the ministers of the cross only, are under a bounden obligation to bring all within the sphere of their influence into the same light and liberty in which they themselves rejoice. And we know that a special blessedness is promised to him who shall turn a sinner from the error of his ways. "He which converteth a sinner from the error of his way, shall save a soul from death, and shall hide a multitude of sins." And just as blessed and happy a thing as it is to bring another soul to the belief of the gospel, — so wretched and wicked and fearful a thing is it when a man who bears the Christian name lives in such a way as positively encourages those around him to contemn and disbelieve Christianity. And alas! how often we find this so! How many a seeming believer, — yea, how many an inconsistent and injudicious real believer, — is "a comfort to Sodom;" that is, by his daily life does what he can to bring religion into discredit, — to make worldly men think it a hypocritical pretence, — a sham and a delusion! Ah, Christianity has received its sorest wounds in the houses of its seeming friends. The infidel cannot damage religion half so much as its hypocritical professor can. The consistent believer, by his entire life, should be a warning to the unbelievers around him. It should be a daily thorn in the flesh for the unconverted man only to see him and converse with him. To do so should make the unconverted man uneasy, dissatisfied with himself; it should make him feel that he lacks something that is supremely needful; it should stir in him a sense of discomfort which nothing can allay, save an instant hearty acceptance of the great salvation which is in Christ. Now, my brethren, is this so with you? There are many of you here who profess that you are Christians. There are many of you who come season by season to the communion table, and there declare that you are the disciples of Christ. Well, and what does your life say? Does that recommend Christianity to all around you? Does your daily life enforce the sermons which the unconverted hear in church; or does it nullify them? Are you people whose conversation and conduct, — whose candor and scrupulous fairness in your dealings, and manifest dread of committing sin, no matter what gain may be got by it, — are a constant witness to all who see you that your religion is a reality; or are you rather a "comfort to Sodom," — something that unbelievers may point to as a proof that religion is all a pretence, — something to encourage them in their neglect of religion, — something that worldly men can point at and say, See, that man is a communicant, —

he is never out of church, — he makes a great profession of religion, — and is he a bit better than we are, who make no profession of religion at all? If there is any difference, is it not that he is worse? Ah, my brethren, surely we have all got sins enough of our own to answer for, without making ourselves thus partakers of other men's sins, by so living that they may find in our example an apology for all the ill they do. But let us look more particularly into this matter, and think of various ways in which professing Christians may lay themselves open to the charge of being a "comfort to Sodom and Samaria."

1. There is one obvious way in which professing Christians may do this, which we mention only to pass it by, in the hope that none of us who bear even the Christian name are so sorely and shamefully guilty. This is the way in which we understand from the prophet that Jerusalem was a comfort to Sodom; and that was, by being actually as bad as Sodom itself. You can easily imagine how wicked men would take encouragement to go on in wickedness, when they found those who claimed to be God's peculiar people as wicked as themselves. If there were such a fearful and wretched sight to be seen, as a church-going man and a communicant, who was a swearer, a drunkard, a liar, a slanderer, and a cheat; if there were such a thing to be found, — as God forbid there should ever be, — would not every swearer and drunk-

ard and liar in the parish quiet his conscience with the reflection that *he* was no worse than that wicked professor of religion? Would not such a man be a comfort to all the Sodoms and Samarias in the district? And it is for this reason that it is impossible to calculate the amount of mischief that may be done in a parish by an unworthy minister, — by one of those degraded men whom every now and then the Church is called to denude of the office which he has disgraced. O brethren, it is easy to say, and it is true to say, that religion is a thing that must be judged of on the ground of its own merits, and quite apart from the conduct of those who profess to believe in it; yet, illogical as it may be, foolish and wrong as it may be, the mass of mankind will always encourage themselves in sinfulness when they find professing Christians going on in sin. True it is, that the right way of regarding such a case is to judge that these professing Christians are no Christians, — that they are only men who are adding hypocrisy to their other sins; and that it would be as fair to reckon darkness as a part of light as to reckon them as men for whom religion is in the least degree responsible. And passing by such a case, as one too miserable to be thought of, and in any case quite hopeless to mend, let us consider whether there may not be ways in which even sincere and good Christians may, without saying or doing anything that is expressly sinful, yet so act as to be a comfort to Sodom, — as to encourage wicked and worldly men in worldliness and sin.

2. And as one of these we mention, allowing sinful conduct to pass without notice or rebuke. If any sincere Christian is present in a company where what is sinful is said or done; and if he permits it to pass without remark, or even appears tacitly to approve it; I do not see how he can clear himself from the charge of having been "a comfort to Sodom." If any clergyman is present in a company of persons who so far forget, I do not say what is in accordance with God's law or with morality, but even what is due to common propriety, as to indulge in profane swearing; and if the clergyman allows that to pass without the least indication of disapproval; I do not see how he can clear himself from the charge of having been "a comfort to Sodom." If any sincere Christian is present when any man avows his intention of doing what is wrong, or mentions with satisfaction that he has already done what is wrong; and if the Christian makes no sign of what his feeling is or ought to be, then that Christian most assuredly is "a comfort to Sodom." If any sincere Christian is present, when a man relates with something like pride how he made an extremely profitable bargain by means which he probably regarded as being decidedly smart, but which right-thinking people would call lying and cheating; and if the Christian expresses nothing of the disgust which such conduct has excited in his breast; then that Christian

is proving himself "a comfort to Sodom." For, my friends, the very worst man attaches, and cannot help attaching, great importance to the opinion of his behavior which a real Christian entertains. His own heart condemns him when he does what is wrong; and he has an uneasy feeling that the Christian is in his heart condemning him too. Depend upon it, all who are real consistent Christians are able by their disapproval, — even by their silent disapproval, — to check a man most materially in his wrong-doing; and they are also able most materially to encourage him and comfort him in his wrong-doing by appearing to approve it. The apparent approval of one true and earnest Christian, — even the very humblest in worldly rank, — will have more influence to comfort the wicked man, — to keep his mind easy, and his conscience asleep, — than the loudest declarations of his own wicked associates that he is a fine fellow and has done nothing wrong. And I am not forgetting, my brethren, the restraints which the usages of civilized society impose upon our telling a man to his face what is our opinion of his conduct. The Christian is not called upon to go up to a man and tell him that he is a bad man, merely because he thinks he is one. The Christian is not called to set himself up as a sort of daily reviewer, a moral critic, of the character and conduct of all he knows. The. Christian is not commanded to tell every bad man he meets exactly what he thinks of him; nor forbidden to be civil and even respectful in answer, to those of whose conduct he disapproves the most. It is not demanded of the sincere believer, in order to his escaping the guilt of being "a comfort to Sodom," that he should make an enemy of almost every man he meets. Nay, my friends, — there is a silent, unobtrusive disapproval, by which the humblest may be a check upon the highest; there is a silent, unobtrusive disapproval, expressed without words or demonstration of manner, one can hardly tell how, which even the most hardened sinner will find it very hard, very uncomfortable, to bear. If the believer in his very heart reprobates and condemns the wicked man's wrong-doing, that condemnation and reprobation will make itself keenly felt, — felt by that electric sympathy which makes us so readily know when a really strong and decided opinion of us and feeling toward us is entertained by another human being. If you truly hate the sin, while yet, so far as that may be, you love the sinner; then, my friend, your manner toward the sinner will involuntarily be such, that you will be quite clear of the risk of being "a comfort to Sodom."

3. Another way in which a Christian may so act as to encourage and comfort an irreligious man in his godless ways, is by seeking his society and acquaintance; — showing him that you think him a congenial spirit, and that you feel it pleasant to be with him. I need not say to you, my brethren, that whatever may be a man's position and occupation, it is almost cer-

tain that he will find it absolutely necessary to be upon terms of kindly and even cordial social intercourse with many persons who he knows are not Christians; and perhaps even with some persons who have violated and are violating the laws of common morality. You cannot entirely decide for yourself what kind of persons shall be your acquaintances, in the way of business, or duty, or social intercourse even; you cannot entirely decide for yourself who shall be your *acquaintances*, — but most assuredly you can decide for yourself who shall be your *friends*. You can choose for yourself, and you ought to choose for yourself, those whose companionship you shall seek, whose conversation you shall delight in, to whom you will tell your secrets and confide your feelings, — those, in short, for words can make the idea no plainer, whom you will make your chosen friends. And we do not hesitate to lay it down as a certain principle, that a Christian man ought never to choose for his special friend a person who he knows has no religion. A man, they say, is known by the company he keeps; — that is, if he keeps it by his own free choice and will. No man will choose for his especial friend one whose hourly conversation revolts and disgusts him. The refined taste, to say nothing of principle, of a cultivated man shrinks from contact with that which is coarse and foul; and if we find a professed Christian whose chosen and intimate friends are found among the profane and godless, I believe the common sense of most men would conclude that such a one's Christianity did not reach far beyond profession. But what we now maintain is this: that if any believer courts, and delights in, the society of those who are not Christians, — no matter how pleasant and elegant and intellectual that society may be, — that believer is incurring the guilt which Jerusalem incurred, when Jerusalem made itself "a comfort to Sodom." That believer is following a course which directly tends to encourage the unbeliever to go on in his evil ways. For what is the natural reasoning of any man who is not a Christian, when he finds a man who is a Christian ever ready to make him a companion and a friend? "How can he think," the unbeliever will judge, — "How can he think that I am going to hell! Is it possible that he should like to be the companion of my walks, — to interchange thought and feeling with me, — to discuss great questions with me, — perhaps often to jest and laugh with me; — and all the while believe and know, that as sure as there is a God above us, I am going down to hell!" Don't you see now what eternal damage you who are Christians may do an unbelieving neighbor? Don't you see how you may so act as to confirm him in all his unbelief? Don't you see how you may so act as to make him fancy that you do not believe the great truths of Christianity yourselves? I do not love, and I do not respect, that Christian man, and still more that Christian minister, who is ready to be as familiar with a bad man, be he rich or poor, as the bad man himself may choose. I cannot imagine how any earnest believer can ever find it otherwise than inexpressibly awful and tremendous to look in the face of an unbeliever, and to think that he is hasting onward to the everlasting flames! O Christians, "make a difference," as St. Paul said. O Christians, be kind — you cannot be too kind — to the sinful and the godless; but be kind with a sorrowful kindness, — as a parent might weep over a son running fast to ruin! O Christians, love them, — pray for them, — do all the good you can to them; but let them ever see, by your whole demeanor, that you never forget that they are in the wrong way. Let them feel that you dare not make those too dear, from whom the grave must part you forever! See that you be not a "comfort" to them! Rather so hold off from them, — so be kind *to* them, but so shrinking *from* them, as that you may be a constant check on them, — a constant discomfort to them, — a warning voice telling them always that they are on the road to woe! So, with God's blessing, you may save them; so, at the least, you will clear yourself, — clear yourself from the awful charge of having "been a comfort to Sodom!"

4. I go on to mention, as a fourth way in which Christians may encourage and countenance ungodly men in their doings, — the cherishing a worldly spirit, — being as eager for worldly advantage, and as unscrupulous as to the means by which it may be at-

tained, as men who make no Christian profession. And, alas! my friends, how much of this there is among professing Christians! We are told that the true believer should walk by faith, not by sight; should set his affection on things above; should seek *first* the kingdom of God and his righteousness; should never forget that a saving interest in Christ is the one thing needful. But is the fact as it ought to be? Are not many professing Christians — even those in whom charity would hope there may be found "the root of the matter" — the most worldly of men? Are not many who bear the Christian name as eager to get money in any way, as if *it* were the "one thing needful?" Do not many who bear the Christian name show that they are far more eager to get on in life, than to prepare for immortality? Is there not as much vanity and pride and grasping at gain and self-seeking and contemptible worshipping of rank and wealth, — even when completely dissociated from worth and goodness, — among many professing Christians and Christian ministers, as in any class of men? True it is that religion repudiates and flings off such unworthy pretenders; and if the only result of their utter worldliness of heart and life were to make them the contempt of all right-thinking men, we should not quarrel with it; but far worse result follows from the worldliness of Jerusalem; it is "a comfort to Sodom" to see it and hear of it all! The sharp bargain made by the communicant may do worse than levy an unfair tax upon his neighbor's pocket; it may damage his neighbor's soul! It may set *him* up to "go and do likewise!" It may lead him to think that there is no difference between the Christian and the worldly man at all! Oh, miserable, miserable, that it should ever, even once, be said, as I read in a religious paper not long ago, that "give many a loud professor of religion the chance, and he will take you in as fast as another!" Oh! what wonder, if *that* can be said with even a distant approximation to truth, —what wonder if the Christian Church is many a time little better than "a comfort to Sodom!"

5. I shall mention, in the fifth place, just one way more, in which a Christian may incur the condemnation pronounced in the text: this is, by never in any way warning his neighbor that he fears or knows he is not a Christian.

My Christian friends, I dare say some of you have some idea that it would be intruding into the priestly office were you to set yourselves to the work of bringing souls to Christ. You think *that* is not your vocation. *That* is the work of the Church; and by the Church many people mean the clergy. But if you saw a friend manifestly stricken by fever or consumption, would it not be your duty to warn him, although you are not a physician? If you saw a friend drowning, would it not be your duty to try to save him, although you are not a member of the Humane Society? Ah, brethren, if a man be really in earnest about religion, he will never bear the sight of a human being whom he daily sees and talks with, going to eternal ruin, without a word of warning or advice! If you are a Christian, and if a man with no religion is accustomed frequently to see you and converse with you; and if you talk of many things which interest you both, yet never of the most important thing of all; if you talk of your common welfare, your hopes and prospects in life, yet never of the world in which you are to live forever; if you never, in any way, say that word which shall imply that your friend and you are resting upon different foundations, — that you believe in Jesus, and that you know and feel that he does not; if you never express or hint the wish, that so far as you are a true believer, he were such as you, — and that thus only can he be happy here and hereafter; what are you but "a comfort to Sodom;" — what are you but something to soothe down your friend's latent fears and cares about his soul, and to speed him peacefully along the way to woe? It is possible enough he may not like to listen to your warning words; it is possible enough you may make yourself an annoyance and a discomfort to him; he may think you are his "enemy, because you tell him the truth;" but oh! better, better *that* than to be a comfort to one, to whom comfort is the anodyne that will drug to death, to whom comfort is the stream that will bear on to perdition! Clear yourself, my Christian friend! let not your friend's blood cry out against you! Oh! let it not be, that on the day of judgment, a spirit condemned shall be able to cry out, that if you had done your duty by it, — if you had warned it as you ought, — it never would have come to that doom of woe! Never tell us, that really you have not opportunity, — you have not moral courage; the thing *can* be done, — done in many ways; and Christian principle, sincere and deep, will not be easily daunted. Who can tell how God's gracious Spirit may carry home to the conscience and the heart the words even of youth and inexperience? I have heard of one who on his death-bed said, that if, as he humbly trusted, he had been led to yield himself to his Saviour, and so to find hope in death, it was by the simple and solemn warning of one, in whom simple earnestness and heartfelt piety gave force to the words of early youth, unsophisticated and sincere. But if it be thus true, that a solemn responsibility rests upon every Christian, what shall be said of that which rests upon the ministers of the cross? How shall they clear their own souls, in the great day of account, if they fail, as each Lord's-day comes round, as dying men speaking to dying, to warn, to rebuke, to exhort, to leave no means untried that shall waken up the thoughtless and regardless from their false peace, — that shall carry such discomfort, such disquiet, such restlessness, such a keen barb to the unbeliever's heart, that he shall never know ease till he has betaken himself to that atoning blood in which alone our sinful nature can be washed and made pure! Can there be a more bitterly bad account of the preaching of any minister, than that an unconverted man should like to hear it? Could worse be said of any preaching, than that an unconverted man finds it pleasing and soothing? Is it not so, if it be so at all, because *that* preaching is "a comfort to Sodom!" No sermon is good, unless it makes a godless man uncomfortable and ill at ease; it is only thus that it will ever stir him to earnest turning to Christ. O brethren, what an awful thing to think of, that perhaps in the place of woe, there may a soul be found, that shall be able to say: I went every Sunday to my parish church,—I listened to the preaching of the parish minister; his sermons were always pleasing and soothing to listen to; they never made me uncomfortable; they never sent me home dissatisfied with myself, and anxious to get peace and pardon; Sunday by Sunday I heard them;—I heard them and I am here! Think of the unfaithful minister,—think of the cowardly minister that durst not preach the truth for fear of giving offence,—think of him entering the other world, and greeted there by such a cry as *that!* Oh, shall the preacher of the gospel dare to preach smooth things, with such a possibility as *that* before him! Shall the fear of man drive him to dare the curse of God! Shall he, bidden as he is to "speak comfortably to Jerusalem," speak comfort to Sodom too! Or shall he not rather, as one bound to "take heed unto himself," as well as "to the doctrine," cry aloud and spare not in the unbeliever's ear; pressing and crushing it home upon him, that he *must* choose between blessing and cursing, between life and death; that so, when his ministry is ended, when his voice is hushed, when he lies down in his winding-sheet, — it never may be said of those cold dumb lips, which shall give out text no more, that when, Sunday by Sunday, they spoke from the pulpit in the house of prayer, they spoke words of "comfort to Sodom!"

XV.

THE RESURRECTION OF THE BODY.

"For this corruptible must put on incorruption, and this mortal must put on immortality." — 1 Cor. xv. 53.

IT is a remarkable change, when we come to think of it, which at death passes at once on the material and the immaterial part of the nature of man. The soul is separated from its mortal tenement; and that spiritual existence, whose warm affections we vainly referred to the material heart, and whose thoughts and fancies we vainly referred to the material brain, now lives apart from both, and independent of either. But the soul was always a mystery; it was invisible before, and it is no more now; we cannot tell how it left the body, but we never knew how it lived in it, or where in this mortal framework was its home; and its departure is no more inexplicable than its existence. It is on the more familiar body, that the more palpable and the more affecting change is wrought. The contrast with that which a little before it was, strikes us painfully and harshly; and an undefined and mysterious awe comes over us, as we stand by the body from which the soul has gone. The heart is there, but it beats no longer; the eye, but it sees no more; and the kindliest and best-loved voice cannot arrest the attention of the dull, cold ear. The color of life has fled from the cheek, and the light of intellect from the brow; the multitudinous machinery of animal life is there, but the vital spark to set it in motion is wanting; and when weeping friends stand round the bed of death, *that*, which once could never see their grief without seeking to soothe and lighten it, remains heedless and still.

But this is not all. The great law of decay, powerless against life, now asserts its authority over the lifeless frame. To that place where the rich and the poor meet together, alike in the helplessness and humiliation of mortality,—to that narrow house, appointed for all living, — the living bear the dead, and lay them to their long repose. And then, decay begins its quiet work; the worm feeds sweetly on that, round which many warm affections clung, and on which many fond hopes were set; that which parents had caressed and cared for; that by which we knew those we loved; that which was so often the eloquent and loved expositor of the mind within, which spoke in the eye, and flushed the cheek. And in a little, the change grows more complete still; and a little dust, not distinguished from the crumbling mould around, is all to show where sleeps what was once a human frame, but is now of the clods of the valley. The trees around send out their roots and pierce it; the long grass waves the greener, nourished by man's decay; and when daisies grow over the grave, and moss has covered the head-stone, there is now beneath it nothing;—sāve earth to earth, ashes to ashes, dust to dust.

And so,—all sense is over. The old churchyard, where every spadeful of earth is mingled with human mould, is as lifeless and feelingless as any common field near it. The heart there throbs no more to the call of passion, nor dances to the song of hope. Over that quiet place there floats the sound of the Sabbath-bell; but many who heard it once, hear it now no more. Lowly grief, and lordly pride, rest here together. The ashes of friends mingle without sympathy; and those of enemies without recoil.

My brethren, all the generations of mankind have seen as much as this; and at this point the informations of sense and of reason cease. *That* is the very last that we see of our fellow-creatures. But we can well believe that through the long ages before our Blessed Saviour "abolished death," and "brought life and immortality to light," declaring that he was "the resurrection and the life,"—many a bereaved heart must have asked in anguish if *this* was the end of all? Was the touch of the vanished hand never again to be felt; was the well-remembered voice hushed forever? Was *this* the sorry ending, in the dust of death, of all the thoughts and purposes, of all the warm feelings and affections, which even in the darkest days of the history of our race, spoke man made at first in the image of God! And have we looked our last, we can hear the mourners asking, upon the features and the forms of those we loved, whose presence once warmed our hearts and brightened our homes? Must it be, that the parting look, when we lifted the winding-sheet aside, and gazed silently and long upon the sharp face, so sadly changed, was indeed the very last? And we can trace, even among those who enjoyed no gospel-light, what look like indications of some dim, confused yearning after the glorious doctrine of a Resurrection, which forms so essential a part of our Christian faith. Perhaps those are right who maintain that at least some vague aspiration, some blind reaching, after that wonderful Christian truth, underlies all doings and observances implying care or respect for man's mortal part after the soul has left it. Perhaps they are right who think they discern in all these some undefined and almost unconscious hope, that at death even the poor body is not done with forever, — that there is something coming yet, in which even the material part of man's nature is concerned. And if this be so, what a meaning and solemnity are breathed through many little things in which we are ready, perhaps, to see nothing more than human weakness; such things as the care which the dying have expressed that they might sleep in scenes, and near friends, they loved;

and that their ashes might remain unmolested, save by the gentle hand of Nature; such things as the sweetness and seclusion of the places where we would wish to lay the dead; such things as the awful inscription which the greatest of philosophers and poets caused to be written over his grave; such things as that last direction of the patriarch Joseph, of which the apostle Paul speaks with such solemn approval; — telling us that "*by faith*, Joseph, when he was a-dying, gave commandment concerning his bones!"

And yet, brethren, we can well understand how, notwithstanding whatever natural longings may be thus indicated, the stupendous nature of the miracle implied in a resurrection of the body baffled the belief of such as walked in Nature's light alone. That propensity to live in the future, — to be always putting off the true enjoyment of life to some indefinite season, somewhere in the days before us, — conjoined with a horror of annihilation, — both of which seem natural to man, had indeed led some who enjoyed no revelation, to wish and to hope that the spiritual part of man were immortal; and it was a great thing to believe that what in us now acts should continue its agency, and that what now thinks should think on forever. Perhaps it filled the philosophic mind with lofty thought; perhaps it yielded some comfort to humbler and tenderer spirits; when the dying man raised himself upon his dying pillow, and said, with an eye that brightened at the belief, and a voice that gained strength from the hope that prompted that last exertion, that what in him truly lived was strong now as in his days of youthful strength; — that his interest in the welfare of those he loved was only growing deeper; — that it would be deeper on the morrow, though he might never see it in this world; — and that his better life only began when men said he died. Perhaps there may have been men whom nature alone guided to such a belief as *that;* let me say for myself that I do not believe there ever were, — that I hold the proofs of our immortality derived from nature alone as worth absolutely nothing, — that I believe that only through relics of God's own teaching had men even the faint inkling of a future life, which some who never heard of Jesus have possessed, — and that only our blessed Lord "brought life and immortality to light." But granting that the man was ever found, who, untaught from above, was able, in the act of death, to declare confidently that he knew he should never die; — surely, even then, the white sharp features; and the tongue that grew palsied with the words of hope on it; and the drops on the rigid brow; and soon the cold senselessness; and then the thought of what was coming in a little longer; would tell friends around that *that* life, so confidently held by, was the immortality of the soul alone. All merely rational belief was staggered by the first thought of what was meant by raising and reconstructing the mortal part of man. It is so yet. The resurrection of the body is an essentially Christian doctrine. Wherever the apostles went and preached, you remember the two distinctive words which they always named together: "Jesus and the Resurrection." I believe we often fail to remember both how essentially Christian this doctrine is, and also how essential a part it is of Christianity. How forcibly, how constantly, the apostles pressed it on all who heard them; and with what wonder, what incredulity, even with what contemptuous derision, their hearers listened!

And it need not surprise us. The doctrine implies a miracle the most stupendous. We know how the poet, looking upon a skull cast out from the heaps of a ruined city, moralized upon the mighty power which would be needful to refit that dismantled palace of the soul, and quicken it to life again. We think of the multitudes who have given back their mortal part to the elements; how every period of thirty years sees the grave close over a thousand millions of human beings. We think in how short a time the mortal remains of man cease to bear a trace of what they were in life. "Dust we are, and to dust we return." It was a quaint but solemn fancy of the poet, to apostrophize a molehill in a churchyard, as containing part, perhaps, of a great company of human beings. It is strange, indeed, to think how many mortals may meet in that small hillock; how winds and rains may there have brought together in death those who never met in life; how the warm blood once ran through that crumbling mould; how every atom of it claims closest kindred with ourselves! And we remember, too, how science tells us, not as a striking fancy, but as a certain fact, that the whole material world is pervaded by the atoms which entered into the material frames of generations that are gone. There is something of them in the yellow autumn harvests, and in the leafy summer trees; something in the dust which our footsteps stir, and which the breeze wafts in play. There is but one generation of humankind alive at once; but there are a hundred slumbering in the dust together. "All that tread the globe, are but a handful to the tribes that slumber in its bosom."

No wonder that men, upon any authority less certain than that of the Almighty God himself, should have failed to believe that what was so widely dispersed and so completely assimilated, should ever be separated, assembled, quickened again. And there was a difficulty hardly less formidable in the very nature of the thing. Human reason has seen, and it can imagine, that gradual series of decay which turns fresh and vigorous youth to weak and faded age, and which then brings the wasted frame to dust and ashes; but how strange to conceive this process reversed, — the steps of this series retraced? To think of dry bones arranging themselves in human form, and knitting themselves together by nerves and sinews; to think of the multitudinous apparatus of animal and intellectual life again appearing about them and within them; and, more wonderful than all, to think of the vital spark returning, to set the whole machinery again in action, — warming the heart, and circling in the blood, and beaming in the eye, — was what the human mind, of itself, could not do. "Can these bones live?" said the Almighty to Ezekiel, in the valley of vision; and the prophet answered, "God, thou knowest!" And till God himself answered the question, *that* was the sum of what man could say.

But the question is answered now. Prophets desired to see the things that we see, and did not see them. Ezekiel, with all his inspiration, durst not say that dry bones could live again; but there is not a child among us but has been taught to say confidently, in that Creed which we have repeated from infancy, "I believe in the resurrection of the body!" There is not a doctrine of the gospel that is more clearly, strongly, and fully declared. You remember how St. Paul, in the chapter in which our text stands, argues the question at length; and anticipates and puts down all objections. "This corruptible shall put on incorruption, and this mortal shall put on immortality." "The dead shall be raised incorruptible." "That which was sown in corruption shall be raised in incorruption; that sown in dishonor shall be raised in glory; that sown in weakness shall be raised in power; that sown a natural body shall be raised a spiritual body." And remembering that the soul is not all the man; remembering that it needs body and soul in union to constitute the perfect human being; remembering that the body is redeemed with Christ's blood as well as the soul;—the great apostle hesitates not to say, that not even the perfect holiness and happiness of the *soul* would content him; that not till the body, wrested from land and sea, and glorified into beauty and perfection, is united to the soul again, would he be willing to confess that Christ's great atonement had proved fully successful in all it aimed at for God's glory and man's salvation; and that only "when this corruptible shall have put on incorruption, and this mortal shall have put on immortality, *then* shall be brought to pass the saying that is written, Death is swallowed up in victory!"

I know, my friends, that a hundred objections may be started to the doctrine of the Resurrection; and a hundred questions may be put as to the rationale of it. We are not careful to answer such questions. It is not wise to go into details as to a truth whose details are not revealed to us, and as to which we might speculate endlessly without reaching certainty or clear understanding. St. Paul looked forward to the question, "How are the dead raised up, and with what body do they come?" and doubtless such questions would be in the mind of the men of Athens when they mocked at the mention of a resurrection; but it is more reverent and more wise, not to try to explain what is manifestly miraculous, and manifestly beyond our comprehension. Some of you may remember how the great Emperor Napoleon, in his exile at St. Helena, was wont to speculate upon this great Christian doctrine; and while expressing his wish to be burnt rather than buried after his death, he said, truly enough, that as for the resurrection, *that* was miraculous at all events; and it would be as easy for the Almighty to accomplish it in the case of burning as in that of burial. It is best to hold, with simple faith, by the great truth, that "this corruptible must put on incorruption, and this mortal must put on immortality." We hold by that truth; and we do not pretend to explain how it is to come true. And we all know that we see daily things we can explain as little. Who can tell us how the oak grows from the acorn; how the golden harvests of autumn grow from the seed which decays in the ground? Let us not perplex ourselves in endless speculations as to the manner in which the dead shall rise; but let us rather repose in the certainty that they surely will. That almighty One, whose voice speaks to us in this text, we may be sure, knows how he is to fulfil it.

The body, then, shall awake; though it be not till "the heavens are no more." The grave is but a place of temporary rest, not of eternal forgetfulness. Great truths are sometimes embodied in single words; and this is so with the word *cemetery*. That word means *sleeping-place;* it is a truly Christian name to give a burying-place; it implies that such as slumber there, sleep for a great awaking. The grave of the righteous is the treasury of the skies; it will hear the voice, "Restore the dead," and every atom of its trust shall be rendered back. From places which we pass with little thought of those who are resting there, human forms will come forth to judgment. From some unknown spot, over which the Deluge rolled its effacing waters, the first of men will rise. Ruth will rise from that place where she was buried by Naomi's side; and Moses from the sepulchre which no man knew. The cave of Machpelah will give up its charge; and David and his fathers will rise from the place where they slept together. Martyrs and patriots will come out from the dungeon where they died, and be brought back by the winds to which men scattered their ashes. The material frame will as certainly be there, which was burnt to ashes, ground to powder, cast into a rapid stream, — as that which lay, in careful seclusion, from the hour of death to the day of judgment. Massive stones and cathedral arches do not keep the remains of royalty more securely than the wide elements of nature are preserving the vestiges of every man that ever breathed. From ocean depths, from mountain-side; from the forest and from the desert; they shall come again!

And thus, the earth is more valuable than you would think it. God has far more to watch over in it than its living population. It rolls on its way, bearing in its bosom a vast freight of that which is yet to people heaven. Let us remember, that the quiet burying-place which we pass with scarce a glance, contains mines which in God's sight are richer by far than ever enriched Peru. Not merely the mouldering remains of organized matter; not something which has seen its day and done its work; but something whose day is only coming, and whose work is not yet well begun; something which rests less in memory than in hope; the "body still united to Christ!" The field of the world is a harvest-field. Not vainly did our fathers call the burying-place God's Acre. It is sown with the seeds of God's harvest; and the day of resurrection is God's reaping-day.

The places on earth that are quietest now will be most bustling on that day of resurrection! When the hum has ceased in the great city's streets, the sequestered walks of its burying-place will be trodden by many generations together. It is a strange thing to stand in the breathless stillness of some populous cemetery, and to think what a stirring amid its dust the voice of the last trump will make!

And thus, the human body is as imperishable as the human soul. These frames of ours, which seem among the most fragile things on earth, are the only immortal things about it. That delicate organization, which any slight accident may destroy, and which a century brings to dust, will outlive far, far more than states and empires. It will see the world out! It will last infinitely longer than the everlasting hills. It will be young and fresh after the material universe shall have fulfilled God's purposes, waxed old, and passed away!

What shall we say, then, to this destiny which awaits such as fall asleep in Jesus? We are ready to think that it would now confer on us a happiness beyond expression, if the Saviour were once more to appear among men, working the same miracles as in ancient days. How it would delight many, if he would now accompany them, as he did the sisters of Lazarus, to the place where lie those so dear, and so missed day by day; and give them back to their homes and hearts! It would delight us, though they were only given back to a world of sin and sorrow, and a life which a few years would close again. How much more, if they were raised to a being in which sin and sorrow were alike impossible, and endued with a life which could never end! How much more, if they came forth from the tomb, not in the pale body worn down by long disease, but in frames which, though yet material, had caught something of the pure immortality of the happy spirit within! How much more, if they and you were no longer to pass your days in the company of sinful men; but in the society of beings all as pure as they are happy, and in the immediate presence of the Blessed Saviour himself!

It is to this latter kind of resurrection that our Redeemer lifts our hopes. It is to a sinless and perfect life that the dead in Christ shall rise. The corruptible is to put on incorruption; the mortal, immortality. The body raised is to be indeed the same; and yet, how different! The eye that will open on the better world will be brighter by far than ever brightened at the view of native scenes, or long-parted friends. The voices that shall swell the hymns above will be sweeter by far than ever sang God's praises here. These poor frail bodies are, to sum up all, to be made into conformity with the glorified body of Christ. And if we should ever feel disposed to envy those to whom the Saviour when on earth gave back their beloved dead, we may comfort ourselves with the hope, that though ours will never be recalled to tread by our side the thorny paths of this world, — though we have parted, till advancing seasons lay us low, — though "our path" meanwhile may be "in these ways we know, and theirs" through scenes strange and far away, — they *may* yet — and if God's grace fail us not, they *will* yet — be our companions in that better land, where tears are never shed, and friends are never parted!

The wisest people of antiquity exerted all their ingenuity to arrest the progress of decay in their beloved dead; and so successful was their skill, that we can even yet draw forth from the sepulchral pyramids of Egypt, forms that two thousand years since walked the streets of cities whose very ruins have disappeared before the touch of time. It was but the other day that I held in my hand the hand of a little Egyptian boy who died two thousand years since; and it *was* a strange thing as it were to touch that hand across that long waste of years. And though, when we look on the decaying features, which in all their fragility have outlived rocks and empires, we may smile at this earnest anxiety to preserve the least important part of man, we cannot but feel a thoughtful interest in the contemplation of that pious care which made men so anxiously seek to preserve the lips they had in childhood kissed, and the knees they had climbed. It was a praiseworthy, even though a futile task, for such as knew of no resurrection, to care for even the material part of man; and though we, in these modern days, may bury our dead from our sight, and yield the battle with decay, it is not because we feel no concern in even the decaying relics of a parent or a friend; it is because we know assuredly that this mortal shall put on immortality, and that God himself will watch over it in the space which must elapse before it does so. Give, then, Christians, the body to the grave; and never seek to arrest its quiet progress to rejoin the elements. Let it decay like all things here, returning peacefully to the dust from whence it was taken; and rather cherish in your memory the pleasant recollection of its health and strength, than preserve in your dwelling the wasted image of its weakness and ruin. Lay it in the grave, in the certain hope of a joyful resurrection; and when you come to die, cling to the same blessed hope. Know that never pyramid kept ancient king so carefully and well as earth and air and sea will keep the mortal part of your friend and of yourself. And anticipate, through Jesus, that coming day, when the blessed soul shall tenant its glorified body, and the glorified body shall be rendered meet for the dwelling of the blessed soul.

It is sad to have to suggest any thought so fearful, in the presence of hopes so bright. Yet, while we contemplate the resurrection of Christ's people, we must not forget that there is a resurrection of those who are not his people, too. "The dead in Christ shall rise first;" but the dead without Christ shall find no hiding-place in the grave. They shall rise too, invested with a woful immortality. And however, in the prospect of the dismal eternity before them, they may long for the peace of annihilation, *that* peace they can never know. There will be no escaping from life and consciousness and perdition. We dare not amplify such a thought. Is there one who will reject God's offered mercy in Jesus, and brave that awful doom?

I am sure, my friends, that we have all felt, in our own experience, what a curious power there is in the human mind, to cast off the thoughts of these solemn realities of death and resurrection which await us all, almost as rain-drops fall from the wings of the water-fowl. We have all an extraordinary power of living in the forgetfulness of our latter end. And it seems not to be God's purpose that it should always be present with us. Even those who have sought to bring these remembrances home to them by means to which we are not likely to resort, have told us that they strove in vain. Some of you may think of that good priest, three centuries since, who tells us that not even the mouldering bones which he kept in his chamber, not even the coffin standing continually by his bed, could make him think, indeed, that he must die. You may know, too, how a certain great poet and humorist, who passed away but a few years since, seeking, as it seemed, to bring the fact of death home to his feeling, spent some time during his last illness in drawing a picture of himself dead in his shroud. In his biography, published by his children, you may see the picture, grimly truthful ; but I think you may see there something of a morbid taste for the ghastly and the physically repulsive ; and it is with far more pleasing imagery that the Christian should seek to invest his passage from this life. Surely in perfect cheerfulness and healthfulness of spirit, the human being who knows (as far as man can know) where he is to rest at last, may oftentimes visit that peaceful spot. The hard-wrought man may fitly look upon that soft green turf, some day to be opened for him ; and think to himself, Not yet, I have more to do yet; but in a little while. Somewhere, doubtless, there is a place appointed for each of us; a place that is waiting for each of us, and that will not be complete till we are there. But our Saviour is "the Resurrection and the Life;" and "this mortal must put on immortality." And we rest in the humble trust, set out in words which have been used in Christian prayer for ages, that "through the grave, and gate of death, we shall pass to our joyful resurrection." It *will* be a lowly thing to lie down there, in the humble repose of mortal dissolution; but oh! never forget, that to the true believer, lowly as that sleep may seem, it *is* a sleep, sent by God, and to be broken by a joyful waking!

XVI.

CHRISTIAN SELF-DENIAL.

"And he said to them all, If any man will come after me, let him deny himself, and take up his cross daily, and follow me." — St. Luke ix. 23.

SO deep an impression did these words of our Saviour make upon the minds of his followers; so great and far-reaching a truth did they appear to convey; so essentially characteristic of the religion of the Man of Sorrows did the truth they imply seem; that three of the evangelists have preserved them in the self-same form. And here they stand, to teach us the necessity and the nobility of Christian self-conquest and self-denial. As for the terms in which the text is expressed, the only thing about them that needs explanation is that reference to taking up the cross daily; and most of you are doubtless aware that the allusion is to the fact that criminals sentenced to the barbarous punishment of crucifixion were forced to carry their own cross to the place of execution; and that sometimes, for lesser offences, the criminal was sentenced simply to carry a cross. And thus the meaning of our Lord's words is, that if any man, then or now, wishes to be his disciple, *that* man must make up his mind to daily self-denial, and to the daily bearing of burdens, more or less painful to be borne. It was not a smooth or attractive account of his religion that the Blessed Redeemer gave. He said frankly that its requirements were hard, that its standard was high, that it might, nay, that it would, lead along paths where it would not be pleasant to walk; and that if its ultimate rewards were glorious, you must go through a great deal to reach them, and they were far away. The founder of a new religion would be likely to repel men anywhere, if he dwelt strongly upon the persecutions and hardships which those who went with him were sure to meet; but the Jews of the Saviour's time were of all men the most likely to be repelled by such statements as these. For, as you know, worldly prosperity was the blessing of the Old Testament, even as worldly adversity is sometimes the promise of the New; the Israelites regarded wealth, long life, and earthly comfort and honor, as marks of the Divine favor; they had not learned, as we have, that sometimes "whom the Lord loveth he chasteneth, and scourgeth every son whom he receiveth." But notwithstanding all this, the truth must be told; the Saviour would not enlist men under his banner as earthly commanders sometimes do, by false representations; — by putting very prominently the ideas of glory and victory, and saying very little of certain privations and perils, of possible defeat and death. No man could ever say worse of the Redeemer's service, than the Redeemer himself was content to do. For "he said unto them all, If any man will come after me, let him deny himself, and take up his cross daily, and follow me."

The Saviour hardly ever said words whose bearing is more direct upon the practical work of our daily living; and though it is a bold thing to make the assertion, we do not hesitate to assert that no words ever uttered by Christ were ever so misunderstood and misinterpreted by very many men, in many places, and in many ages. You would say that nothing could be more plain, than that what our Lord meant when he said these words, was, that whosoever earnestly tried to lead a Christian life would find it needful to make many sacrifices of feeling and inclination for duty's and religion's sake; to do many things which would be painful and difficult, and to turn away from many things attractive and alluring. Our Lord plainly meant that no matter how difficult and painful any duty might be, we must do it, if our allegiance to him demanded that we should; and that no matter how dear anything might be, though it should be our most cherished hope or possession, we must give it up, if it stood between us and our salvation; yea, that we should be willing to cut off a right hand or to pluck out a right eye, if these *offended* us in our heavenward career. And I need hardly tell you that when our translation of the Bible was made, the word *offend* did not bear the meaning with which we are now familiar, but meant *obstruct* or *prove a stumbling-block*. So that Christ's teaching was that the earnest believer must be ready to give up anything, though it should be a right hand or eye, that tended to obstruct him in his Christian course; and that he must be ready to fulfil every Christian duty, however painful, — and to bear every burden laid upon him by the hand of God, though it should press upon him heavily and sorely, as the weighty cross upon the poor criminal who bore it to the place of doom.

Well, *that* was Christ's teaching in the words of the text; and that is the spirit that breathes from the whole New Testament. The spirit of Christianity says, Deny yourself everything, however pleasant, that God disapproves; Bear every cross, however painful, that God lays upon you: Do every work, however hard, that God allots you; Suffer, labor, endure up to martyrdom, when your Redeemer's voice calls you to do so. And the farther teaching of Christianity on the subject, is, that in those ways to tread which God commands, we may look for the kindly guardianship of angels; and better far, that through all these trials a Divine Spirit will go with us, giving us the strength, guidance, comfort, light, we need; and that all these things shall be made to work together for our eternal good; — that all shall go to mature in us a nobler character, to develop all in us that is most Christ-like and divine; — and so that the "much tribulation" of this world shall tend to make us the more meet for the glorious "kingdom of God."

I have thus sought to set before you in a brief form the great lines of Christian doctrine concerning self-denial and self-sacrifice. It may be added here, that this doctrine has proved sufficient to produce many instances of the purest heroism that this world has ever witnessed. Many a time it has led men to make a sacrifice of feeling that demanded a sustained resolution more than equal to the fiery, feverish courage that bears the forlorn hope to the deadly breach. Many a time it has gained victories, silently won, in struggling hearts, to which earthly battle-fields are nothing. Many a time has it led the martyr to the stake, and nerved him to abide in calmness the too slowly-rising flames. What incalculable, what inexpressible things has it brought men to do, to suffer, to resign! It does its work, even yet, amid the trimness of modern society. Ah, my brethren, sometimes the thin cheek, the deep-lined brow, the languid step, are indications of a heroism every whit as noble, of a strife every whit as fearful, as ever were hinted by the empty sleeve, the scarred face, the cross of valor over the brave heart! Truly said the wise man, "Better is he that ruleth his spirit, than he that taketh a city."

And now, my brethren, what has man oftentimes made of this Christian doctrine of self-denial and bearing the cross! What a wretched, what a foolish caricature of the simplicity and truth of the gospel! I should lament very much if I were in any way to exaggerate or misrepresent the teaching of many Christians on the subject of self-denial; but I appeal to all of you who are acquainted with the history of the Christian Church in early ages, with the doctrines still taught by the Church of Rome, and with the spirit than runs through a large portion of contemporary literature, if I am not correct in saying that there are many men and women who fancy that it is a Christian thing to seek out painful and disagreeable things, and to do them just because they are painful and disagreeable, although God never sent them to us, and although no good whatsoever is to come of our doing them. They fancy that it is pleasing in the sight of God, that it is ennobling as regards our own character, that it is carrying out the spirit of the text, to seek out voluntary and self-inflicted sufferings; to cut off the hand and pluck out the eye, though they are doing nothing whatever to *offend* and obstruct us, merely because to part with the hand or the eye is a very sad and painful thing. You all know quite well that the great thing which in the Middle Ages caused a man to be regarded as a marvel of holiness was not the amount of good he had done to the souls of his fellow-men, but the quantity of needless and aimless suffering which he had inflicted on himself; the great things which were told to his honor were such matters as the number of years he had slept upon sharp flints; the bloody stripes he had daily laid upon himself; the irksome garments he had worn; and the nearness to starvation which had been reached by his daily diet. They fancied then that the more repulsive and revolting anything was, the more like Christ you would be if you resolutely faced it. They forgot that though Christ was the "Man of Sorrows," he did not bear his sorrows just for sorrow's sake; but because a noble work was to result from them, — the work of man's salvation in consistence with God's justice and glory. And such of you as are conversant with the literature of the present day must know how much of the old spirit of Romish austerity — the spirit that idolized Stylites on his pillar — runs through a great part of it. There is a current idea that it is a fine thing to go through self-imposed trials, — to do what is disagreeable just because it is disagreeable; it is noble to climb Alpine heights — not because the slightest good is to come of your doing so, — not because you have the faintest idea of what you are to do when you reach their summit; — but just because it is difficult and dangerous to climb them, and most men would rather not. Some people nowadays appear to think that when our blessed Lord uttered the sublime words which form the text, he meant that we are to be always seeking out a tribe of petty disagreeables, — constantly finding out something we don't like to do, and then doing it; some people, I do believe, have a vague impression in their minds which they have never put into shape, but which really comes to this, that God would be angry if he saw his creatures cheerful and happy. Oh, the wicked delusion! God is love! When will men believe that grand foundation-truth! You may see something like God's feeling in the kindly smile with which the kind parent looks on at the merry sports of his children, delighted to see them innocently happy. But believe it, brethren, there is nothing the least like God in the sour, morose look of the gloomy fanatic, as he turns with sulky indignation from the sight of people who venture to be harmlessly cheerful. Let us try to feel it, that God loves us; — that God wishes us to be happy; — that it was because he loved us and wished our happiness that he sent his Son to die for us; — and that he does not desire or intend that in this life we should endure any suffering or sorrow, except that which for wise reasons he himself sends us, — sends us for our spiritual good, and would not send us if that end could be attained without it; — for "He doth not afflict *willingly*, nor grieve the children of men!"

You now see, my friends, what is the Christian doctrine of self-denial; and what is the perversion of it. Christ says that whosoever would be his disciple must be prepared to deny himself, and take up the cross, because it will oftentimes be duty and necessity to do so. But those who misapprehend Christ's meaning, put the case in this way: they say, Christ said that if any man will come after him, he must deny himself and take up his cross; it therefore appears that Christ thought painful self-denial a good thing, a wholesome discipline, — perhaps a work of merit; and if self-denial be such a good thing, we cannot have too much of it; the more of it the better; and so, let us seek out pain and suffering for ourselves. In short, here is the point at issue: Christianity says, Deny yourself, cut off the right hand, if it be your duty; if God call you to do it; and if your soul's salvation and sanctification are to be advantaged by your doing *that.* But Bhuddism, Romanism, Puritanism, and modern Asceticism, say, Deny yourself, find sorrow for yourself, although there is no end or aim whatsoever to be gained by these; for self-denial and self-inflicted suffering are good things in themselves. Ah, we meet them here with a flat denial. We say that it is the teaching of Jesus, that all the glory of work and self-sacrifice is reflected back on them from a noble end. It is noble, it is heroic, it is martyrdom, to go to the stake for the cause of the blessed Redeemer; it is folly, it is wrong-headedness, it is self-murder, to give your body to be burnt, merely because to be burnt is something terribly painful and abhorrent. The self-denial required by Jesus does not lie in seeking needless suffering for ourselves, but in bearing humbly and submissively what should come in the discharge of Christian duty. "Let a man," says Jesus, "deny himself, and take up *his* cross," — *his own* cross, — the cross God is pleased to send him, and no other! Let him bear the sorrow allotted to him in love and wisdom by the Almighty; let him not tempt the Lord by trying to take the reins of providence into his own puny hands. Let us ever seek, my brethren, to hold unswervingly on our Christian way; and let us seek to mortify every evil propensity, every worldly lust, that would turn us aside from it. And *that* will give us enough to do! If we take the trials God sends us; and strive faithfully against the temptations from within and without that God permits to assail us; we shall find that we need not go out of the way to create trials for ourselves. The world, the flesh, and the great Adversary, are hourly seeking to mislead us; and if any man will come after Christ, he *must* deny himself, and take up his cross daily!

And now, brethren, lest any of you should fancy that it is setting up a low and an unworthy standard of Christian self-sacrifice, to say that it never should be attempted merely for its own sake; let me remind you of a case in point. Not one of those romantic persons who are represented in modern literature as almost afraid to breathe God's air and look on God's sunshine lest *that* should be a sinful self-indulgence, — not one of them, I suppose, will pretend to exceed the great apostle Paul. And you know that although he, like the other apostles, was ready to suffer even to death in the way of duty, and for the gospel's sake, he never did so gratuitously; he never suffered as though there were anything good in the mere suffering itself. He avoided suffering whenever he could avoid it without making a sacrifice of principle. You remember how on two different occasions he pleaded his rights as a Roman citizen, to escape bonds and stripes. Yet he bore these cheerfully when they came in the way of duty; he could say, sincerely, that he "rejoiced to be thought worthy to suffer the shame of stripes for the name of the Lord Jesus;" — that is, when they could not be avoided but by the giving up of Christian principle.

But as regards suffering of any sort, it is a fearful responsibility that rests upon the man who wilfully brings it upon himself, with the purpose of thus disciplining and forming his character. It is intruding upon the special province of the Almighty God. When God sends you sorrow, you may hope that he will send you the grace to bear it and profit by it; you have no right to expect *that*, if you presumptuously bring it upon yourself. You have sometimes known of a mother, perhaps, who was making an idol of her child, saying, long after, that it was in kindness and love for her soul that God took that little one to himself; that the sore affliction was sanctified for her good; that it served to turn her affections towards the better world. Yes; it was well for her when God took away her child. But suppose any human being had thought to do her good in this way: suppose any man had dared to say to her, You are making an idol of your child, — it is injuring your soul, and therefore I shall kill it; would you not say that *that* man was a profane intruder on the province of Deity; would you not say that he was a blasphemous madman? It is so of all disciplinary suffering; it is not for us to seek it; it is for God to send it, and for us to bear it when God has sent it. If indeed it were so, that suffering never came without seeking it, *then* perhaps occasional acts of uncalled-for self-denial would be a good spiritual discipline; just as those gymnastic exercises which exert the muscles when there is no necessity for exerting them, tend to keep them fit for use when they are needed. But, O brethren, God sends us trial sufficient! We have crosses enough to bear, to keep our souls ever in training; we have occasions enough on which God calls us to deny ourselves, without seeking supererogatory woes. There is no need that we should seek out flints to sleep upon, and hair-cloth to wear, scourges for our discipline, and vigils and fastings to keep down our fleshly nature; there is no need to seek out petty vexations that may daily sting us like insects, nor weightier disappointments to crush out the spring from life. No; so long as we are in a world where our hearts cleave to the dust and worship the creature, we shall find it needful to mortify and crucify the affections which gravitate towards earth; so long as we are in a world where there is work to be done and temptation to be met, so long shall we have to deny and hold down a hundred feelings within, that shrink from work and side with temptation. And even in a world where "godliness has the promise of the life that now is;" and where the true believer is the truly happy man, the Saviour's words have never ceased to hold good, that "if any man will come after me," he must "deny himself, and take up his cross daily!" Not that there is merit in any suffering of ours; not that by sufferings inflicted upon ourselves, we have to eke out anything that is lacking in those mysterious sufferings of the Lamb of God that took away sin; not that God grudges us the cheerful enjoyment of life, or that it pleases him to see his creatures wretched; not that there is anything noble in crucifying affections which are beautiful and right, or in denying ourselves happiness which God meant us to partake; not that the noblest specimen of human kind is the emaciated eremite, with the haggard face and the wasted frame, who (for God's sake, as he fondly fancies) has weeded out all save bitterness from life; who has resolutely denied himself everything that he ever loved, and accumulated upon himself all that our nature shrinks from; who has no home, no hope, no love; not that God would have us deny ourselves anything that is right, or take up any cross save that which he himself imposes; but simply and entirely because from the very make of this universe, you never *can* follow Christ without finding that in following him you *must* deny yourselves many things, or you will stray from the right path; and you cannot, except by denying your Lord, miss taking up your cross daily!

And it is a far more difficult thing, a thing demanding far more faith and prayer, to live in the daily practice of true Christian self-denial; than to heap upon yourself those foolish though terrible austerities in which even the Romish anchorite has been beaten by the Hindoo fakir; and which seldom have failed to foster a deep-set spiritual pride, and to produce a most repulsive and unamiable temper. No doubt, there is a factitious pleasure in self-imposed suffering; no doubt there may be an acquired taste for it; no doubt there is in human nature a capacity of coming to feel a positive satisfaction in thinking how much you are denying yourself, how much you are taking out of yourself; no doubt there is a prejudice, very hard to get rid of, that all this is in some way noble, beneficial, pleasing to God. No doubt this erroneous belief has not been confined alone to the disciples of the Man of Sorrows; it runs through all religions; India, Persia, Arabia, have known it, no less than Rome and Scotland; the fakir, the eremite, the hermit, the monk, the covenanter, have erred together here. The Church of England and the Church of Scotland are no more free from the tendency to it, than the Church of

Rome; and the grim Puritan, who thought it sinful to smile, was just as far wrong as the starved monastic and the fleshless Brahmin. It shows how all men, everywhere, have been pressed by a common sense of guilt against God, which they thought to expiate by self-inflicted punishment. But we, my brethren, know better than *that.* Jesus died for us; Jesus suffered for us; *his* sufferings took away our sins; our own sufferings, how great soever, never could; Christ's sacrifice was all-sufficient; and any penance on our part is just as needless as it would be unavailing. Take, then, brethren, without a scruple or a misgiving, the innocent enjoyment of life. Let your heart beat, gladly and thankfully, by your quiet fireside; and never dream that there is anything of sinful self-indulgence in that pure delight with which you watch your children's sports, and hear their prattle. Look out upon green spring fields and blossoms, upon summer woods and streams; gladden in the bright sunshine, as well as muse in the softening twilight; and never fancy that though these things cheer you amid the many cares of life, you are falling short of the ideal sketched by that kindly Teacher of self-denial who said, "If any man will come after me, let him deny himself, and take up his cross daily!"

XVII.

THE GREAT VOICE FROM HEAVEN.

"And they heard a great voice from heaven saying unto them, Come up hither." — REV. xi. 12.

THIS is a world, my friends, in which there is no standing still. Ceaseless progress is the law of nature. Everything is going on. Time is going on; life is going on; among all visible things there is nothing that remains always the same; everything is either wearing out or growing better; some things indeed more slowly than others; but even the living rock crumbles in the lapse of ages; and the everlasting hills wax old.

And in our lives, my brethren, we feel it often, and sometimes we feel it sadly, there is no pause nor cease. We have all of us, perhaps, known quiet and happy days that we would have liked should never have gone over; seasons when it would have pleased us if time would just have stood still. But whether it be the school-boy, who wishes the day would never come that is to take him once more from the love of the home fireside to the cold indifference of strangers; or the youth, doomed to long years of Indian exile, who lingers, with a sinking heart, on every moment of the last days he is to spend among dear ones whom he may see no more; or the man condemned to die to-morrow, who wonders what makes the hours fly so fearfully fast when he most longs for their lingering; all men feel that there is no making life stand still. Indeed, it is more especially on the life of man, and the formation of his character, that this law of progress lies; it has been suspended to many things else, but to these never. The sun once stood still, but human life never did. The shadow on the dial went back, but all the time the shadow of death was stealing lower on the brow of man. The Jordan was arrested in its course, but the stream of Time flowed on. There is indeed in human life sometimes an appearance of standing still. We have all observed that many a man among us remains for years very much the same in external appearance; we see little outward difference in him from what he was this time last year, or what he was five or ten years since. But he has not been standing still; to the eye of God he is a very different man; he has moved away from the point where he stood before; he is so many years more confirmed in the service of God or the service of Mammon; so many years more bent on the things of time and sense, or elevated to the interests of eternity; so many years more grown into that habit of mind in which he will live forever. Here, in truth, we have no continuing city; our feet are not set upon solid land; from birth to death we are carried on by a rapid current against which there is no striving. We are cast, at birth, upon the stream of Time; and we must grow and decay as the stream flows on with us. Sometimes it bears us as it were through happy fields, where flowers grow along the banks, and green leaves are reflected on its waves; by a motion so calm and quiet that we hardly feel we are advancing. But the current goes on yet; goes on in the quietest country-place, where the pulse beats calmest, no less than in the throng and excitement of the great city; and in fast fleeting strength, and fast fading beauty, in the silvering hair and the withering cheek, in anticipations sobered and tempers mellowed or perhaps soured, in the soul more earthly or more heavenly, we see the work it is doing. You and I, my friends, are going on; and the great question then is, Whither?

Now there are just two ways in which men can advance. Advance they must; and there are just two great tracks along which all possible progress is bearing all human beings. The one leads upwards, and its end is heaven; the other leads downwards, and its end is perdition. In one of these ways every man is walking; every one of us here is advancing either to heaven or to hell. Yet a little while, and we who are here met in one place, may be parted by a gulf which all eternity can never bridge over. In far less than a hundred years you will have walked your last mile along the path in life you made choice of; you will have reached either the glory or the grief in which the two paths end. And God knows there are voices enough to invite us along the downward road to ruin. Pleasure, with her siren voice; Fame, with her trumpet tongue; Worldliness, with its choking cares; Temptation of every kind, with its varied allurement; all tend to lead men on in a way which is not heavenward. And man's own weak heart, with its vain affections, lends a willing ear to these congenial invitations, till the whole soul is engrossed by things seen and temporal; and then the unseen realities of eternity are forgotten, till death rends the veil of flesh away!

But let us, my friends, this Sunday afternoon, try to bring in our minds from the cares of our daily life; and listen, in thoughtful attention, to a Great Voice from heaven which says to us, Come up hither. Let us consider whether there be not a voice around us, not speaking indeed to the outward ear, but speaking all the more solemnly to the heart; stealing gently upon us in our thoughtful hours, and breaking rudely in on the busy whirl of life; blending with our own serious moods, and sometimes checking the power of folly. And if we never observed it before, let us listen now; let us think whether there be not near us another voice than that of birds and winds and waters; a voice that harmonizes with these, and yet stands apart from them; a voice from God's dealings and

God's word, from Christ's cross and Christ's throne, from the Blessed Spirit the Sanctifier and Comforter, from angels and apostles, from saints and martyrs, and from our own dear friends who once trod by our side the thorny path of life, and who have gone before us.

First, then, the voice of God comes to us from heaven, and says to us, Come up hither.

We need hardly say that none of us who are here now has ever heard God's voice with the outward ear. We have listened to the thunder, as it rolled above us, but no articulate words were there. Where the wind rustled the leaves, their sounds were not those of our English tongue; and where great sea-billows thundered their anthem of praise, it was the mind of those who listened that clothed their stormy music in meaning. The true voice of God speaks not to the ear but to the heart; for wherever God does that in which man can make out deep meaning; — wherever what happens to us teaches us a great lesson; — wherever in nature, or providence, or revelation, we can find out what is the mind of God; — there is God speaking to us. And it is in this fashion that God says to us, Come up hither. He says these words to us, in very truth, in a voice more solemn, though it be more still, than any which this world of sense could make. Get the key to the cipher in which the Almighty expresses his purposes, and you will find that from every quarter to which our eyes can be turned, from every thought on which our minds can rest, from every event that befalls us, from every joy that cheers us, from every grief that saddens us, from every care that perplexes, from every disappointment felt, from every hope deferred, from every friend that fails us, from every man that dies, — we can discern and discover that God never meant that man should take any path but that which leads to heaven. In what a multitude of ways he has shown us that it is upwards he would have us go; what hosts of things and events and circumstances and actions, stand like guideposts of God's own erecting along the way of life, pointing us away from this world, inscribed in great letters — To Heaven! There is the vanity which God has impressed upon all earthly objects; what means *that*, unless it be, that the place of our affections, and the home of our heart, should be somewhere else, amid purer and holier things? Would a Being of infinite goodness have placed men, with their capacity of infinite happiness, in a scene where every rose has its thorn, every blessing its canker, and where every imagined source of enjoyment, if compassed to the utmost, would still leave an aching void within, — if he had not meant, thus disheartening them with things seen, to make them think, May there not be something more satisfying and more real that is not seen as yet; and since there well may be a better world than this, may we not take God's word that there is; — should we not bestir ourselves, and seek out the way, and go up thither? And then, death and change; the mutability of the most permanent things, the fleeting character of the most precious things, the evanescence of the happiest feelings; — what mean *these*, but to turn our thoughts to a place where "every loveliest thing lasts longest," where joy is eternal, and decay never comes? And when God resumes the friends he gave us; — when the sudden stroke, or the slow decline, has snatched or has worn down those we love to the house appointed for all living; when the ties that bound us to earth seem almost parted, and we feel "the bitterness of death," and the soul turns weary away from all things here, and longs for the rest and the meeting which never can be in this world; — is not all this God's sharp discipline to turn us into the upward way; God's solemn voice saying to us, Come up hither, — where anguish is never felt, and friends are never parted?

But we are not left to read, by the light of reason, the pages of nature and providence alone, to find which way God would have us go. Elsewhere God's voice is heard more plainly; heard in the thunders of the law, and the invitations and promises of the gospel. The whole Bible is a great voice from heaven, saying, Come up hither. For, what is the Bible, but the history of that plan of redemption, but for which all men must have trodden one broad way, the downward way to ruin? It is revelation that furnishes us with convincing proof that it is the upward path which God would have us choose from the two that lie before us. Had he willed that we should take the downward path, he had but to leave us alone; and then the curse of that law which we have every one of us broken would have crushed us down to final woe. There was but one road before us by nature; only one road, save for the work and sacrifice of him who said of himself, "I am the way." And could there be more certain proof that God would have us choose the path to glory rather than this, — that he made that path where before there was none; that path which begins as it were from every poor man's door, but ends in glory which no mortal eye hath seen! And lest the doubting spirit should fear that such a path was not made for it, in its unworthiness, the Bible is thronged with declarations of God's desire, that "not any should perish," but that "all should come to repentance;" that all should "forsake their wickedness and live;" that "the wicked should forsake his way, and the unrighteous man his thoughts; and return to the Lord that he may have mercy upon him, and to our God, for he will abundantly pardon."

Nor should we forget, that although the upward road to life is so free to us, — open to us "without money and without price," — it cost the Almighty an infinite price to make it; and in the price he paid — his dear Son's life — to make this upward road, you may see how sincerely he desires that men should have such a way, and should avail themselves of it. You have heard of great roads made by human hands, for the passage perhaps of armies, or for leading the commerce and civilization of milder regions through rugged and desert tracts. You have heard how the everlasting hill has been pierced through, and the living rock blasted, and the mighty river bridged, and the far-stretching valley spanned over; how all the wealth of kings and states, and all the energies of thousands of men and decades of years, have been bent on the great beneficial work, that was to increase men in wealth and comfort. And even yet, it is fine to look on these unperishing monuments of the industry and skill of past ages; these hoary relics of an ancient race of gigantic strength and gigantic energy; and then to think how long man's works may outlive man's self; — to think where are now the hands that quarried these huge stones, and reared these time-worn arches — where the feet that trod them first, and the eyes that saw them when they were fresh and new. And our own modern days have seen roads more wonderful still link distant cities and provinces, making space almost vanish, and perplexing our old notions of time, making the bustling city a near neighbor of the sylvan quiet, and bringing the deep hum of crowded men almost close to the still music of nature. But oh! how infinitely little all these ways which man has made, — how utterly insignificant the price they cost, — compared with that mighty way which bridges the space between earth and heaven, — the time between now darkly and then face to face; which it cost Christ's sufferings to make, Christ's death to open; — which the feet of patriarchs and prophets, of saints and martyrs, have trod; — and along which the Saviour invites us to follow! Oh, brethren, if it proved the military commander's intense determination to convey his army to a point he had fixed on, when through Alpine solitudes and snows he cut his onward path, with lavish expense of labor and of life; is it not fair to reckon that when the Almighty at the expense of his dear Son's blood, opened the way to heaven, and made it plain for man to tread, he did by that very act call from heaven to man with affectionate, earnest entreaty, and say "Come up hither!"

A second voice that invites us up to heaven is that of our Blessed Saviour.

We have spoken hitherto of the First Person in the Trinity, — of God the Father; and we have seen that in many ways he is calling upon men to turn their steps into the path to glory. But we are now to speak of One whose name makes appeal to deeper and tenderer sympathies than even that of God; of that beloved Divine Person who has learned by experience what it is to be a man. He was whatever we have been, sin only excepted. And the same gracious voice which spake so kindly to the least deserving while he dwelt on earth, speaks to our hearts yet from the glory where he dwells, and says to us, "Come up hither." For even now he says, as before, "I am the way;" "Follow me;" "Come unto me, all ye that labor and are heavy laden, and I will give you rest;" "If any man serve me, let him follow me; and where I am, there shall also my servant be:" "and if I go and prepare a place for you, I will come again and receive you unto myself; that where I am, there ye may be also:" "Father, I will that they also whom thou hast given me be with me where I am, that they may behold my glory which thou hast given me." And what mean all these gracious words but this, that Christ would have men choose the upward way, though the gate be strait and the path be steep? "I am the way," says Christ: and whither, but to heaven? "Follow me," says Christ: and whither, but to heaven? "I will that where I am, there ye may be also:" and where is that, but heaven? Does he not thus cry to us, "Come up hither"? Oh, may it be the answer of our hearts, Lord, we come; for, blessed be thy name! whither thou hast gone and where thou art, we know, and the way we know! And putting out of view altogether the many invitations to sinners to repent and be saved, which our Saviour uttered, and which his apostles uttered in his name; putting out of view altogether the fearful representations he gave of the place of woe and the miseries of its tenants, and the beautiful pictures he drew of the rest and happiness of the blessed, — all calculated in the highest degree to startle and to invite sinners to thought and repentance, — what was the Redeemer's whole appearance on earth, but one earnest, unceasing, life-long entreaty that men would turn to God? It was all that men might "wash their robes and make them white in his blood, and therefore appear before the throne" on high, — it was all for *this* that he lay in the manger at Bethlehem; it was all for *this* he went about doing good; it was for *this* he preached his every sermon, and wrought his every miracle, and withstood his every temptation, and bore his every pang of pain. It was all for *this* that the sun was darkened, and the rocks were rent, and the dead came back, and all nature shuddered at the sufferings of the expiring Son of God! And the Saviour even yet appears to remind us of all his earthly travail and sorrow; and to whisper to our hearts, As ye would not that all *that* should prove in vain, — "Come up hither!" I died that ye might have leave to come! And will ye not "come unto me, that ye might have life?"

The Blessed Spirit, too, adds his voice to that which invites us towards heaven. The whole scope and object of his working, meant as that chiefly is to make us fit for heaven, is an indication of his design and his wish that we should go up thither. The Spirit the Purifier, as he makes us holier and better, thus fitting us for a clearer atmosphere and a nobler company, is ever whispering within us that it must be a higher life in which virtue shall be perfect, and another world in which hearts shall be pure. As his gradual influences, like gentle rain, steal into the soul; as the fruits of righteousness appear, and the work of sanctification progresses day by day, — what is this for, but that we may be made meet for the place where God is seen, — fitted for the society of the spirits of the just? It is not for time that his seed is sown; it is not for time that his harvest grows; and though his blessed influences may rear up virtues which shed a fragrance over this sinful earth, and breathe a blessing on the weary hearts of suffering men, and make Christianity a name to be revered, and the true Christian one whom the eye sees and blesses, — yet it is in a more genial clime that this gracious work is made perfect; and thus the Holy Spirit, as he works to make us fit for heaven, is not uncertainly calling us up thither.

And the Spirit in his great work of comfort, too, is calling to us from heaven, "Come up hither." If you consider, you will see that there is a reference to heaven in every part of the Comforter's work. For, is not the great comfort when dear friends die, that we may meet them yet, where farewells and partings are a sound unknown? Is not the great comfort under the pressure of suffering, that there is a place where there is no more pain? Is not the great comfort in the night of weeping, that God tells us of heaven, that there is no night there? Is not, in short, the great comfort of earth, that there is such a place as heaven!

Is it fanciful to think that the angels, too, concerning whom we know that they rejoice when a sinner repents and prays, and thus gives the first sign of choosing the heavenward path, add their voices to the great call thither? And surely the apostles and martyrs, who first preached the gospel of Jesus, in labor and peril and much tribulation, until the fiery or the bloody baptism sent them from their work to their reward, — seem, in no fanciful sense, to be even yet pointing to all they did and suffered that men might know a way to heaven was made, and asking if all that shall have been in vain. Even yet, from the pages of the inspired history, the burning zeal of Paul reproves the lingerer; even yet, the proto-martyr Stephen, from where his dying eye saw Christ standing, says, "Come up hither!" And the whole of the noble army who from that day to this, have borne a martyr's testimony to the faith of Jesus, — from the first whom Jewish stones crushed, and Roman lions tore, and Greek philosophers laughed at, — to the last whom the clubs of savages slew, and the racks of the Inquisition silenced, and the venomed shaft of polished ridicule assailed, — seem to cry in one vast voice from their place of rest, — "Come up hither!"

And now in the last place, brethren, there is one voice more that invites us up to heaven; one voice more, that adds itself to that great call, to the several parts of which we have been listening. It is the voice of those dear friends who have fallen asleep in Jesus, and gone before us from the place we knew together. There are few, indeed, who have lived long in this world, and have not stood by the bed of the dying; and let us hope that there are many who have seen a Christian friend or brother depart:—who have looked on such a one as life, but not love, ebbed away,—as the eye of sense grew dim, but that of faith waxed bright and brighter. Have you heard such a one, in bidding you farewell, whisper that it was not forever; have you heard such a one tell you so to live, as that death might only remove you to a place where there is no dying; and as you felt the pressure of that cold hand, and saw the earnest spirit that shone through those glazing eyes, have you not resolved and promised that, God helping you, you would? And ever since, have you not felt, that though death has sealed those lips, and that heart is turning back to clay, *that* voice is speaking yet, *that* heart is caring for you yet, *that* soul is remembering yet, the words it last spoke to you? From the abode of glory it says, "Come up hither!" The way is steep, the ascent is toilsome; it knows it well, for it trod it once; but it knows now, what it knew not then, how bright the reward, how pleasant the rest that remaineth, after the toil is past. And if, my brethren, we go with interest to the grave of a much-loved friend, who bade us, when dying, sometimes to visit the place where he should be laid when dead; — if you hold a request like *that* sacred; — tell me, how much more solemnly and earnestly we should seek to go where the conscious spirit lives than where the senseless body moulders? If day after day sees you come to shed the pensive tear of memory over the narrow bed where that dear one is sleeping; if amid the hot whirl of your daily engagements, you find a calm impressed, as you stand in that still spot where no worldly care ever comes, and think of the heart which no grief vexes now; if the sound of the world melts into distance and fades away on the ear, at that point whence the world looks so little; if the setting sun, as it makes the gravestone glow, reminds you of evening hours and evening scenes long since departed; and the waving grass, through which the wind sighs so softly, speaks of that one who "faded as a leaf," and left you like "a wind that passeth away and cometh not again;" — oh, how much more should every day see you striving up the way which will conduct you where the living spirit dwells, and whence it is ever calling to you, "Come up hither!" It was the weak fancy of a dying man that bade you come to his burying-place; but it is the perpetual entreaty of a living seraph that invites you to join it *there!*

Mothers, who have seen your little ones depart, believe that from that glory in which there are far more little children than grown-up men, they are calling you to join them. Listen, wherever you go; and your heart will hear a little, familiar voice, saying, "Come up hither." Parents, who have seen your children die in the bloom of youthful hope and beauty, and in the faith and hope of the gospel, — remember that you can now reckon an angel among your family; and believe that he or that she whom you remember so well, remembers you not less; and believe, too, that the dear voice, which you sometimes hear in dreams, is coming down from heaven to you with a thousand others, and bidding you hasten there. And, aged pilgrims, who can remember yet, with a quivering heart and a tearful eye, how, long, long since, you knelt at a pious mother's side, and said your evening prayer, — till on one sad evening you said your prayer alone, and thought, at "Our Father which art in heaven," that now you had a mother there too; — think that she has watched you all through your course in life, and that now from her place of rest she speaks and says, Son, "come up hither!"

You are going away, my friends, from this house of prayer; and no one here can tell how these words now spoken may affect you. You may regard all that has been said of this Great Voice from heaven, as nothing more than the fancy of the preacher; or you may hereafter keep your attention awake to that mighty sound, which in sober earnest is about your daily path, and which mingles in your ear with the voices of your daily companions. You have heard the like a hundred times before, on a hundred previous Sabbaths; and you may fancy that you are now just what you were then; and that hereafter, just as you are now, you may hear and consider the gospel invitation elsewhere. But, my friends, you are *not* the same; you have used up so many weeks' or months' quantity of your little allotment of life; and now there remains so much the less, and you are so much nearer the end of whatever path you are treading. Since every night you must pitch your tent a day's march nearer some home, oh that through the wilderness of this world you may be striving upwards to the promised land! And there is another thing in which you are not the same. You are more grown into good or evil, more bent upon heaven or earth, than when you heard the gospel-call last; for every time you hear it and resist it, you are encasing your heart in a flinty armor, that will turn off the arrows of conviction when they reach it next. If you care less for what has been said to-day, than you did for the last appeal you heard like it, — then fear, my friend, lest by an insidious progress, the great Adversary is leading you downwards to his realm of woe. And if so, plant your feet as on the rock, and take not one step farther; for to-morrow may end your path, and to-day is the accepted time. Repent, believe, obey; praying for the Spirit's aid, and trusting in the Saviour's grace; and it may be that you are not yet too late, if so you continue in the downward path not one moment longer. But if, treading the upward way, you listen to the voices that float around it, till they grow familiar to your ear as your mother's voice, and sweet like that of your native river; — till the habit of attention grows into your soul, and their ever-regarded sound always warms and cheers and swells your heart; — oh, what a happy meeting *that* will be, when your sun is set and your journey finished, — when the voices that called you coming shall welcome you come, — when the voices which came sweetly from afar, and sounded pleasant even amid the world's din, shall be sweeter yet close at hand, as they stir the leaves of the tree of life, and melt away upon that tranquil sea; — when many holy ones and dear ones shall crowd around you, and greet you now grown pure and holy as themselves, — in accents so familiar and friendly that you will feel you are now at last *at home*. And then, more conscious of the soul's great worth, and more bent upon the bliss of others, you will add your own to that Great Voice which from heaven calls to all on earth, and says, — "Come up hither!"

THE END.

CPSIA information can be obtained
at www.ICGtesting.com
Printed in the USA
LVHW100442110522
718424LV00003B/196

9 783375 003814